SO
HELP
ME
GOD!

Other Books by Herbert Tarr

The Conversion of Chaplain Cohen

Heaven Help Us!

A Time for Loving

SO HELP ME GOD!

HERBERT TARR

Times
BOOKS

Third printing, October 1979

Published by TIMES BOOKS, a division
of Quadrangle/The New York Times Book Co., Inc.
Three Park Avenue, New York, N.Y. 10016

Published simultaneously in Canada by
Fitzhenry & Whiteside, Ltd., Toronto

Library of Congress Cataloging in Publication Data

Tarr, Herbert.
  So help me God!

  I. Title.
PZ4.T1915So 1979   [PS3570.A65]   813'.5'4   79-10905
ISBN 0-8129-0827-9

Manufactured in the United States of America

To

FLORENCE MEYER

and the *lamed-vovniks*,

wherever they may be hiding.

1970-1

ONE

If all's fair in love and war, label the Class of '70 Exhibit Aleph. Nixon having welshed on his promise to end the war if elected, the poor and uneducated continued to be shipped off to Vietnam, while the well-connected stayed home to make a killing. America became Dodge City, millions scrambling for deferments, fatherhood, psychiatrists, Canada, obscene tattoos, *anything* to elude Selective Service or jail.

Unable to escape into the National Guard or reserves, the route taken by pro football players, I auditioned for conscientious objector, quoting Albert Camus: "No, I didn't love my country, if pointing out what is unjust in what we love amounts to not loving, if insisting that what we love should measure up to the finest image we have of her amounts to not loving." But I was turned down as lacking in sincerity when the head of the draft board called me a yellow-bellied radical comsymp, and I hit him in the mouth with my application form.

A Protestant chaplain tipped Columbia University students off to Union Theological Seminary's treasure trove of 4-D's. By then, Union was booked solid through World War Three by hordes for God instead of Country. But one classmate, inquiring at rabbinical school, was invited by return mail to apply at once, proving there is a Jehovah or Jews look out better for their own. True, Levi Simon qualified for the divinity ploy, having graduated from a Hebrew college (which he attended evenings and Sundays while matriculating at Columbia) in addition to being the university's most decent person.

I know. You're wondering what we had in common. Looks,

for one thing. People were always confusing us, being that we are both shaggy brunet six-footers, with thick eyebrows and mustaches camouflaging thin faces, and the same rangy build that enabled us to use each other's clothes in a pinch. Whenever we ran out of clean underwear, we borrowed each other's rather than do as those who turned theirs inside out.

Levi, however, also dug godliness. "Yes, I pray," he acknowledged shamelessly, unwinding from his head and left arm the thin leather straps of a self-flagellant. "I pray as devoutly as those who expect everything from God, and I try to act as if everything depended on me."

Slowly, my skullcapped friend rewound the kinky leather strips—phylacteries, he called them—on two tiny top hats. These, he carefully placed inside a red-velvet bag, possibly beside a ritual Fred Astaire doll. "When people don't believe in God," Levi remarked, "they don't believe in nothing. They believe in anything."

Spoken like a natural for divinity school—right? Ah, but he was afflicted with principles. After filling out his application, he decided against submitting it! "*God* knows I never intended to become a rabbi."

"As long as He doesn't blab to your draft board."

Levi turned on me. "How can I cheat God!"

I'd have argued the point if I had the foggiest notion of what God is. The Lord and I have never had a meaningful relationship. Hell, I find it tough enough making it with the flesh, let alone the spirit. Disillusioning, all my elders who dragoon youth into an undeclared war. Not that the young should be idealized. When Bobby Kennedy, speaking at Columbia, asked for his audience's views on the Vietnam War, the majority voiced approval. Only after cancellation of college deferments did undergrads turn belligerently antiwar.

"I can't do it!" My friend discarded the application. "It just isn't right."

"Levi, fifteen million draft dodgers can't be wrong. Not to mention forty million parents and sweethearts aiding and abetting. Why, beating the draft is one of America's oldest traditions. And didn't Bud Whitfield piss on the psychiatrist at his physical?"

"Judaism means everything to me," Levi maintained. "It's sacred. Using it would be unforgivable."

"Don't be silly. That's God's business, forgiving."

He heaved a sigh. "Drew, *I* could never forgive me."

Nobody but Billy Graham could say that with a straight face. Only, Levi meant it. "How can I pretend to be something I'm not? Rabbis are very special people, different. There's nothing holy about me," he said. "And refusing to serve my country. I can't go through with this, Drew. Certainly not as a Reform rabbi. It would kill my Orthodox parents."

As you can see, Levi already talked like a clergyman. He was humble, patriotic, spoke in non sequiturs, and he was full of crap. "Isn't there a rabbinical school that's unorthodox and unreformed?" I asked. "Something neither here nor there."

He nodded. "Conservative. The Jewish Theological Seminary. I'm graduating its Hebrew College now. But everyone there *knows* I had no intention to become a rabbi. And how can I forget that America liberated both my parents from concentration camps?"

"America is my country too. But there must be better ways to serve than by fighting an immoral war." No, it was not dying that terrified me, but killing. That's akin to committing suicides.

My friend measured himself against every virtue—duty, truth, integrity, honor—and judged himself unholier-than-thou. In short, no deal.

I saved the application. And when Father Daniel Berrigan, sentenced to jail for burning draft board records, fled instead of surrendering to authorities, I demanded of Levi what could be sinful about holing up in rabbinical school until the war blew over. Placing the application on his desk, I noted, "After all, houses of God *are* called sanctuaries."

Levi now reasoned with the brilliance of a scholar who had received an A in Logic 1.1 and would later flunk Life, "Drew,

[5]

anyone entering rabbinical school for ulterior motives is unworthy." (Yes, my friend also believed that all doctors go into medicine to heal, all lawyers hunger for justice, all congressmen work for the general welfare.) Into the wastebasket went the precious application.

I rescued it.

My friend slumped into a chair. "I *can't* attend the Rabbinical Institute. Isaca Zion is applying there because the Jewish Theological Seminary, being Conservative, doesn't accept women."

"Who?"

"My Bible professor's daughter. Didn't you meet her once? Isaca *wants* to be a rabbi. Me, I'd be an imposter. How could I face Isaca in class day after day, her knowing that?"

Levi was adamant. Nothing I said could budge him. But being cogent, there was someone my arguments did convince. Myself. So they shouldn't be a total waste—the application and the war—I asked the Rabbinical Institute to send an application to me.

Well, why not? Okay, so I wasn't a thoroughbred like Levi. But as much Jewish blood flowed through my veins as royal blood through Prince Charles', the only difference being that he was trained from birth for the throne and I was more like Queen Elizabeth's father, King by accident. But King George made do through World War II, and so would I until Vietnam War's end. Divinity student for the duration—where was the harm?

The Rabbinical Institute of America was located midway between "Needle Park" at Broadway and Seventy-second Street and the Dakota apartment house on Central Park West. The matter-of-fact building of slick white brick had not a trace of Gothic, which I always associate with religion and other mysteries that never intrigued me. A receptionist directed me to an upstairs lounge, where dozens of other candidates were waiting to be interviewed.

Most were legitimate, presumably, but none couldn't be

taken for teachers, accountants, used-car salesmen, social workers, or full-blooded Gentiles. Would true men of God ask each other, as several there did, "You think they'll ask if we believe in God?" And surely none would reply, "That wasn't on the application."

Someone kept inquiring who was the greatest prophet in the Bible until he was told "Irving." Another wisecracked, "Isn't Irving what lots of people wanted to name the new State in 1948 because Israel sounded too Jewish?" and everyone had the decency to groan.

After cracking my knuckles one by one, I chewed my fingernails down to the quick. Wisely, I had told nobody of my plan. So if it flopped, at least I wouldn't be *doubly* embarrassed.

Frequent mention was made of exactly three dozen people being there. When I asked what was so special about that, someone explained that thirty-six was the number of unknown saints. On account of their acts of unselfish goodness, legend had it, the world continues to exist. These *lamed-vovniks* themselves don't know who they are, virtue being their only reward and not infrequently an untimely death their fate. Whew! *I* was safe.

The inquisition got under way when a blue-haired lady with a lisp entered the lounge and asked for Mr. Seth Astrachan. Sly fellow. To make a pious impression, he carried a bible.

What would the admissions committee ask? Me, I never could take religion seriously after learning that everyone is descended from Adam and Eve, whom the Bible records as having only male children, and that Christianity originated with a heavenly whisper, "Don't be foolish, honey. I'll respect you like crazy afterward." And the neighbors telling Mary later, "Yes, the baby does look exactly like Him." Religion called to mind a huge dry river bed I saw out West through which trickled a tiny stream. Try as I did to imagine the torrents that once gushed there, I failed.

"If they do ask about God," someone nagged. "What's your position?"

I had my own problems. Suppose I *passed* the interview! What, then?

A sudden hubbub. Two girls who had entered proceeded to a couple of empty chairs, looking neither to the left nor to the right. Something familiar about the pretty redhead; just shy of six feet, she had long legs, slim hips, and bouffant breasts.

To the unasked question heavy in the air, she responded, "Yes."

Someone behind me whispered, "When did the army start drafting women?"

"That's Rabbi Zion's daughter," said another.

I glared at the tall redhead, who had ruined things for Levi. She was likely to do likewise for other Jews as well. Not that I opposed women's liberation. Every woman should have the same right and opportunity as any man to be a sonofabitch. Still . . . a *female* father figure?

"Mr. Andrew Baron." Return of the lady with the lisp.

I bounded to my feet. "Just a minute." I ran past her to the john, which turned out to be only partially furnished.

"We've had nervous applicants before," lisped the blue-haired thmart-ath on my return. "But never one who ran into the ladies' room. Why, Mr. Baron, you're sweating."

"Recurrence of malaria . . . contracted in Israel."

She recoiled.

"Haven't told anyone," I said. "Wouldn't want to hurt tourism."

She pointed toward a conference room and hurried off in the opposite direction.

Inside, a genial, fiftyish, round-faced man with horn-rimmed glasses introduced himself as Dean Diamond, and asked me to take the one empty chair at a table surrounded by a dozen men. *"Baruch ha-ba,"* he said.

Baruch ha-what? I sat down, mopping my brow. Flop sweat? Not that I was completely unprepared, having read the entire Bible through the night before. Fortunately, years of higher education teach one, if nothing else, how to fake exams. Ask Teddy Kennedy.

The dean tapped the papers before him. "Your college transcript is very impressive. Your application, too."

"Thank you, sir." He'd have loved Levi's application, which I had adapted.

He noted, "You have a distinguished name."

"Yes, sir. Andrew was one of the twelve apostles."

"I was referring to Baron. A contraction of *Bar Aaron,* 'son of Aaron,' first High Priest of the Jews."

"Of course, of course." *Really?*

Dean Diamond then took it from the top. "Tell us, Mr. Baron. Why do you want to become a rabbi?"

"What else is there?" I held out both hands, palms upward to indicate openness. "A rabbi is a Jew squared, isn't he?"

"And what does being a Jew mean to you?" asked a well-groomed man with silver hair.

"Just . . . everything, that's all." Hardly responsive. But I wasn't a *practiced* prevaricator.

A mild-mannered man beside me pulled at my sleeve. "What other vocations have you considered?"

Tricky question. To see whether my other choices would jibe with the ministry, as usury would not. "Only teaching."

"Jewish studies?"

"Naturally." My ears rang. When everyone refrained from speaking until the ringing stopped, I realized the committee heard it too. A bell had marked the end of the period.

The dean drummed his fingers on the table. "Why become a *Reform* rabbi? Why not Conservative?"

For all I knew, the two denominations differed from each other the way Sodom differed from Gomorrah. "Conservative is too, well, Orthodox for me. That left Reformed. So I chose Reform School, naturally—"

Chuckles cut me off.

Dean Diamond explained. "Reform school is for delinquents. And ours is Reform Judaism, not Reform*ed.* That's Dutch, and a church. True, some of our brethren say that Judaism is what Reform Jews reform because we don't wish to reform ourselves. Still . . ."

Mistake one. "Sorry, Rabbi."

"Oh, *I'm* not a rabbi," said the bald chairman. "I'm Professor of Bible here. What's your favorite book?"

"That's easy," I pulled on my right ear. "The Old Testament."

Dr. Diamond gave me a quizzical look. "That's Christian terminology. Or the adman's. Old Testament to contrast with the New and Improved Testament. I meant *which* book of the Bible. Nobody expected you to say *Portnoy's Complaint.*"

Probably Roth's novel stimulated another goof. "Song of Solomon." I should have named one of the prophets instead of biblical erotica, but at that moment only Jeane Dixon sprang to mind.

"Interesting," said an elderly man with a cloud of white hair across the table. With his penetrating gaze, haughty eyebrows, aquiline nose, and unwrinkled olive skin, Dr. Tchernichovsky looked like King of the Jews. "Song of Songs was Rabbi Akiba's favorite book too. He interpreted it as a portrayal of the love of God for His bride Israel."

No joke! "My favorite rabbi, Akiba."

The mild-mannered man tugged at my sleeve again. "What *did* you think of *Portnoy's Complaint*?"

I stopped fiddling with my ear. "My friend's mother"—that was Mrs. Simon, as quoted by Levi—"when she heard the novel was about a thirtyish Jewish bachelor who savagely condemns his parents for having ruined his life, she said, 'Well, Portnoy was a fool to let them do it.'" The group's chuckles encouraged me. "The mother of another classmate was Philip Roth's grade-school teacher in Newark. She said she wanted to leave him back. But she didn't. Because, she said, 'Philip has such a nice mother.'"

Roars of laughter. One of the men repeated the punch line to himself. But another asked grimly, "Exactly how anti-Semitic do you think Philip Roth is?"

"Oh, he isn't anti-Semitic," I said, though I doubt that if positions were reversed, Roth would have stuck out his neck for me. "He's an enormously gifted writer who sees *all* people through shit-colored— Shorry! I should've shaid—"

The mild-mannered man grabbed my hand and pumped it. "So far as Philip Roth is concerned, shit fit, Mr. Baron."

"Well, if you say so. I'm sure you're an expert in such matter . . . s." I then declaimed, "We know only too well man's failings—and today's writers are only too proficient in exposing them. But we need one to tell us how a man may transcend himself by sheer force of will."

The aristocratic elder remarked, "That sounds familiar." (Uh-oh. Gide, a goy as well as a gay.) "Were you paraphrasing Rabbi Kook's poem?"

I nodded with such force that my teeth banged together. "A favorite of mine."

A man with a nose like a church key remarked, "We don't usually ask applicants their theology, Mr. Baron. But since you yourself raised the subject . . ."

What a liar!

". . . and as a professor of theology . . ."

A sociology prof of mine had characterized the philosopher and the theologian as blind men searching a dark room for a black cat that isn't there. With this difference: the theologian finds it.

"Mr. Baron, do you believe in a personal God?"

"You mean, one-to-One? Well, personally . . . it is my devout belief that when a man doesn't believe in God, he doesn't believe in anything. He believes in nothing. I therefore pray to the Lord as devoutly as if I expected everything from myself, but I try to act as if everything depended on God."

That impressed the hell out of the committee. Silence enveloped the room.

Dr. Tchernichovsky spoke up finally. "Would you please repeat that? It didn't make any sense."

I couldn't have then repeated my own name. What had I said? Jesus! Why was I born?

"Better yet, Mr. Baron, let me ask you this," said Dr. Tchernichovsky. "Do you believe that in the end good will triumph in the world?"

In the end everyone would be six feet under.

"Your silence is very telling, Mr. Baron. You don't believe in good's winning out, do you?"

"Well, that depends."

"On what?"

I thought of Vietnam, but said, "On whether the Rabbinical Institute admits one Andrew Baron."

Dr. Diamond stood up, smiling. "Thank you, Mr. Baron. Very nice meeting you."

That was it? No toughies such as girls are forever asking whenever one tries to score: What do you *really* want out of life? Somehow I made it to the door without tripping over anyone. "When may I expect to hear . . . ?"

"Since our purpose at this interview," said the dean, "is to weed out *obvious* misfits and draft evaders—"

I gulped. *"Drafty waiters?"*

"Draft *evaders.* They're flooding every divinity school in the country. Not that anyone here doubts *your* sincerity, Mr. Baron. Notifications will go out next week. *Shabbas shalom.*"

I had made it! Wasn't that enough to make you believe in God? You, not me. I required the Second Coming.

Waiting for Levi in the dorm, I fell asleep. Next thing I knew it was dusk. Still no Levi. He'd probably gone home to Manhattan Beach. No chance of calling him there, because Orthodox Jews, he had told me, don't answer the phone on Friday nights and Saturdays.

I drove out to Levi's, determined to get him into the act.

But at the very mention of the Rabbinical Institute, he cut me off. "My father would have a fit!"

A pretty, middle-aged woman in her Sunday best appeared in the foyer. "Just in time!" Mrs. Simon exclaimed, and swept me into the dining room. Her husband was seated at a table that looked set for a dinner party—embroidered white linen cloth, flowers, wine in a cut-glass decanter, candles.

"Am I interrupting?"

"Impossible on *Shabbas*." Mr. Simon handed me a skullcap. "The Sabbath isn't complete without a guest."

Levi's father had a face like tapioca pudding, with a lump for a nose and crinkly brown raisinlike eyes. Mrs. Simon was a dark, shapely beauty with high cheekbones and delicate features so perfectly proportioned that her profiles were identical. Smiles flitted back and forth between her full lips and sparkling brown eyes, as if exchanging happy secrets.

While she fixed me up with a place setting, Levi put a napkin over my knife. "Symbolic of bloody weapons," he said. "So we hide them from sight during prayer."

"Better, would be hiding weapons during warfare," Mr. Simon commented. "But what fun would wars be without bloodshed?"

"*Baruch ato adonai. . . .*" Levi sang a long prayer, after which we all drank wine and ate braided bread. Platter followed platter—the only pauses were for seconds—until I protested, stuffed.

"It's true." Mrs. Simon nodded. "Where there's *too* much, something is missing." Then she served another round of kugel.

Out of respect for Levi's wishes I mentioned nothing but the story of my life—at Mrs. Simon's request. Not that she pried. She was so genuinely concerned about people that news of my parents' divorce upset her as much as if it had happened that moment before her very eyes. Both had remarried, I hastened to add, omitting the number of happily-ever-afters. To Terri and Dad marriage was a stage that adults went through often.

Mrs. Simon said, "The divorce must have hurt terribly."

"Yes." Demoralized me, too. For the longest time I couldn't understand how Terri and Dad could have done it to each other. Had my parents ever been in love? "Of course, very much," they told me. "You're the proof." So all through boarding school I saw myself as the remains of a love that had expired.

A sneeze during dessert provoked something long and unintelligible from Mrs. Simon.

Even more effective than his wife's Yiddish blessings, Mr. Simon said wryly, were her curses, to which he attributed his last two operations. "My husband takes his troubles like a man," she commented with a wink. "He blames them all on his wife."

The good-humored banter seemed all the more remarkable after I noticed matching blue numbers tattooed on the couple's left forearms. Horror must have registered, for Mrs. Simon said, "Please don't look at us like that, Drew. The concentration camps and all. That was so long ago, I can't believe it really happened. Must have been a nightmare. And since then, the State of Israel was born."

In the middle of Grace—Jews say it *after* meals; that way, I suppose, if God doesn't deliver, they don't—the lights suddenly went out. On Friday nights a timer disconnected the dining room's electricity thirty minutes after dinner. Evidently, Orthodox Judaism also had something against Con Edison, as who doesn't?

Levi was right about his parents' antipathy toward Reform. Mr. Simon wouldn't be caught dead inside a temple of theirs. "Reform is *tref*," he stated, then translated for my benefit. "*Tref* means feh."

Didn't he accept Reform as part of Judaism?

"Do you think," said Mr. Simon, "there's such a thing as hot ice?"

When I left, Mrs. Simon gave me half a chicken and four pieces of gefulte fish with all the trimmings, and Mr. Simon offered the use of their home as a locker room whenever I went swimming at Manhattan Beach. "Come back soon," both said. "Don't be a stranger."

On the way to my car, I begged Levi to reconsider R.I., refraining now from telling of my ruse lest he talk *me* out of it.

"No way, Drew." He spoke of a Rabbi Zusya, who burst into tears on his deathbed. Asked why, the man said, "When I'm ushered into the Presence of God, He won't ask why I wasn't Moses. After all, I am not Moses. Nor will God ask why I wasn't Isaiah, because neither am I Isaiah. Why am I crying? Because God *will* ask, 'Why on earth weren't you Zusya?' "

I hit Levi with Golda Meir. She could forgive the Arabs for killing Israelis, the premier stated on "Meet the Press," but she'd never pardon them for forcing the Jewish state to teach its youth to kill.

"Only one in five or so get sent to Vietnam. Me, I'll never spill a drop of blood anywhere," Levi said. "On my honor."

That remark—on my honor—had me checking out possibilities in Canada. But then came May's demonstration at Kent State to protest Nixon's incursing Cambodia and the National Guard shooting four innocent students to death. During their televised funerals, a sudden revelation struck me as a rabbi read the memorial prayer. How idiotic to let myself be chased away by an Administration that, with any sense of honor, would exile itself. For ignoring the majority of Americans who, according to the latest Gallup Poll, considered U.S. intervention in Vietnam a dreadful blunder. No, I wouldn't desert to Canada, forever despising the country I love in order to justify my flight.

So when R.I. sent a provisional acceptance, joy reigned. But briefly. The final word now depended on the school's screening trinity: a medical doctor, a clinical psychologist, and a psychiatrist. Uh-oh. *One* strike and I was out.

My father's attitude toward Judaism was, I pass, let someone *else* be chosen. So irreligious were he and his friends that I sometimes wondered if the Jewish people had not introduced monotheism to the world so much as palmed it off, in the manner of the ex-husband who marries off his former wife to spare himself alimony payments. Dad's religious identification derived mainly from a Jewish country club, the Christian ones having denied him entry, whereas my mother identified with the Human Potential Movement in all its varieties. They had left it to me to choose my own religion when I came of age, though table manners were strictly enforced at home.

With that nonsectarian background to hide, I studied loads of psych books over the weekend, only to learn that it was impossible to fool tests like the Rorschach. Whatever one said, the texts warned, was a dead giveaway. Any wonder that I reported to the clinical psychologist a caffein-sodden mass of jitters, idiotically apprehensive of his ability to read my mind through my eyes?

"Nice meeting you, Doctor," I said, then watched my sweaty palm skid off his and slide toward his cuff.

Dr. Kohler, a man thin enough to be his own shadow, hmmmmed and gave me a *verrrrry significant* look. Eyes unblinking, he laid out pictures of eight people and asked me to select my two favorites. A collection of drooling mouths, menacing stares, running noses.

"Something's wrong with these people," I noted.

"Oh?" resounded through the office.

"They're all very disturbed."

"You think so, Mr. Baron?"

A bead of sweat started its clammy descent of my spinal column.

Handing me pencil and paper, the psychologist asked me to draw a person. Clearly a trap. How should I know which was the rabbinical sex to draw?

Happily, the phone rang, and during Dr. Kohler's conversation I sketched swiftly. The result pleased him, however, not at all.

He waggled a finger at my creation. "What on earth is *that*?"

"Adam and Eve."

"I asked you to draw a *person*. Adam and Eve are *two*." He held up, inadvertently, one finger.

"Oh, I thought you said, 'Draw a *pair*, son.' Your accent." As Dr. Kohler responded, I rushed in with "Well, that explains it" before realizing he had said, "Mr. Baron, I was born in Milwaukee."

I had not made a friend. That was apparent from the way Dr. Kohler snarled, "Describe the weather."

I turned to look through the window.

He stabbed my drawing with his index finger. "*Here.*"

"But I didn't draw *weather.*"

Never before had I seen spittle dribbled by a grown man. Well, if that was the way he wanted to play. "Sunny and clear. Eighty-one degrees Fahrenheit, thirty-two Celsius, sixty percent humidity."

". . . now"—Dr. Kohler introduced the Rorschach—"to uncover the *source* of your hostility toward me, Mr. Baron." In my projections, the sun always broke through, God was in His heaven, and all was right with the Far East. At test's end, the psychologist volunteered, "But you're not at all like what I thought! That's good. I mean, healthy." He caught himself. "But I'm not supposed to reveal anything to you applicants."

"Good and healthy—*me*?"

For the first time that morning Dr. Kohler smiled. "*Everyone* taking these tests gets nervous. That's—dare I use the word—normal."

I was so elated until depression set in. Elated to have succeeded, I grieved to have succeeded at fraud. Yet according to the psych books, it was impossible to fool the Rorschach. Could someone be a genuine phony? a sterling fake?

I arrived at the psychiatrist's office, thinking now I could relax. My mistake. This was Dr. Bayliss' opening query after checking his watch: "When did you first hear the call, Mr. Baron?"

"I never heard any call." Did he expect me to come on as Joan of Arc with heavenly voices?

"I meant"—to underline his words, the psychiatrist scratched his bulbous nose arrhythmically—"to become a rabbi. You say you never had one?"

See what happens when you let down your guard? "It's

your terminology I never heard of, Dr. Bayliss, in connection with things Jewish," I said. " 'Call' and 'calling' were coined by John Calvin."

Dr. Bayliss glowered, as he beat a swift retreat to my sex life.

Uh-oh. To err is human, but to fornicate hardly divine.

". . . You didn't reply, Mr. Baron."

Sure, I was stalling. "Have I ever enjoyed sexual intercourse? Well, yes and no."

Dr. Bayliss' finger went up his nose. *"Yes and no?"*

Jewish novelists portray guilt as more potent than libido. "I didn't enjoy it."

"I see. Why not?"

"We were merely engaged, Heidi and I."

"What did you do?"

"We broke it. After four weeks. The engagement, I mean."

"I mean, what did you *do*? *Please* be specific."

"You know. First we undressed. Sometimes I her. Sometimes she me. Sometimes I myself. Sometimes—"

"Yes, yes. Go on, go on. And then? And then?"

". . . snack."

"Snack?"

"I like to eat afterward. Sandwich, milk, Devil Dogs . . ."

"Oh, a nosher." Bayliss reached for a sourball and went on. "Tell me, Mr. Baron, what you like most about Judaism."

From out of the blue popped an honest answer. "Sabbath Eve. The family around the table, the candles and flowers. The warmth." Not till then did I realize how much that Friday night at the Simons' had affected me.

Walking off with a 4-D after that was as easy as crossing the street from the psychiatrist's office to Dr. Jacoby's for my physical. The physician, whose hairless head resembled a bowling ball, was a kindly, humorous man. As I stripped to my shorts, he alerted me that more rabbis died from overeating at circumcisions, bar mitzvahs, weddings, and dinner meetings than from all other causes combined. "They ignore the Psalmist's warning: 'Too much oil quenches the wick.' So take care. Don't dig your grave with your own teeth."

Why did a warning bell suddenly sound in my subconscious? A word of Dr. Jacoby's cited a clear and present danger. Which one? Overeating? Hazard? Grave? Died? Nothing scary about *them.*

"Okay, drop your shorts, Baron, and bend over."

Circumcision. Uh-oh. Born during Terri's back-to-nature phase—whole grains, no additives, no subtractions—this idiot had prepared for the wrong exams! Yet I couldn't have reported to Dr. Jacoby with a freshly bandaged member. Would he have believed I had stubbed it on a toilet seat?

"Baron, I asked you to drop your shorts and bend over."

"Bend over *what,* Doctor?"

He chuckled. "Come on, Baron."

No way out. Hoist by my own peter. Nothing to do but give up. Foiled by a foreskin! Damn, damn, damn. . . . Defeated, I doubled over abjectly before fate.

There was a ripping sound, and Dr. Jacoby howled. The abrupt jacknife had split my shorts.

He took a peek, then, still laughing, told me to straighten up. "*Now* drop your shorts. And cough."

I uncovered my crotch like a coy stripper, while maintaining the privacy of my parts. "Peekaboo."

Dr. Jacoby doubled over with laughter till he could have jabbed my groin with his nose instead of poking it with his fingers. Which he did without, thank heaven, dislodging anything incriminating.

Twenty-three days later I was awarded a draft deferment. *Hallelujah.*

Second thoughts weren't long in coming or difficult to withstand. But those third, fourth, and fifth thoughts! That damn war in Vietnam *had* to end by fall. Yet I had already written hundreds of letters to Administration officials, gotten out the vote, contacted every congressman, paraded in peace marches, demonstrated incessantly. Who was listening? Only other people.

The Kent State tragedy did change things. Some students, convinced that the revolution was at hand, used an old recipe from the front page of a chic intellectual journal to cook up a batch of bombs, while many anti-students stockpiled guns. The middle ground between the two arming camps was a quicksand of meetings.

Levi and I attended scores, eager to support any movement short of blood-in-the-streets. There weren't many, however. Take APPLE PIE (Americans for Perfect Peace and Love on Earth—Permanent, That Is), which wanted to blow up the Pentagon and a dozen colleges before final exams.

"These cures," Levi noted, "are diseased."

Nor did revolutionaries help with statements like "First we'll make the revolution. Then we'll decide what for."

At one Friday night meeting, in a living room high above Park Avenue and almost as wide, somebody called for mass self-immolations on the Upper East Side, whereupon several would-be celebrities turned to neighbors over cocktails and canapés as if to say "I will, if you will." Nobody would, knowing he'd miss his notices in the morning papers.

Exasperating charades. So, impulsively, I stood up and declaimed, "Take me! I'll be happy to self-destruct."

The crowd, mistaking sarcasm for passion, burst into cheers. Several sobbed, while somebody broke out a chorus of "For he's a jolly good fellow."

Promise not to laugh? Tears started to my eyes. In my whole life nobody had ever made me feel breast-fed. So I didn't even care why I was being serenaded.

Alas, someone pricked my balloon with a cry of "Bullshit."

The speaker, a slim man with long salt-and-pepper hair and a shiny black suit, pushed his way through the throng and strode to the center of the room with the authority of a stage star who has a percentage of the gross. When he faced front, many gasped, seeing his Roman collar. Several called him by the wrong name.

A boyish grin scampered across the sensual mouth of the fortyish man whose outsized dark eyes seemed to have been charcoaled into his pale face. "You think all priests look alike?" Laughter from the crowd. "And didn't you hear? The F.B.I. caught Dan Berrigan on Block Island the other day."

A pall fell over those who hadn't read the newspapers that week. Everyone admired Father Berrigan. Me, I considered him a saint and Dr. Martin Luther King, Jr.'s successor.

Introducing himself as Father Charles Jovak, the elfin man added, "I suspect Dan Berrigan *let* himself be caught. He could easily have disappeared. But at the cost of no longer witnessing against this country's evildoing."

Some difference. A godly priest on the half-hearted lam, and myself the atheist in a half-hearted dodge into the ministry.

Father Jovak addressed me. "Sorry, fella. No disrespect intended, God knows. I think you're beautiful. Absolutely Christ-like."

Uh-oh. Here come them nails. Hungry though I was for approval, starving is preferable to burning. Yet how does one gracefully withdraw an offer of suicide? Surely not by remembering a previous engagement.

Happily, the priest continued, index finger punching holes in the air. "But I won't *allow* you to immolate yourself."

"Okay," I said, and swiftly sat down to the pumping of a dozen hands and scores of "Nice going's" and only a "Quitter" or two.

The way celebrityhood changes a person. All of a sudden I found myself thinking of what to do for my *next* number. O Lord, I nearly prayed. Let this spotlight not pass from me.

"You see"—Father Jovak was addressing the crowd now— "self-immolation isn't *original*." It would go unrecorded by the mass media. The tree that falls in an uninhabited forest might just as well remain upright and I unsinged.

What to do instead? Father—"Call me Chuck"—Jovak's

answer was immediate. Either he had pondered it for weeks, or it came straight off the top of his head. "Immolating *another* person for peace." His coal-black eyes glittered, but he didn't rub his hands. "It's never been done, killing for peace. Except, of course, in Vietnam."

Nobody threw a net over him. Several people did request elaboration, however.

"Entirely simulated, of course," he said. "What I have in mind is a *mock* immolation. I'll be the immolator, along with exactly three minutes of copy to fit into Walter Cronkite." The priest's eyes focused on me. "How about it, fella? Will you be my make-believe burnt offering?"

Doing something just for the sake of not doing nothing was never my idea of doing anything. Yet last minute's hero couldn't very well announce now that he worked only as a single. "Meaning no disrespect, Father," I said without gagging. "Pretense goes against my grain."

Father Chuck was very understanding and not at all discerning. He thanked me for my honesty, then appealed for another volunteer.

This time a dozen hands shot up in the air.

"Hey, Father Baby!" A burly young black in a dashiki and an Afro waved a well-muscled arm. "You can light *my* pyre."

Laughter and applause.

There was no question which volunteer Father Chuck would select. After checking each other's calendars, the two men agreed on August 24. A self-appointed public relations man advised that black and white televised poorly, then stopped—he didn't mean *people*. "No black suit and white collar. Wear blue. And it'll make a good contrast to the flames."

With the business concluded, the meeting turned into an office party. Me, I was buried in the cheese dip and canapés, when—"Lord love you!"—a clap on my shoulder propelled caviar from my mouth like BB's. It was Father Chuck, who lauded my virtues while staring me in the eye, his own cavernous enough to look out the *back* of his head. I had experienced less intimacy during winter's shack-up with Heidi. "You're really *something*," he concluded.

How did one respond to such passion? Well, my parents are very cool folk. For a graduation present Dad, who anticipated my being drafted, sent me his World War II medals. And Terri's generous check was accompanied by a tape of a new television commercial that showed her performing such outlandish things, for her, as cleaning a bathroom and wearing an apron. Other commitments had kept both from attending graduation. So not wishing to feel like an orphan, I had stayed away too.

The priest, heedless of my squirms, extolled my offering. "It was prompted, contrary to popular opinion, out of love."

"Love?" The closest I'd ever come to love was self-love, which I had in very short supply.

Love, the priest repeated, like the Lord God's in sacrificing His only begotten Son.

Shame swept over this long-time shuttler between skepticism and disenchantment. "Father," I cried, "make it a doubleheader on August twenty-fourth, okay?"

But I'd had my chance and blown it. Father Chuck didn't say that, being too gracious. "More is less," he remarked, "Except for audiences. So come to the demonstration and bring a friend"—he winked broadly—"who has a blue suit."

I didn't count the days until August 24. Too busy finding myself a furnished apartment and wheedling R.I.'s tuition with a made-up abortion. (Accompanying Dad's check was a joyful note: "It's about time!")

Levi, receiving his orders to report for induction, accepted with the equanimity of one who believes that getting screwed is also part of the divine plan. With such disciples, it was a snap being God.

He accompanied me to the rally at the United Nations Plaza, festooned with banners demanding America's immediate withdrawal from Vietnam. The presence of dozens of people soon attracted more—all it takes to draw a large crowd in New York is a small crowd.

My friend pointed to a verse on the U.N. Plaza wall. *They shall beat their swords into plowshares and their spears into pruning hooks* . . . "I wonder why the U.N. omitted the name of the author."

"Everyone knows it's Jesus," I said.

"Really?"—with a rueful smile—"That must come as a big surprise to Isaiah."

Everything was going according to plot that afternoon, except for the media, who had stayed away. After all, the Vietnam War had been running longer than *Fiddler on the Roof.*

Suddenly, several members of APPLE PIE appeared with signs proclaiming violence as American as it and began hurling obscenities. When this tactic failed to ingratiate them with the crowd or to end the war, they beat their placards into heads and their signs into bodies until cops dragged them off amid cries of police brutality.

"Those fools ruined the demonstration," Levi exclaimed.

"Think so?" The P.R. man in front of us turned around. "Look." Men with cameras and sound equipment were crossing First Avenue.

As soon as the last APPLE PIEnik was carted off, Father Chuck entered in good old black and white, his eyes swiveling from side to side as though something were amiss with his vertical hold. Who could blame him for being nervous? Me, I'd sooner skydive without a parachute than speak in public. And what if something went awry and the priest's match wouldn't light? Or if the young black accidentally did.

"You never told me," Levi said. "How does one *pretend* to burn somebody alive?"

"Don't know," I said, "but they do it all the time in my mother's movies."

"With the same stunt men each time?"

Father Chuck made his way through the throng, numbering in the hundreds, and mounted the stone steps beneath

Isaiah's words. There he raised his arms and held them aloft as if in benediction. When the crowd quieted down, he lowered his outstretched arms to his sides until they paralleled the ground. Then from nowhere produced a sword that as it flashed at the crowd made people exclaim in surprise. A sleight of hand transformed the sword into something else.

"This," said the priest, "is a plowshare."

Oh's and ah's and wha'?s.

Next, Father Chuck held up a spear, and a wave of his hand made the spear's point take a sharp U-turn.

"Pruning hook." As the crowd applauded, he cried out, "That's what we expect from that United Nothingness!"

Cheers. Father Chuck had made his point neatly and entertainingly.

"For my next feat," he said, "I'll need an assistant."

Scores volunteered, with the nod naturally going to the Afro'd young black in a dashiki. The priest had him kneel and bow his head. After a moment of concentration or, perhaps, prayer, Father Chuck, making like Rowan and Martin's *Laugh-In,* emptied a flask over the supposedly startled black.

Howls from the audience. Only the P.R. man didn't laugh. "O my God!" he cried, and headed for the stage.

A cigarette lighter materialized in the priest's hand. He lit it and held it over his partner's wicklike hair, then announced, "Gasoline."

Though that was not believed, some people stirred uneasily. But as the wind wafted gas fumes our way, or the power of suggestion overcame us, a woman shouted, "It *is* gasoline!" At that moment the black faked an escape try. He couldn't run very far on his knees, however, with Father Chuck holding him down.

Uproar. Screams and milling around and cries for help. Police moved in, but fearful of provoking a tragedy, they didn't rush Father Chuck. Instead, they called for him to drop the lighter.

That was the cue for Walter Cronkite's three minutes.

"How shocked all of you are," Father Chuck exclaimed. "It hurts to see anyone so young and innocent harmed, right?"

Several people ventured onto the stone steps. To rescue the young black, I assumed, incorrectly. They snapped his picture. Except one man bent on saving his film for the precise moment of ignition.

Slowly, for maximum effect, Father Chuck moved the flame closer to his partner. "Why, then, have you allowed boys like him to die every night for a decade in Vietnam?" His voice cracked. "Why have you dispatched such boys to kill other boys for reasons nobody fathoms? Why haven't you stopped *those* killings?"

Several boos! Evidently, there were those who resented Father Chuck's interrupting himself for a commercial.

Levi remarked, "Some actor, that black."

Actually, the fellow was overacting. Eyes bulging, face sweating, body trembling, he caricatured terror. But the scene was going well, and the T.V. cameras were whirring it up.

The priest raged on as he turned toward the camera marked CBS-TV.

His shaky hands made me nervous. Any sudden movement by either man, and the lighter would ignite the Afro. Probably what the P.R. man, now on the second stone step, was frantically calling to the priest's attention.

A young black woman climbed the stone stage. "Please, mister," she begged. "Let my brother go."

Several people rushed up to snap her picture.

Father Chuck burst out, "Aren't they *all* our brothers?" And he began to cry. Real tears. That scared me. Clearly, he had lost control.

So did the crowd. A collective keen swept them, transforming us into a single mourner. I closed my eyes.

Screams made them fly open. The black was grappling with Father Chuck for possession of the cigarette lighter. When they toppled off the stage, the lighter dropped into the liquid. Suddenly, flames shot up a foot high.

"Terrific climax," I exclaimed. "How do you think it will play on television?"

Levi looked pensive. "Like a race war."

Prophetic words. For instead of focusing on black and white uniting to oppose the war on yellows, the local media spoke of white *versus* black when the young black testified *through an interpreter* that he had never seen the priest before in his life!

Mea culpa, I wrote Father Chuck in jail. Offering to testify, I asked why the black had lied. Was he a crazy—or what? Did he really expect to get away with pretending not to speak English well? Presently, the charge was reduced to reckless endangerment, and the priest released on bail with trial set for October.

To add up to a perfect .000, Father Chuck never made Walter Cronkite. He was upstaged by what happened that same day at the University of Wisconsin. To protest the Vietnam War, several youths had packed a truck with bags of fertilizer soaked in oil and sent it crashing against a building. In addition to causing damages of six million dollars and wiping out years of research, the blast wounded four people and killed a thirty-three-year-old professor.

At which point the overwhelming majority of students and over-thirties withdrew from the apocalypse. Fighting fire with fire would lead only to total conflagration. So the revolution did not take place that summer of '70.

That finally decided me on enrolling at R.I. Not as weird as you think. It would enable me to remain in the land I love, unmolested, while taking a doctorate in sociology concurrently at Columbia, where attendance wasn't compulsory. So none of that time would be wasted.

True, a lie is a poor substitute for the truth. But who ever invented anything better?

Stopping by to say good-bye to Levi that Saturday night, I interrupted a seance. The family was gathered around the dining-room table by the light of the lamppost outside. Levi held an unlit candle that looked like a braid of human hair preserved in colored wax. Only the Ouija board was missing.

"*Havdalah,*" Mr. Simon explained after welcoming me. "Separates the Sabbath from the secular week." He filled a silver goblet with wine and lit the candle. It revealed shadows groping the walls, a Rorschach test in fast motion. Raising the goblet, he chanted and drank, then gave us all a snort.

A second prayer was recited over a perforated silver box, which Mr. Simon sniffed before passing around. Delicious smells, like a bouquet of incense. Another prayer, over the plaited candle, as he counted his fingers in the candlelight and chanted anew. Then the family sang a hymn and kissed one another and shook hands, mine among them, and wished everyone a good week, and peace for Israel and Vietnam.

Tears filled Mrs. Simon's eyes.

That made me feel as if I had pointed Levi out myself to the draft board. After all, I was staying behind, a civilian. "I'm 4-F," I blurted out. "You know Joe Namath? I have his knees."

"Mazel tov!" Mrs. Simon clasped both my hands. "I'm so happy for the two of you."

Her lack of resentment made me feel guiltier. Yet what could I do, aside from the right thing? And who knew what that was any more? A devout believer in the trickle-down theory am I. Wrong at the top leadership inevitably trickles down to the people.

"I'm sure, though," Mr. Simon added after a moment's hesitation, "God will soon provide the world with peace."

Mrs. Simon looked dubious. "So why doesn't God provide *until* He provides?"

"Maybe," Mr. Simon said, "if all of us prayed hard enough."

But if prayer were that effective, I mused, governments would draft people to pray.

Over coffee and cake, we talked of everything but Levi's imminent departure. Unhappily, the conversation—about good old times with no mention of the future—resembled a wake for the living. Only, everyone at a wake knows nothing worse can happen to the departed.

"What a country, America," Mr. Simon remarked. "Unable to stand injustice anywhere except at home."

Mrs. Simon, citing Europe's appeasement of Hitler, defended the United States. "Isn't it awful! Having to make excuses for being loyal to your own country."

"Awful," Mr. Simon said, "that people who came to America to escape the Russian draft now have to send their sons and grandsons to fight in Asia."

She chided her husband. "Life is still the greatest bargain, dear. We get it for nothing, don't we?"

"True, there's no down payment." He nodded. "But some people never stop paying afterward. Sometimes with their sons."

Mrs. Simon's face sagged.

A chair scraped the floor. Abruptly, Levi stood up and invited me to join him for a swim. Since I felt like drowning myself, the Atlantic Ocean would come in handy.

"Take bathing suits," Mrs. Simon called after us. "You don't want to catch colds."

While we were changing in his room, Levi spoke disjointedly. "It's hard on them, my leaving. . . . My mother has a heart condition, my father bouts of depression. Legacies of the concentration camp. They rarely speak of those days, and I never ask. Both families wiped out. I'm named after both grandfathers. . . . I guess you'd call me an overprotective son."

We took towels and a blanket and jogged the few blocks to Manhattan Beach. Since it closed at nine, we jumped the locked gate, then raced through the sand. I beat my friend to the water and dove in. When I came up for air, he swam over.

"You're so fast, Drew. You *must* have Joe Namath's legs."

I squirmed like a fish on a hook. "Last one to London is a rotten egg," I said and swam off.

We raced each other from buoy to buoy. His winning each

time made me happy. It was high time nice guys finished first. After exhausting ourselves, possibly the water too, we staggered out and stretched out on the blanket.

Levi raised his right arm overhead and pointed to the expanse of black velvet. "See those pinpricks of light, Drew? Once I believed them emanations from a world of pure goodness that existed on the *other* side of the sky. The original Garden of Eden. It glimmered through those tiny holes. Split the sky open instead of the atom, I thought, and peace and love would spill down and flood the earth." He dropped his arm, embarrassed. "Now for the second chorus of 'Over the Rainbow.'"

I grew melancholy. College graduation . . . end of summer . . . my friend's going away . . . sad, sadder, saddest. To me good-byes represented small deaths. But at least Levi's departure distressed people. "Your mother and father love you very much, don't they?"

Levi stared at me. "They're my parents. Don't yours?"

"Of course," I said, too loudly. "My mother and father say they love me. All the time they say that."

"Not my parents. But we see love."

"See?"

An emphatic shake of the head. "The correct translation from the Hebrew of 'Love thy neighbor' is '*Do* love to your neighbor.' Meaning, love is not what you feel or say, but how you act. Actually, you are what you do."

"Sort of like, 'You are what you eat'?"

Levi laughed. "To old-fashioned Jewish mothers, you are *if* you eat. Probably on account of the Jews being so poor when they came to America. Only the slaves were poorer."

"My father put another twist on that. A lemon twist. You are if you drink. Over*eating*, Dad considers unkosher."

Levi eyed me curiously. "You're a paradox, Drew. You sound Jewish. And yet . . ."

"Well, my father is Jewish. So is Hollywood, where I grew up. All those agents, producers, writers. . . . You should hear Mary Tyler Moore, and she was educated by nuns."

"Oh," Levi said. "Must have been hard on you, the inter-marriage."

"You mean the divorce," I blurted out. "Makes a person stateless."

My confession embarrassed him. And what could he say, "Come on a my house"? Levi stood up, uncomfortable. "Guess I got a home for the next two years, the army. If—" He checked himself.

If he stayed lucky for two years. I grabbed him by the arm and exclaimed, "The war's sure to end long before then. Levi, I'm *betting* on it."

A crooked smile. "I'll be damned if I bet against you, Drew."

The Simons had retired by the time we returned. On top of my pants lay a large box of goodies. When I showed reluctance to accept the gift, Levi said, "My mother loves to give. Accepting will be *your* gift." Then he asked me a favor, to report to him on the Simons' health. "My parents are terrible. Every once in a while when I ask how they are, Mom or Dad will answer, 'Better.' So be sure to ask one about the other. That way you may get the truth."

Well, it took all kinds of liars to make this world.

Finally the good-byes with me feeling what Congress should have felt, sending surrogates to war. Of the 234 draft-eligible sons of congressmen, forty-eight served in the armed forces, but only twenty-six in Vietnam and only eight in com-bat. One of these was wounded, none killed. Sheer coinci-dence, of course.

Levi gripped my hand in his. "*Shalom*, Drew. *L'hitraot*. That's Hebrew for 'Till we meet again.' Meanwhile, my thanks. Worrying so about me, trying to save me from the draft. Those too are acts of love."

Apparently, there is retribution. It zapped me on registra-tion day, starting in a coffee shop near R.I., when a fellow interviewee sat down beside me, pointing to my breakfast. "How's the bacon and eggs here?" he asked.

I looked him square in the eye. "This is *lox* and eggs."

He stared at the curling bacon. "*Crisp lox?*"

"There's nothing worse," I assured him.

In the school lounge other augurs of debacle to come. R.I. had accepted one third of the male applicants and half the females. Yes, that made me number thirteen. And then the very tall redhead, who looked more like the farmer's daughter than a rabbi's, approached to inquire after Levi. "Didn't he introduce us once at Columbia?" said Isaca Zion.

I spilled coffee over my pants and excused myself.

Dean Diamond, entering with the aristocratic old professor, called for attention. The seat nearest the door didn't make me feel less surrounded. Maybe I'd already blundered by saying yes to "Do you think Spiro Agnew is a *dreck?*"

The dean introduced Dr. Tchernichovsky, whom he described as a *mentsch* among the mechanical people, a believer that whereas ethics teaches the difference between right and wrong, only religion can instill the faith that good will triumph in the end. "Dr. Tchernichovsky never talks over anyone's head," Dr. Diamond said. "He talks to where your head should be."

The professor, a tall, ramrod-straight septuagenarian with broad shoulders and a stern visage—Michelangelo's *Moses* come to life minus the horns—surveyed the students for a long moment. "Let me confess," he began. "Every teacher encountering a new class feels envy. While he ages year by year, finally day by day, they stay forever young. Add the teacher's realization that he's arrived at his final destination prior to the eternal one. So I envy your limitless opportunities too." He smiled. "Happily, there's a cure.

"Mythology concerned itself primarily with the question 'What is my fate?' and paganism with 'What are my desires?' But the authentic Jew asks, 'What is my role? my task? my obligations? How can I fulfill God's will?' That means, irrespective of whether the Lord Himself can fulfill it."

Amazing. Was he calling God inept?

"My task now, for as long as God gives me strength, or for

as long as I can wrest the strength from Him—the faculty's task is to light in you, while fanning in ourselves, the will to challenge and to overcome the obstacles and the negativity that reality always presents to the ideal, to value, to God."

Some of that sailed overhead. So I sat up straighter in my chair.

"What is *your* task these coming four years? In the words of Martin Buber, '*You yourself must begin*. Existence will remain meaningless if you yourself do not penetrate it with active love. Everything is waiting to be hallowed by you, realized by you. God created the world, drew it out of Himself so that you may bring it closer to Him. Meet the world with the fullness of your being, and you shall meet Him.' "

A beautiful talk. It would surely have inspired me, were I inspirable. When was the last time I'd been inspired? . . . Oh, yes. John F. Kennedy's inaugural address.

> Now the trumpet summons us again—a call to bear the burden of a long twilight struggle against the common enemies of man: tyranny, disease and war itself. . . . The energy, the faith, the devotion which we bring to this endeavor will light our country and all who serve it, and the glow from that fire can truly light the world.

Who knew then that meant Vietnam?

Doom struck with distribution of the reading list. Half of it was unintelligible, being in a foreign language, *Hebrew*. Even the Holy Bible! HEBREW. Till that moment it hadn't occurred to me that the Virgin Mary never spoke with Siobhan McKenna's Irish brogue. A plague on Cecil B. De Mille and George Stevens!

Demoralized, I evacuated the building.

Blocks away I found myself trailing a little pigtailed girl with a foreign book in her hand. Levi had taught at an afternoon Hebrew school—now I was considering mugging for a Hebrew *Dick and Jane*. That seemed wiser than stopping a child on the street and offering her money.

Such was my confusion that only when she paused to look both ways before crossing the street did I notice that she was not Middle Eastern, but Far. There and then I gave up the rabbinical ghost.

Stopovers at a few bars eased the pain. Also my equilibrium. When I staggered up to my door, I almost broke my neck stumbling over something large enough to be self-pity materialized. It turned out to be a package, however. The accompanying note read:

> Since I baked too much to fit into the trunk we just shipped to Levi, would you kindly do us a big favor and take these extras off our hands?
>
> With love,
> Mr. and Mrs. Simon

The Simons! Hadn't Levi asked me to do him the immense favor of looking them up? And weren't there three full weeks to go before the semester started? If the Lord could create an entire universe in less than a third of that time, why then O why couldn't I fly over the goddamn rainbow?

THREE

Night fell before I was sober enough to call at the Simons'. Once inside I hardly knew where to begin. It wasn't as if everyone was dying to know Hebrew. More New Yorkers spoke Swahili.

"Happened to be swimming by—"

"You were swimming?" Mrs. Simon said. "In the rain?"

I inquired after Levi. His *Kaddish*, Mr. Simon said, was now being trained in basics like maiming and killing.

"*Kaddish?*"

"A son who'll recite the *Kaddish* memorial prayer for his parents," Mrs. Simon explained. Seeing me wince, she hastened to add, "Nothing morbid about that. It's consoling. Makes my husband and me and our parents . . . unbroken. Few among the Six Million are so fortunate."

"Who but the living can the dead trust to carry on for them?" Mr. Simon picked up my cup of wine. "So *l'chaim*, to life." He forced the hair of the dog on me. Exactly what I needed to do without.

Something puzzled me, I remarked, as the room slowly revolved on its axis. The New Left Jews at Columbia. Why did they battle for every cause under the sun except the Jews'?

A wry smile appeared on Mr. Simon's face. "In my native Czechoslovakia, everybody identified himself as either a Czech or a Slovak," he said. "Only Jews called themselves Czechoslovakians." The smile suddenly vanished without a trace. He lit a cigarette. "Only in dreams are all men brothers. Sometimes I wonder if we did right, not telling Levi more about the concentration camps. *All* the details. He's as good as gold, our son. But gold needs an alloy, to harden it."

Mrs. Simon flared. "Of course we did right! I would never raise a child of mine to be a hater. Nobody can make a life out of bitterness."

Mr. Simon put out the cigarette without having taken a second puff. "Who said anything about hate? I'm talking about immunizing *against* hate. Levi went off without knowing in his bones what people are capable of. That's like traveling the world without inoculation shots. Sometimes I think what killed the Six Million was Jewish optimism, our incorrigible faith in the goodness of man."

"Not so," Mrs. Simon said. "Optimism and faith pulled me through."

Mr. Simon faced me. "You know what my wife also believed at one time? That when the Americans liberated the camps, they'd jail all the inmates. Someplace we'd never be seen again."

I didn't understand. "Why?"

"To prevent us from telling what had happened inside the

camps. Because nobody in the world would be able to stand the horrifying truth. Once the facts were known, my wife thought, people all over the world would go mad."

"So I was wrong. I'm not sorry. The world is *mashuga* enough as it is," Mrs. Simon said. "But is this how to treat a guest? To arguments?" She left the room, to invite me into the kitchen some minutes later for a late snack.

Playing with the rib steak before me, I asked how Levi was managing in the unkosher army.

Losing weight and helping the chaplain to conduct Sabbath services for Jewish personnel.

"Tough language to learn, Hebrew. Isn't it?"

"Oh, I don't know," Mr. Simon said. "In Israel even the dogs understand Hebrew."

"A language that's read backward? Would be impossible for *me*."

Mr. Simon rose to the bait. In a moment he brought out Levi's aids for beginners. Since Hebrew is as phonetic as Spanish—for which *muchas gracias*—it didn't take long to memorize a dozen cards and read makeshift sentences like "She sells sea shells by seashore" and "Bye-bye, Baby Bubie."

Just as I was beginning to feel I had a future as a civilian, Mr. Simon gathered up the alphabet. "You don't really want to learn all this, Drew."

"Never wanted anything more!" My vehemence startled the Simons. "I mean, all the great men spoke Hebrew—Moses, Freud, Jesus."

Mr. Simon shook his head. "Jesus spoke Aramaic, the *lingua franca* of the day."

I was surprised. "Nobody wished the Virgin Mary mazel tov on Christmas Eve?"

Apparently not. The Roman Empire celebrated December 25 as the Birthday of the Unconquered Sun. Because few pagans would renounce its drunken revelry, Christian missionaries converted that date into Jesus' birthday.

I spent the night in Levi's room memorizing all the letters, dots and dashes, and (Hebrew being indeed backward, with no capital letters) special *final* letters. But how to check my accuracy? On the top of one bookshelf lay a Hebrew pamphlet on top of a record, which I played until dawn, chanting all the while à la "Sing Along with Mitch Miller."

Mr. Simon had already left for work in the diamond center when I awoke, and Mrs. Simon laughed at my request to monitor my reading. "But that's Levi's bar mitzvah portion." Seeing I was serious, she slipped a skullcap on my head, even as she protested.

I tackled the unintelligible paragraph with all my might and plenty of mistakes. At chant's end Mrs. Simon exclaimed, "I can't believe it! Drew Einstein."

Elated, I tossed the pamphlet in the air. Mrs. Simon scrambled to catch it. Failing, she picked up the pamphlet and kissed it, then waved aside my apology. "How could you know this is from the Torah? But a few more lessons, Drew, and you'll read as well as any bar mitzvah boy."

"Where *does* a person learn Hebrew?" I said casually. "In a *hurry*." She recommended the Ulpan at the Jewish Agency on Park Avenue.

"Is that where you learned?"

Mrs. Simon closed her eyes as if to summon up a memory. Or was it to blot it out? "I studied Hebrew in concentration camp," she said quietly. "That was my way of fighting back."

"*Study* in concentration camp?"

On the evening before five thousand Jews were scheduled to die, four hundred attended the library. She also told of ghettos that, until their liquidation, organized religious celebrations, schools, choirs, plays, concerts, poetry readings. Noting my amazement, Mrs. Simon said, "For grieving there is always cause. The religious person seeks out causes for rejoicing."

"But why didn't the Jews fight back, *really* fight back?"

"Is *that* the question?" A sigh so deep it seemed to drain all the color from her cheeks. "I always thought the real question is, Why did Christians torture and murder?"

Even before the start of the semester, the freshman class was appointed to serve as adjunct rabbis on the High Holidays. Can you imagine in a synagogue pulpit on Rosh Hashonah and Yom Kippur someone whose entire Hebrew repertoire consists of "She sells sea shells by seashore" and "Bye-bye, Baby Bubie"?

Dean Diamond responded to my demurral with: "So?"

How do you argue with a So? A Why, you can counter with Why *not*? But So not? And then you risk running those two words together.

He removed his black horn-rimmed glasses and searched my face. "You can't read English, Baron?"

Huh?

"That's about all a High Holidays student-rabbi does. So what's troubling you?"

Only sacrilege. I knew how *I'd* feel if Pope Paul turned out to be Golda Meir in drag. "Mediating between God and man," I said. "That's no job for freshmen."

"Baron, we Jews eliminated the middleman thousands of years ago. Any *thirteen*-year-old may lead a Jewish service." The dean fixed me with a baleful eye.

"Still and all. Long Island is *full* of thirteen-year-olds."

Dr. Diamond spoke slowly, as if telling a pubescent the facts of religious life. "That temple needs you, Baron, for the same reason delicatessens hang salamis in their windows. Symbols are the only universal language. Every institution, every profession, every person displays something up front to indicate what or who it or he is. Only the *mohel* doesn't."

"Why doesn't the *mohel*?" I hoped to claim his prerogative.

"A foreskin in the front window?" Dr. Diamond slammed his glasses down on the desk. "What is it with you, Baron?"

Sometimes the safest lie is the truth. So I told one. Getting up in front of people and speaking scared the hell out of me. Whenever called upon for a speech, I always feared that as soon as my dry mouth opened, dust would fly out and rigor mortis set in. Only stomach cramps kept me breathing throughout.

The dean walked around the desk and placed both hands on my shoulders. "Why didn't you say so in the first place?"

Everyone loves a confidence. Had I confessed a long history as a pulpit-wetter, Dr. Diamond would have hugged me to his bosom.

"You don't have a phobia, do you? Because if you do, Baron . . ." He cleared his throat. "Moses had his brother Aaron act as his spokesman. But that's not feasible here. Much as it would pain us, the Rabbinical Institute of America would have to turn Moses away."

You can see—well, *can't* you—I had no choice.

When people had convictions, they built cathedrals. Now that they have concepts only, they build Temple Shaloms. A showpiece of rubbed aluminum steel, with a baked enamel coat of pink and a huge door of aluminum finished in bronze and flanked by Venetian-glass mosaics, the temple with a heart-shaped façade sat on a raised plaza at the head of a landscaped mall.

"Gorgeous?" A middle-aged man had sneaked up on me, gleaming in a pomaded razor haircut, black silk suit, silver tie, and colorless nail polish. The pinky of his left hand glittered with a diamond ring as large as a boil.

I introduced myself and my mission with all of the aplomb of one terrified lest he live to fulfill it. "Why the heart shape?" I asked. First building I'd ever seen with a cardiac condition.

"Most people do take it as symbolic of 'Thou shalt love the Lord thy God with all thy heart'"—the man's teeth flashed in a broad smile—"or for somebody bending over to wash the bathtub. But seriously . . . it's the Ten Commandments."

The man volunteered to show me around what he called "the plant." Inside the marble lobby, he kept repeating my name like a tic. Of enormous help should I suddenly come down with amnesia. "Two and a half million, Andrew. And today, Andrew, it'd cost twice that."

"They thought God wouldn't be able to locate anything smaller?"

"Heh-heh," said Nat Gwirtz without baring a tooth. He pointed to the left—Commandments One through Five. "Offices and the youth lounge." Six, he showed me, was the sanctuary, and Seven through Ten all flocked wallpaper, satin drapes, and crystal chandeliers. "Where we have the finest affairs, Andrew. Elegant?"

"Elegant isn't the word." Gaudy was. Mirrored walls and ceilings? What kind of perverts liked to watch themselves eating? "Why is the ballroom five times the size of the sanctuary?"

"Let's face it. Which gets the more play?" To accommodate the overflow on High Holidays, the wall between the two rooms was raised. He demonstrated by flicking a switch.

Whereas the ballroom suggested a harem out of the *Arabian Nights*—a sign heralded a future congregational Sabbath dinner: "*Sure to be a fun evening!*"—the modernistic sanctuary was modeled after the State Theater at Lincoln Center. In a pinch, I suppose, people could pray there.

The second floor was classrooms, plus cozy meeting rooms for bridge, folk dancing, woodwork, painting, ceramics, landscaping, dramatics, Weight Watchers. Welcome to the suburban afterlife.

"Now, Andrew, for the *pièce de résistance*." Nat Gwirtz ushered me into the health club with a gymnasium, basketball court, locker room, showers, exercise rooms, handball court, steam rooms.

"Ever see anything to match this temple, Andrew?"

Back on the first floor, I asked the obvious as we passed a door emblazoned THE FINEST. "Muhammad Ali trains here?"

"The Finest," growled Nat Gwirtz, "is *the* caterer of Long Island, Andrew." He shot his cuffs, revealing a pair of winking diamond cuff links. "And I, Andrew, am its manager."

"Inside the temple?" Oh, wow. What would Jesus say? Two thousand years, and those Jews are still at it.

"Know how much we paid for an exclusive? And we kick back five percent of the food and liquor bills on every affair. Why, The Finest keeps this temple afloat."

And what was to stop caterers, once they got the hang of the religious game, from muscling out the Father and opening up chains of synagogues across the country, like Kentucky Fried Chicken? Still, you had to hand it to Temple Shalom. No promises here of pie in the sky when you die. This synagogue, thanks to The Finest, delivered.

Nat Gwirtz held out a finger sideways. "The rabbi's study is the fourth door on the left, Baron."

I wondered which kind of clergyman Brownmiller would be. The few Christian ones of my acquaintance were either religious belligerents with X-ray stares, who treated everyone like a potential Luther, or Clark-Kent mild with light voices and tentative demeanors, whose knees seemed to buckle whenever we shook hands. That made me feel brutish and sinful, but good. As for rabbis, I never saw one who wasn't congratulating some bar mitzvah kid on the magnificent accomplishment of having reached his thirteenth birthday.

The secretary scanned me up and down. "You're tall," she noted.

"I'm wearing socks." (I always try to meet non sequiturs halfway.)

In the adjoining office between columns of books on a paper-strewn desk, peeped Rabbi Brownmiller, framed by a dozen plaques on the wall behind him. He greeted me warmly, adding as he started to rise, "You're tall."

"The only people who think so are shor—" The rabbi hadn't started to rise. He was already risen to a height of about five foot two. "—ly observant." I executed half a deep-knee bend and lurched forward, like Groucho Marx on the prowl.

A boyish face belying his grizzled curly top, Rabbi Brownmiller offered me a seat, then perched atop his desk. "Hope things have changed at R.I. since my student days," he said. "In four years there the subject of the rabbi's role never arose. The faculty consisted of scholars who never held pulpits, except for one, Dr. Furth. But whenever asked about his experiences, his eyes glazed over. You know what one sage said? 'A rabbi whose congregation doesn't want to drive him out of town isn't a rabbi, and a rabbi they do drive out isn't a man.' . . . Or maybe Dr. Furth was just a poor electrician."

"Electrician?"

"Today's congregants expect their clergy to turn them on. Come, Andrew."

Inside the sanctuary, Rabbi Brownmiller, almost apologetic, recounted an ancient rabbinic tale of a flute of reeds that dated back to Moses. Its sweet tones delighted all the worshipers in the ancient Temple in Jerusalem. Then the priests inlaid the flute with gold. It looked exquisite, but now it sounded metallic and its tones jarred. "To the children of starving immigrants, this affluent edifice is the living end," he said. "But to children raised in luxury, it's merely overkill."

He handed me a book entitled *Union Prayer Book II*. "The choir opens the service with the hymn on page seven. You, Andrew, continue with page eight." (Every blessed word was in English.) "Responsive reading on page nine." (More heavenly English.) "Read the *Borchu* on the following page."

Uh-oh. Entirely in Hebrew except for *(Congregation rises)* and *(Congregation is seated)*. "I read all that Hebrew on page eleven?"

"No, no. Just the first two lines." (Only nine Hebrew words, praise be.) "Same procedure with the *Sh'ma*." (Only a dozen words in Hebrew.) Page after page of English readings were assigned to me—solo, responsively with the congregation, in unison with them, and best of all, silently—leaving the majority of the Hebrew to the choir.

"Now, then. Let's roll the Torah."

Ascending the pulpit, the rabbi went up to the huge front closet over which hung an Eternal Light patterned after Catholic incense vessels. The curtains, when parted, revealed six Torahs, crowned and dressed in velvet, like kings and queens holding court on pale blue satin. He took the purple Torah from the Ark.

"Would you undress it, Andrew?"

The silver adornments and scepter in the form of a tiny sculpted hand came off easily enough. But where was the zipper located on the cover? Finally, I yanked it off over the twin posts to which the scroll was attached, then unbuckled the girdle that held it together.

Rabbi Brownmiller laid the scroll on the altar, and, taking hold of one post, motioned me to hold the other, then unrolled the parchment, which was two feet high and hundreds long. An exquisite work of calligraphy, but I could more easily read a Picasso.

"Here's the place, Andrew. Read from here"—he pointed to a spot thousands of letters away—"to here."

"You're *kidding!*"

He looked up in surprise.

"I mean, if I read nearly the entire service and the scroll too, what will your congregation think? I mean . . ." Usually, cold sweats hamper my power of expression. Somehow I managed to inquire what Rabbi Brownmiller planned to do during my Rosh Hashonah service.

"Is this your first High Holidays?" he exclaimed. "I, of course, shall deliver the sermon."

The blowing of the shofar on Rosh Hashonah says to us: Awake from your slumber and rouse yourselves. Search your deeds and turn ye in repentance. Remember your Creator, ye who forget truth. Look to your souls and mend your ways and deeds. Let everyone forsake his wicked path and his evil purpose.

—Maimonides

Unnerving, that preface in the High Holy Days prayer book. What scared me though was the Torah portion, virtually unreadable with its stylized lettering and neither vowels nor punctuation. Remember that subway ad for speedywriting, "F u knt prkts shrthand frgt it"?

The Ulpan's Mr. Fish helped. Asked for coaching in the Torah version, he nodded, opened his mouth, and out came *Pagliacci*. Well, maybe not the opera, but neither was it a reading.

The Torah was always chanted, he noted, pointing to a score of different melody marks above and below the Hebrew words. As an aid, Mr. Fish loaned me a book with a facsimile of the Torah portion, curlicues and all. As if I could work a miracle that not even Caruso could have pulled off. Singing the unreadable.

You know what they say about perseverance, how stick-to-it-iveness always pays off in the end? After two bleary-eyed days, I was still confusing the vowel-less, unpunctuated words. Easy to do when a simple *I lv hm*, for example, can be read as *I leave home* or *Olivia, hum!* or *I love Him* or *I love ham*.

At my next Ulpan lesson, I taped Mr. Fish chanting the Torah portion. Did that help when I next took on Genesis? Is the Pope Irish?

As Rosh Hashonah closed in on me, I found myself praying. How mortifying. Mystifying too. So far gone was I that when the doorbell rang fifty-one hours before the holiday, I raced to admit my prayer answered.

On the threshhold stood a sprite-like middle-aged man, who had nothing at all together. His faded blue jeans and tie-dyed T-shirt went as well with his crew cut as his dyed black hair with his lined face, or his shiny new American Tourister overnight case with his scuffed black laced shoes. Only his deep-set charcoal eyes matched—each other and nothing else. "Andrew Baron?"

I nodded.

"You don't recognize me? Father Chuck." He gloated. "Fooled you, didn't I?"

My mouth fell open.

"You wrote that if ever there was anything you could do. Well, I'm hiding out."

I invited the priest inside and gave him a cup of coffee and vanilla wafers before inquiring who was after him.

"Don't you read *The Daily News*, page four? I jumped bail." His face lit up with a grin, which vanished as he told of being framed by a black agent provocateur. So *that* accounted for his pretended ignorance of the mock immolation! No, the priest explained, that was *another* black. Father Chuck had selected the other by mistake.

How did he know the first black was a provocateur?

It was his idea to use real gasoline and he never came to the police afterward. Yet Father Chuck thanked God for his predicament. An indicted fugitive priest was good copy, especially one who'd surface regularly to speak out. "Meet the Catholic Pimpernel," he concluded with a mock flourish, before asking to stay. "The cops know nothing about *you*."

Unless, like Father Chuck, they had made a note of my letter to him. But what could I say—whither thou goest, I fleest? "Okay, just so long," I quipped, "as you don't insist on hearing my confession."

His eyes lit up. "You're Catholic? I should have guessed." Gravitating to my desk, he picked up the *Union Prayer Book II*. I had carelessly left it open, never dreaming a priest would be rooming with me. "What are you doing with this, Andrew?"

"Practicing," I said without moving my lips.

"On a Jewish prayer book?"

"Well . . . you see . . ." (Forgive me, Father, for I never do stop sinning.) "Well . . . I'm a rabbinical student. My mother, she was, among other things, Catholic for awhile."

"Oh. What made her fall away?"

"Marriage. The church wouldn't recognize all of hers."

The priest was surprisingly sympathetic. "Everyone has a cross to bear." He told of being chased away by the rector of a famous Fifth Avenue church while begging money for Vietnamese children and refugees from parishioners arriving in chauffeured limousines for the Christmas choral service. "If anything outrages Christians more than an attack on Christianity, it's the practice of it." Father Chuck snorted. "That fancy church wasn't the Church. The Church is the *Beth Emeth*. You look so blank, Andrew." When I confessed ignorance of Latin, the priest said, "But *Beth Emeth*, house of truth, the name of so many synagogues, is Hebrew."

"Oh, *that* Beth. You see, Father, there's this Long Island synagogue in the town of Shirley. The Shirley Temple. *Also* very confusing."

Rabbi Brownmiller invited me to dine with his family on Rosh Hashonah Eve, but I went to temple instead to battle it out with my nemesis Genesis. Some practical joker there had hung up a fringed fuscia banner over the grand marble entranceway:

```
Keep Your Heavenly Cool
with AIR CONDITIONING
By JULE
```

After dumping the streamer into the Judaica Boutique Shoppe's trash basket, I entered the empty sanctuary. But my bad luck held steady. The door to the Torah's blessed repository wouldn't open. Any horror-movie buff knew there had to be a secret switch. So I felt up the Ark and its surrounding marble frame, then stomped the pulpit floor and banged the lectern from top to bottom. That got me nothing but sore knuckles. But lo! On the inside of the lectern I spied a pearl button. When pressed, it opened the doors of the Ark and, happily, not the floor beneath me.

A race for the purple Torah ended at the starting line. All the covers had been changed to *white!* The Torahs were now as indistinguishable as a giant set of buck teeth.

My quarry had to be the middle one, the most convenient. But with six Torahs, there were *two* in the middle. Certain that the correct one was on the right, I chose the left, because I was sure to have guessed wrong.

After undressing the Torah, I laid it on the altar and opened it with fingers crossed. The scroll wasn't divided into chapters. Nor even sentences. So even if I happened on the right Torah, it would be difficult to locate Genesis, 22. With the wrong scroll, as this turned out to be, impossible. As if that weren't enough, one end of the scroll rolled off the reading table and, hitting the floor, unwound like Rapunzel's hair. And with nobody holding the opposite end, the Torah couldn't be rewound tight enough to fit inside its cover. It was like stuffing a girl in her eighth month back into her wedding gown.

By then, parishioners were arriving. So I shoved the Torah into the farthest corner of the Ark, buckled the white cover to its bulging front with the belt, then crowned it and closed the Ark. Mission delayed—the Torah was read the following morning. Before noon that mother Necessity would have to come through for me.

As I was entering the rabbi's study, a florid-faced man elbowed me aside. "Well? well? well?" he cried. "Found it yet?"

Rabbi Brownmiller shook his head and explained to me. "Jule here graciously donated the air conditioning for the sanctuary. You know how hot it often gets on the High Holidays."

"Somebody lost the air conditioning?"

"The streamer that went with it."

"Oh. Why do you need that? People can *feel* air conditioning."

"Yes," growled Jule, "and stained-glass windows can be *seen*. But donors still get their names on them, don't they?" He stormed out.

I donned the long white gown handed me, feeling bridal. Me pure as the driven snow? Somebody up there must still be snickering.

Rabbi Brownmiller ran his hands over his own white robe trimmed with white velvet. "I love the whiteness of the High Holidays," he said. "During my first Days of Awe as a rabbi, I imagined the white Torah behind me was the sun, using me as a prism to refract its precepts to the congregation."

Enter the temple president. Dark eyebrows meeting over the bridge of a weak nose, as if to guard against an advancing low forehead, Mr. Sheridan wore the black suit and white boutonniere of the head floorwalker in a department store.

Jule, he reported, was threatening to turn off the air conditioning.

"Are you suggesting," said the rabbi, "I work *Air Conditioning by Jule* into my sermon?"

"I'll do the honors," said the president. "Know how many Conservative families joined our temple because of the air conditioning?"

At precisely eight o'clock we left the office, me sweating like one on the outskirts of hell, and stepped through a side door onto the pulpit. There we were hit over the ears by a deafening pipe-organ prelude, which stopped abruptly when the Phantom of the Opera spied our entry. The sanctuary plunged into silence. As my companions took seats on either side of the Ark, two thousand eight hundred and forty-six eyes focused on me treading up to the lectern on knees suddenly turned to club soda.

"He's tall," several people in the front row whispered to each other. "Twitching," one observed.

Who had a better right? Aside from my deathly fear of public speaking, I had just noticed the words inscribed over the Ark in dancing letters of flame, "Know before Whom you stand." What, it suddenly hit me with the force of a fist to the pit of my sinking stomach, what if there really was a God and vengeance truly His?

Oh, wow! I had almost forgotten my skullcap. Swiftly, I sneaked it on my head. When the choir finished the opening hymn, I forced my jaws apart and intoned what I had written in red ink in my prayer book for fear of going up on the line. "Our. Service. Continues. On. Page. Eight." One hand held the book to my nose, the other pointed to each syllable lest I lose the place. "In the twilight of the vanishing year . . ."

Without once lifting my eyes to the congregation, I finally reached the word *Sermon*. My sense of relief would have been greater if not for the leather-lunged woman in the first row. Always a few words ahead of me during the readings in unison, she had caused me to proclaim, "Hear O Israel, the Lord our God, the Lord is Love."

Otherwise, I hadn't shortchanged my audience. Surely,

nobody since the Flood had prayed more ardently. When I took my seat, Rabbi Brownmiller leaned over to say, "Very nice, Andrew. But at tomorrow morning's service, read with *less* feeling."

Mr. President stepped up to the lectern with more commercials than the "Johnny Carson Show." For Israel Bonds, the Yom Kippur Ball, sisterhood's theater party, a rally for Soviet Jewry, men's club father-and-son night with a Green Bay Packer, the Adult Jewish Education program, Jule's heavenly air conditioning.

Afterward, in the rabbi's study, the president expressed his own feelings with an emotional *"Why the yarmulke!"* Oddly, a sincere "Same to you" enraged the man. "I asked you, Baron"—Mr. Sheridan snatched the skullcap off my head and shook it in my face—"why did you wear this?"

Evidently a blunder to use a black one when the color scheme was white.

"Are you trying to subvert us, Baron? This temple is *Reform.*"

"Nobody told me—I mean—"

The rabbi took the skullcap from Mr. Sheridan and returned it to me. "Looks like the one my father wears," he said. "Well, *gut yuntiff*, gentlemen. May both of you be inscribed for a sweet year."

How to thank the rabbi for his graciousness? "Jule's streamer," I confessed. "It's in the trash basket in the Judaica Shoppe."

Rabbi Brownmiller sighed. "So who asked you?"

Father Chuck had waited up with an idea that had come to him while reading brief excerpts of Rosh Hashonah Eve sermons in the early *Times*. "Suppose tomorrow a Rosh Hashonah preacher condemned the Vietnam War in the strongest language."

"It would still get only a paragraph."

"Even if the Rosh Hashonah preacher was an uninvited Roman Catholic fugitive priest?"

"The first pulpit hijacking!"

"How about your temple?"

I could never object to a proposal of Father Chuck's. Familiarity, instead of breeding contempt during our two days together, had fostered its opposite. That doesn't mean I believed in all he said. But *he* did. And how many such people are there?

"You have doubts, Drew?"

"All the time, Father. What about you?"

"Never when I'm right," he said without hesitation. The prophet Amos burst into the sanctuary at Beth El during the great fall festival to warn the well-dressed pilgrims of impending destruction. "Ever since those days, your own Rabbi Zion told me, tradition has let anyone interrupt a Jewish service to protest injustice."

Since Father Chuck's surprise appearance was scheduled directly after the sermon at noon, he slept late. Me, I went to the temple at eight o'clock to write crib notes into the correct Torah. The one from the night before looked so *en déshabillé*, I asked the caretaker's help in rolling the scroll back into shape. Together, we unwound, then rewound. All the while, he exclaimed over the many months it took the specially trained scribe to write a scroll. With erasures forbidden, any mistake, or malicious or impure thought, meant an entire panel of several chapters had to be redone. "You know what Rabbi Brownmiller calls the Torah?" said the caretaker, departing. "God's love letters."

An examination of the other middle Torah proved my first guess of the night before correct. Pony in one hand, pencil in the other, I was about to insert the vowels, punctuation and melody marks, when the caretaker's words stayed me. It wasn't right to treat anyone's love letters as if they were subway cars. So back into the Ark went the scroll. I would lip-sync the Torah portion to Mr. Fish's tape, as singers in films always do to prerecordings.

In the rabbi's office, Mr. Sheridan was still exercised over my head, which he wanted bared. I donned my yarmulke anyway. Unable to defy the President of the United States, I could at least stand up to a temple's.

The service opened at ten o'clock, people straggling in. Having survived the evening service, I expected this one to be less nerve-racking. But why should panic subside when it can just as easily mount? What if the tape deck got stuck!

Finally . . . Torah time, the Ark opening after "And they shall beat their swords into plowshares. . . ." A good cue for Father Chuck. But his intention was for after the sermon.

Rabbi Brownmiller removed the Torah from the Ark and held it high. "Hear O Israel, the Lord our God, the Lord is One," he cried with particular emphasis, it seemed, on the number. After the scroll was undressed and spread out on the altar, while the choir sang a paraphrase of the Lord's Prayer, he took a seat.

Mr. Sheridan recited the opening blessings over the Torah, but instead of taking a bow and leaving, rooted himself next to me. How could I switch on the tape recorder! He moved yet closer. "What are you waiting for, Baron? Read."

With him on top of me to note my dumb show? "As soon as you sit down, Mr. Sheridan."

"What?"

"I can't read with somebody looking over my shoulder. Makes me nervous."

After Mr. Sheridan withdrew, muttering, I groped between the Bibles nearby for the recorder. Soon we were off, my lips moving to Mr. Fish's aria. Almost at once the congregation started to buzz. If they were noticing the difference between my speaking and singing voices, afterward I would cite Maria Callas and T.V.'s Gomer Pyle. Otherwise, no problems with mouthing, except for the temptation to sing along with Mr. Fish.

No sooner had we finished, the tape and I, than Mr. Sheridan returned for the closing blessing. Rabbi Brownmiller appeared too, and, helping to dress the Torah, asked anxiously if the president required medical attention. Since the giving of the Ten Commandments, it seemed, nobody had ever sat down between blessings.

Mr. Sheridan snarled, "You think *I'm* the sick one here?"

Afterward, I read a chapter in English from I Samuel. Then came the shofar service, during which someone blew a genuine ram's horn, which sounded threatening when heard in conjunction with "Naught is hidden from Thine eyes, O Lord." Another perfect cue for Father Chuck, which remained unseized.

"Wars." Rabbi Brownmiller's sermon was a mixture of sorrow and outrage. "They always begin with parades and promises, and they always end with widows and orphans."

Father Chuck never did appear, not even during the Pater Noster-like *Kaddish* at the close. The possibility I didn't want to consider: the police had nabbed him.

The final Amen was still echoing in the sanctuary when I rushed to apologize to Mr. Sheridan, showing him my fingernails bitten down to the quick.

"Why did you *chant?*" he demanded. "It's not done in Reform."

"Ah," said Rabbi Brownmiller, "didn't it bring back pleasant memories?"

I raced back to my apartment. Father Chuck was coming out when I drove up. Carrying his suitcase, he never broke stride despite all the honking of my horn. I double-parked and ran after him, calling his name.

He wheeled around. "Why didn't you tell me I needed a ticket, Drew?"

"Ticket?"

"The Irish guards wouldn't let me inside."

"What Irish guards?"

"Those hired guns at the door. You never mentioned them, Drew. No one could get in but paid-up members and those who had bought a ticket for fifty dollars. And when I think of the mobs St. Patrick's lets inside—"

News to me, I said, stunned, being the first to arrive at temple.

"If you were afraid of my jeopardizing your position, Drew, why didn't you say so?"

That wasn't so!

Why, then, the neglect either to mention the guards or to sneak Father Chuck inside the temple *before* their arrival? "Well, Drew?"

I couldn't bear his contempt for the one sin I hadn't committed. "Father, I didn't know about the guards because, well, I can't recall the last time I attended High Holiday services."

"Jesus Christ!"

"That's the *truth.*"

Father Chuck swore at me and stalked off.

FOUR

Classes at R. I. began the day after Yom Kippur with a debriefing. "Fine, just fine" was my reply to all queries about how I spent my Day of Atonement. Wiser than chronicling stage fright and cold sweats and, for the grand climax, throwing up.

Fine, the holy day did start out, Rabbi Brownmiller having relieved me of the Torah reading. So I gladly accepted his invitation to Yom Kippur Eve dinner, where I was plied with honey (sympathetic magic to induce a sweet new year), a fish head (so that the new year would be tops and never hit bottom), and eight delicious varieties of cholesterol. Whenever I refused a helping, Mrs. Brownmiller said, "Remember, you're eating for two."

No, she didn't think me pregnant. After skipping breakfast the following morning I realized, too late, I had been eating for two *days*. Yom Kippur is a fast, and with services all day, there was no chance to run out for lunch. As I starved, Rabbi Brownmiller grew nostalgic. "When I was a kid, we used to bet on how many people would pass out on Yom Kippur. But nobody faints in this temple. Pity."

During an afternoon appeal for funds, I left the sanctuary and headed for a water fountain. About to take a swig, I was stopped by a little girl who yanked at my robe.

"No drinking," she cried, as if rehearsing for the role of alcoholic's wife. "It's Yom Kippur and you're a grown-up."

With Mama nearby, I thanked her instead of retorting that Gandhi, a devout grown-up, drank gallons of liquids while fasting. Why couldn't I have been impersonating a Hindu! The constant traffic in the men's room made it impossible to fill up. And how long could I loiter at the sink? Finally, I made do by licking my fingers dry inside a stall and making a meal out of five Chiclets.

During the lengthy afternoon service, I smuggled the remaining Chiclets into my mouth while faking coughs. One every thirty minutes. But that didn't prevent my developing a first-rate headache on noting Mr. Sheridan's jacket bore a big mustard stain that hadn't been there that morning. No chance of *his* keeling over.

When my saliva ran out, there was nothing to moisten my dry lips but a parched tongue that felt like an emery board. Presently, light-headedness set in, and I began to trip out on the prayers, then to hallucinate about freshly brewed coffee and hamburgers. O for a MacDonald's!

Twenty-five hours and fifteen minutes after my last brush with food and drink, exhausted and dizzy, I followed the rabbi out into the lobby to find half a dozen tables set with coffee and cake, meatballs and other hors d'oeuvres. A nosh before dinner, said the sisterhood president, prior to returning to temple for the traditional Break-the-Fast Ball. Unfortunately, I ate so much too fast that minutes before arriving home I threw up over my dashboard.

Studies at R.I. proved easier than my bout with prayer, also harder. All that Hebrew. And I wasn't the only one it oppressed. Those with little more than Sunday-school education also had difficulty. So much so that the dean announced that starting in 1971 all entering classes would spend their freshman year in Israel to gain proficiency in Hebrew. A great idea whose time had come too late to help me. So to avoid translating aloud in class, I pleaded conjunctivitis, while continuing afternoon courses at the Ulpan.

R.I. held no classes on the holiday of Simchas Torah. After sunset I went to the library of the Jewish Theological Seminary, where nobody from R.I. would spot a student, excused from reading aloud in class on account of an eye infection, studying himself blind. The library was closed, however, and the holiday continuing. A seminarian explained that, outside of Israel, Conservative and Orthodox Jews celebrate each one-day holiday for two days as in olden times when Jews, unsure about exact dates, observed each holiday twice as long to play things safe.

With modern calendars to ascertain dates, why didn't everyone now celebrate each holy day for twenty-four hours, as the Bible ordains and all Israelis indeed do?

The seminarian shrugged. "Why do assimilated Jews say, 'Eat,' while real ones say, 'Eat, eat'?"

I entered the chapel, which had been cleared of seats. Remember the deference of the caretaker for the Torah? Forget it. Here, scores of sweaty men, many without jackets or ties, were dancing in a circle with Torahs held high, like Indians around a campfire.

Visits to poor black churches for civil rights demonstrations had convinced me that people's emotions run in reverse proportion to their bank accounts. Funerals of the wealthy resembled corporate board meetings, and condolence-calls-afterward cocktail parties whose host had stepped out of the room for a moment. Remember Jackie Kennedy's deportment at the President's funeral? Very rich indeed. Me, I'd tried for years to unlearn that good manners are more important than honest feelings. So this explosion of emotion among middle-class whites quickened me with hope.

"Hey! No bystanders here."

Two men suddenly pulled me into the midst of the chant-
ers. Soon I too was running around in circles with a Torah in
my arms.

"Israel and the Torah are one," sang everyone, hugging and
kissing his scroll like a honeymooner, while I behaved as if on
a first date. Very proper. Still, I ended up with a good sweat
before my Torah was snatched away. Then off to the sidelines
to wipe my brow.

A woman's voice behind me said, "Your secret is safe with
me, Andrew."

It was Isaca Zion.

I had to dry myself all over again. "Which secret?"

"Dancing up a storm at R.I.'s rival school."

What, I asked swiftly, about her own presence?

Her father taught at the seminary, she reminded me, then
took me to meet him. A man no longer young, with wild mane
and beard and bristling eyebrows still reddish, he seemed
formed from hair and fire.

"Papa," Isaca said. "Andrew knows Levi Simon."

"A *lamed-vovnik*, I suspect," said the rabbi. "Once, by accident, I repeated a lecture. Levi Simon took a million notes
and asked almost as many questions to distract my attention
from the snickers. . . . Perhaps it's just as well he didn't become a rabbi."

"Why do you say that?"

Dr. Zion pointed across the chapel to a child trying to blow
out a candle atop an apple stuck on another's flag. The kid,
who shielded the flame as if it were his soul that were
threatened, burst out crying when the bully succeeded. "Why
did that youngster extinguish the other's candle? Only because it was lit. So it is sometimes in synagogue. It takes a
tough rabbi to keep his flame kindled. Being the pre-eminent
symbol of Judaism, the rabbi automatically antagonizes many
marginal Jews, incurs their displeasure, sometimes enmity."

As Isaca hurried to the distraught child, I said, "*You're*
a rabbi, Dr. Zion."

"A rabbi teaching in a seminary is like a fish in water. Not the same thing at all as leading a congregation today. When I was ordained, rabbis did nothing but study. Now, congregants expect rabbis to have *completed* studying."

What about Isaca? Red hair flying, she was now chasing after the bully.

"Tough enough, that young lady, to override objections to her becoming the first or second woman rabbi in history." No legal barrier, for the *halacha* never considered that possibility. "Rabbi means teacher. Anyone learned in the Torah qualifies."

Then why wouldn't Orthodox and Conservative rabbinical schools ordain women?

"The Jewish Theological Seminary will. Eventually. As for the Orthodox—" Dr. Zion shrugged. "They have a horror of doing *anything* for the first time. If Adam and Eve had been Orthodox, I'm sure they'd have remained childless."

Adam and Eve were orphans, I noted. They had nobody to teach them.

Dr. Zion stroked his beard, then faced me, as if going from the general to the particular. "Isaca tells me you're different from the others in class, Mr. Baron."

I grew wary. "Oh?"

"Your attitude, she says, is that of a visiting anthropologist."

I countered, "Thorstein Veblen attributed the Jews' position in the vanguard of progress to their being *in* Western society, but not *of* it. That enabled them to remain detached, the trait essential to a critic." So here I was being called, in essence, the Jew of Jews!

"Jews," said Dr. Zion. *"Them?"*

"Andrew, you blow hot and cold." Isaca had returned. "Sometimes so aloof, other times enthusiastically discovering something novel in the most familiar subject matter."

"Well . . . you're different too, Isaca."

"In what way?"

Warm and bright, sunny and sexy. But I said, "Everyone else in class is male." She made a face. "What's the matter?"

Dr. Zion observed, "My straightforward daughter doesn't realize there's more to quips than meets the ear. Some reveal a great deal by what they conceal."

Isaca invited me home for coffee. But she was far too attractive to guard against for any length of time, and her father too brilliant. Already Dr. Zion almost had my number. So reluctantly, I begged off. A good thing too. When they spoke of giving me a *check-geshem*, I responded, "Thanks all the same, but I've just eaten." The funny looks on the Zion faces sent me to my Hebrew dictionary, which defined *geshem* as rain and *check* as check.

You know how public appearances terrify me. So who is volunteered to speak at a fund-raising breakfast?

"It will be my pleasure," I told the dean.

He eyed me in disbelief.

Of course, I had no intention to stick to "Why I Entered the Rabbinical Institute of America." Only a matter of switching pronouns. So with the ready co-operation of my class, I pulled a religious Dr. Kinsey.

Dr. Diamond didn't stop me when he discovered why I was huddling with fellow freshmen. He only shook his head ruefully. "Nobody was ever inspired by a crowd."

True. One man at R.I. inspired me—Dr. Tchernichovsky. Once, referring to his wife and son, he used the present tense until someone interrupted, saying, "But aren't they—" Others shushed him. "Was I speaking of my wife and son as if they were still alive?" said the aristocratic elder. "Well, remember the law of the conservation of energy. There's a similar law in the universe, I believe, that applies to the good. Goodness never gets lost. Like energy, it is conserved forever. My faith in this law of good's conservation is my faith in God."

As for my classmates, they had one thing in common: all were ists. Deist, nationalist, theist, polydoxist, traditionalist, humanist, naturalist, Reconstructionist.

Samson Finn had coined his own religion, Jewmanism (for

Jewish humanism). Overhearing him call God empirically meaningless and spiritually obsolete, Dr. Tchernichovsky observed, "Atheism has a legitimate basis for temporary existence. It's needed to purge the dross that attaches itself to religion. But you are not atheistic. You're just an ignoramus."

Twenty-year-old Bernie List said that in the Old Testament, *mishpat* (justice) appears 513 times and *tzedakah* (righteousness) 157 times, with no word for "beggar," since caring for the needy is compulsory and not left to goodwill or charity. Nice guy, Bernie, but who goes around counting words?

Donald Stein, short and retiring, was asserting himself against well-to-do-parents and on behalf of the Jewish masses. Ezra Farber, the oldest at twenty-nine, hailed the concept of *gemiluth chesed* (acts of loving-kindness). Physical culture enthusiast Gary Himmel pounded his armrest and said, three times, "Never again."

"One creates his own rabbinate," exulted Perry Davis, the blond, handsome former captain of Harvard's fencing team. "You can focus on preserving Judaism. Or social action. Or counseling. Or providing leadership for the Jewish community. Or teaching. Or preaching. Or representing the Jewish community to the Gentiles. Or even scholarship."

Isaca Zion was a special case. With pride she cited nine successive generations of rabbis, a line that seemed to have ended. Her barren forty-year-old mother had begged Rabbi Zion to divorce her, so that he could marry again and father children. But he had refused. Three years later the Zion daughter was born. Hence her name (after the biblical Isaac, born to the aged Sarah) and her determination. "I'll be the tenth-generation Rabbi Zion," she said, "and my son the eleventh."

Nearly all shared the desire for a profession that would involve them totally instead of piecemeal. "Your life is your congregation's, you're constantly involved," rejoiced Ezra Farber. "That's what I call living." But his wife, Roberta, termed that living other people's lives, if not vice versa.

Most viewed the rabbi's primary role as teacher. Next in importance came counselor, pastor, and priestly officiant at hatchings, matchings, and dispatchings. Jane Austen's neighborly village curate, it would seem, had supplanted the Prophets.

Only Stanford Price responded, "It's a damn good living." A Reform rabbi has thirty times as much chance as a Protestant minister to earn over fifteen thousand dollars a year. One third make between fifteen and twenty thousand, the top third, twenty thousand or more, and one out of twenty over thirty thousand. "No," he replied to a follow-up query. "My father isn't a partner with Price, Waterhouse. Why do you ask?"

Only Isaca turned the tables and asked what had propelled *me* toward the rabbinate.

Caught off guard, I said the first thing to come to mind. "There's a passage in Genesis that's stayed with me ever since I read it." (The night before my interview.) " 'Jacob loved Rachel more than Leah, and when the Lord saw that, He opened her womb, while Rachel remained barren. Leah conceived and bore a son, and she said, The Lord has looked on my affliction, for now my husband will love me.' Now, there's a deity after my own heart. Defender of the unloved."

Isaca's eyes opened wide. "A man who can empathize with a woman? That's a surprise."

I looked deep into her hazel eyes, which were flecked with gold, and said, "Sexist."

Rabbi Brownmiller had grown since our last encounter. Unless nervousness affected my aim. When I stuck out my hand for shaking, it hit the rabbi in the navel. Happily, I retained enough presence of mind not to say kitchey-koo.

"Well, Andrew, what's your opinion of R.I.?" He answered his own question. The curriculum, which focused on the linguistic and historical understanding of sacred texts rather than on their contemporary relevance, had been designed for a Reform rabbinate that never existed. Though scholarship was the least important requirement of the modern rabbi, R.I. still steeped its students in scholasticism. The school should offer a choice between professional scholarship and the practical rabbinate. "What do *you* think, Andrew?"

Naturally, I agreed wholeheartedly. Which curriculum would the rabbi have chosen?

"That's just the trouble!" He threw up his hands. *"Both."*

I took out my speech. "About the guest of honor. Anything special you want me to say?"

"That he should cough up plenty. Hey!" Rabbi Brownmiller grabbed my arm. "You wrote that down."

"Of course." I wrote down everything. From "Ladies and Gentlemen" to "Thank you for your kind attention," with words underlined, inflections marked, pauses inserted. All I could memorize for a public speech was to stand before starting and to open my mouth wide enough for the words to fall out.

Rabbi Brownmiller erased his dictation. "Is this your first fund raiser? No girl gives her all to a man who reveals exactly what he's after."

(So there *is* a generation gap.) "Maybe a list of the guest of honor's accomplishments."

The rabbi looked pained. "Oscar made a killing in real estate." Apologetically, he added, "By rights we should be honoring Jewish scholars. Unfortunately, they have as much money as the Pope has battalions. But . . . that's shul business." He relented at once. "Meaning no slight to Oscar. One of the last of the big-time givers. Today's children of affluent Jewish producers prefer being affluent consumers. And compared to their businessmen fathers, even professionals earn little. So they won't be contributing nearly as much. Big problem for the future: more cultured Jews, less philanthropists."

We proceeded to the auditorium, whose front wall was covered by a huge backdrop of what Nat Gwirtz identified as the Bronx. "Our guest of honor owns garages all over the borough," he explained.

While someone waylaid the rabbi to discuss the temple's

proposed indoor swimming pool, a woman complimented my High Holidays reading. "You sounded exactly like Richard Burton," she whispered throatily.

"*Richard Burton?*" So affected, so soon?

She moistened her lips. "I could hardly keep my mind on my prayers."

Rabbi Brownmiller asked everyone to take a seat, and me to lead the group in the singing of "am-o-see." I begged off as a monotone, but he insisted.

So I took a deep breath and sang out, "O say can you see . . ."

People exchanged glances as they stood up and joined in.

The rabbi muttered, "You think this is a baseball game?" When the singing ended, he intoned, "*Baruch ato adonai eloheinu melech ha-olam* ha-mo-tsee *lechem min ha-aretz.* Blessed art Thou, O Lord our God, King of the Universe, Who brings forth bread from the earth."

Everyone helped himself to the buffet, exclaiming over a three-foot smoked salmon branded with the guest of honor's initials.

Nat Gwirtz accepted congratulations. "It's the personal touches," he said, "that make an affair."

After the meal, business associates arose to shovel praise on Oscar, who still looked hungry when they had finished. Poor guy must have felt cheated. If half the encomiums were true, what was he doing there with bagels and lox? Oscar should have been sitting in heaven at the right hand of God.

President Sheridan then touted wills and life insurance policies whose beneficiary would be R.I. His impassioned "Is there a better way to achieve immortality!" made me wonder whether the man could be trusted not to cash in a benefactor should a mortgage payment fall due.

Though no nails could have grown back overnight, my fingers gravitated toward my mouth. I couldn't help thinking of public speaking as a strip without the tease. No wonder the Lone Ranger always wore a mask.

Introduced with "You all remember Student-rabbi Baron, don't you?" I thanked the president profusely "for his overly generous introduction," because that's how my manuscript read. After excerpts from my class's most idealistic responses, with nary a mention of Stanford Price, I elaborated on: "Render unto Caesar that which is Caesar's and unto God that which is God's." And concluded with the saying of Rabbi Hillel quoted by most freshmen: " *'Im ein ani li, mi li? Im ani l'atzmi, mah anochi? Im lo achshav, eimatai?'* "

You could have heard a hand clap.

Rabbi Brownmiller stood up. "Student-rabbi Baron forgets that everyone doesn't share his expertise in Hebrew," he said, then addressed me. "Won't you translate for us?"

Singing the *second* stanza of "The Star-Spangled Banner" would have sounded fishy. So recalling Dad's teaching me to swim by tossing me into the deep end of his pool (the reason I avoid baths to this day), I closed my eyes and went for broke. "If I am not for myself, who will be for me? But if I am for myself alone, what good am I? And if not now, when?"

Then came applause, lots of it.

Up shot President Sheridan, index cards in hand, to take attendance, while announcing the amount of each gift the previous year. Everyone pledged—a variation on locker-room bragging. Conspicuous contribution!

Oscar himself got carried away. "I was planning to double last year's donation," he said. "But after this outpouring, I'm tripling."

A round of applause during which President Sheridan hissed, "Triple, Oscar, your brother-in-law Sol offered. From you we expected quadruple."

Oscar held up his hand for attention. "In honor of my wife's dear brother, I pledge an additional single."

"That's a home run in any man's league." Sheridan called for a standing ovation. "Oscar's upped his contribution. How about upping yours?"

One happy outcome, aside from Rabbi Brownmiller's making no stink about my inadvertent quote from the New Testament. Leaving the temple, I relinquished conjunctivitis forever. If not then, after all, when?

FIVE

As part of our pastoral training, the school assigned Bernie List and me to a hospital emergency room. I respected him. On their own, he and his social-worker sister had organized a group of college students to minister to senior citizens trapped in decaying, crime-ridden neighborhoods. Members of Connect & Sustain shopped for the elderly, took them on outings, fixed meals, ran errands. "Do you know what it means to feel that nobody cares?" Bernie said. "To fear senility and lose self-confidence? To be lonely, unnecessary?" To hear him talk, one would think Bernie as old as Methuselah. Yet he was the youngest in the class, with the freckles and slight build of an adolescent.

Too bad he wasn't directing the emergency room, too. The nurse in charge devoted more attention to her daily Ethel Merman-voiced concerts in the lounges, hoping to be discovered by a sick or visiting talent agent.

In contrast, Margarita Rivera, a part-time Puerto Rican clerk, though only eighteen years old herself, mothered frightened patients. "I treat people the way I'd like to be treated," she said. So wistfully, it made one wonder whether the bruises on her arm were indeed the result of a fall, as claimed.

Frequently, the elderly Catholic chaplain stopped by. Father Joyce blamed the mass media for increasing violence, the drug epidemic, wholesale divorce, more sex outside of marriage than in. His prescription: uphold the sanctity of the family. "But not immature premature family," he said.

"Teen-agers going steady. Leads straight to premarital sex—or worse."

What was worse?

"Marriage."

Marriage sinful?

"Teen-age marriage is. It so often ends in divorce."

"Sometimes," Bernie interjected cryptically, "it's worse when it doesn't."

Possibly because of his fluency in Spanish, Margarita took to Bernie. He responded. Surprising for one so shy.

Yet Bernie could be forward. Once, I got into an argument with a resident determined to tell a patient, over the objections of his wife and daughter, that he had been operated on for a malignancy, successfully. My classmate audited the resident's insistence on reporting nothing but the truth. This from a doctor romancing three nurses with the same line and inquiring of senior staff members how to cheat on income tax. Quietly, Bernie said, "Do as you're told, Doctor. Else every time we meet in the hospital, I will throw my arms around you and personally kiss you."

The resident was startled. "You wouldn't—"

Bernie put his hands on the doctor's waist.

Several doctors, nurses too, were guilty of telling patients nothing. Too bored to explain what were to them routine procedures, some left patients to stew in ignorance. So Bernie and I took it upon ourselves to alleviate fears such as of being electrocuted by the EKG machine and, since plasma is yellowish in color, being intravenously fed urine.

Otherwise, Bernie offered counsel only when solicited. But Margarita's talk of quitting high school for a full-time job upset him. He insisted on her graduating.

Carlos, a tough young orderly, scoffed. "I finished school, and look at the job I have. There's no graduation from being Puerto Rican."

"Train yourself for something," Bernie said. "You've got a head. Use it."

Carlos replied with a swagger that he enjoyed using his body more. "How about you, man?"

Though Margarita's shift ended at eight, she often stayed on to do homework. "It's quiet here," she explained.

Why anyone would consider an emergency room quiet became clear one night when her stepfather came roaring into the hospital. Spying him, the girl cowered behind Bernie.

"*Prostituta*," the drunk yelled. "Spending all her time in the hospital, *she* says, but coming home with a different man every night."

"Orderlies *escort* Margarita home," Bernie said.

The man only knew that Margarita stayed away too much, and when home, ignored him. "I demand the respect due a father!" But the embrace he forced on the struggling girl was distinctly unparental. And when she broke away, he slapped her.

Before Bernie or I could intervene, Carlos with one blow knocked the stepfather to the floor. Then kicked him in the side. "You touch Margarita again," he vowed, "I'll kill you."

Suddenly all sobriety, the stepfather got to his feet and slunk away.

Carlos sneered at Bernie. "I bet you'd have *talked* to him, right?"

From that night on Margarita always appeared cheerful and unmarked. Now only Carlos escorted her home. Before long the couple announced wedding plans.

Instead of congratulating them, Bernie asked why the rush. The draft. Carlos wanted to get married before being inducted. To my astonishment, Bernie appealed to Father Joyce.

Together, the priest and Bernie marshaled arguments. Only, what Bernie considered the most important reason of all he confided to me later. Margarita was much too good for Carlos.

No postponement, said Carlos. But Margarita, persuaded, prevailed on him to delay the wedding until he received his first assignment. If one of her reasons for marrying was to escape a drunken stepfather, what good would it do if she had to remain at home?

After Carlos' induction, Bernie began spending more time at the hospital. Not that there could have been anything improper. Margarita never so much as addressed him by his first name. And he never gave her anything but college catalogues.

One evening the girl remarked, "You don't think I should ever marry Carlos. Do you?"

Bernie hesitated a long time. "My own parents married young—and I lived to regret it." Not that Mr. List wasn't a good man. But Mrs. List outgrew her husband intellectually—both were embittered. "I want a better life for you, Margarita."

Bernie's relationship with her continued. Indeed, deepened. Who wouldn't have been flattered by his attention? Yet he seemed oblivious to his effect on the girl.

Somehow, word reached Carlos. Home on a pass, he barged into the emergency room. "Why," he demanded, "is that List sniffing around?"

Margarita became indignant. Yet she looked pleased too.

The singing nurse reported the quarrel to Father Joyce, who came down at once to lecture Bernie. "It's harmful, involving oneself completely or permanently in anyone's problems," he warned. "Sometimes dangerous."

"But you're the one," Bernie protested, "who preaches against being unfeeling."

"You never heard of the Golden Mean?" said Father Joyce. "I know personally, for example, that sometimes the most dangerous task in the world is drying a widow's tears."

Could anything be sweeter than passing off truths as good humor? Every winter the student body put on a Purim *spiel*, or play, that poked fun at the faculty. "Remember," Dr. Diamond cautioned, "it's a *mitzvah*, commandment, never to lie. But it's no *mitzvah* to tell the truth."

Dashing Perry Davis, the intellectual jock, drew the plum role of R.I.'s president. Worenz of Awabia, as students called him, ran the school between digs in Israel. Periodically, he'd empty his shoes of sand and return to the United States to excavate the pockets of rich Jews. Straight yellow hair falling over cornflower-blue eyes and a Greek-coin profile, this charismatic archaeologist in his late fifties, who had lived most of his life in the desert like an Arab, was not only Jewish, but also a rabbi. So much for stereotypes.

Despite an expensive custom-tailored suit and elite manner that attested to an upbringing amidst privilege, Dr. Worenz's eyes welled with tears as he spoke of the values of the Bible and the wonder of treading the same ground as the Prophets. Yet when Dr. Tchernichovsky commented afterward in what sounded like broken German, the president responded coldly, "I don't know Yiddish."

(In the skit someone asks why a scholar accomplished in a dozen dead languages disdains Yiddish. The student portraying Dr. Tchernichovsky replies, "You ever see Sammy Davis, Jr., eating watermelon?")

Whoever found it difficult after the Holocaust to believe in a God both omnipotent and good was grateful for Dr. Tchernichovsky's concept of a good but limited deity. "God did not die at Auschwitz. Man did. Or rather, man's utter and idolatrous belief in himself," he maintained.

"Everyone should regard his merits and failings as equally balanced, while regarding all mankind as half-deserving and half-guilty. One more sin, and he weighs down the scale of guilt against himself and the whole world, thereby destroying both. On the other hand, by acting justly, he weighs down the scale of merit in his own favor and mankind's, thereby saving both. For God grows whenever man grows, just as the world grows whenever God grows."

(Mimicking Dr. Tchernichovsky, the diminutive Donald Stein was to blow up a balloon labeled "guess Who" until it hid him from view. Then former weight lifter Gary Himmel would switch places with him.)

If the balloon burst, an off-stage voice would exclaim, "So Dr. Furth was right, after all!" For months that instructor had been reading us God's obituary notices. Built like a tall butter-fish, Dr. Furth claimed Heinz Kissinger as a Hebrew school classmate and the Lord nonexistent. To Dr. Furth, Judaism was doing your own thing religiously. Dr. Tchernichovsky, who disliked Dr. Furth, had observed sardonically, "The sinner's goal is to do away with God in order that he himself might become God."

(As Dr. Furth, Hank Brenner would sashay onto the stage in levis and cowboy hat, twirling a lariat. "Which ranch do I hail from?" he'd drawl. "The Bar Nothing.")

The only Jew to work on the Revised Standard Version of the Bible, Dean Diamond gained fame for, in his words, deflowering the Virgin philologically. That is, correctly translating the Hebrew word *almah* as "young woman" in Isaiah's "Behold, *almah* shall conceive and bear a son," thereby shattering the biblical basis for the concept of the Virgin birth. Yet he never criticized Jesus, whom Dr. Tchernichovsky called the master of the parable, an art form invented by the Pharisees. Dr. Diamond stated it was no religious crime in ancient Israel to declare oneself the Messiah, that being a claim to the Jewish throne, not divinity. The religion of Jesus was always Judaism; Paul's religion *about* Jesus became Christianity.

(In recognition of his manifold contributions to all mankind, a posthumous Ph.D. is awarded to Moses, thenceforth to be known as *Dr.* Moses.)

The show's climax had Satan complaining to God just before the birth of the saintly Levi Yitzchak of Berditchev: "O Lord, this soul will turn all men to goodness, and Satan won't stand a chance of luring them into sin and corruption. If Levi Yitzchak is born, I might as well retire." With a sigh the Lord replies, "Have no fear. Levi Yitzchak will become a rabbi, and he'll be so busy with committees and meetings and communal bickering, he'll never have time to hinder your work."

During dress rehearsal, Stanford Price took me aside. "How do you feel about Purim?"

By now, neither Hebrew words nor exotic holidays intimidated me. Not even the recently observed New Year for Trees. (Yes, trees.) So I risked an insouciant "Why?"

"Don't you think Purim a heartless holiday? Too blood-thirsty for civilized people."

"The Jews were saved, weren't they?"

"Yes, but Haman and his sons were hanged instead," said Price. "And drowning out Haman's name with noise during the public reading of the Scroll of Esther. So barbaric. Won't you join us this year in boycotting Purim?"

The "us" made me hesitate. No sense in my fighting a lone rear-guard action in defense of a losing holiday. Bad enough to be considered a latent Orthodox since automatically kissing a dropped book, which turned out to be the collected essays of William James.

Price also sought to enlist pacific Isaca Zion with "In Hebrew, remember, the words for *compassion* and *womb* both come from the same root, *rchm.*"

She got indignant. "You want to abolish the only holiday that stars a woman?"

Next, Price turned to Samson Finn, the Jewmanist, whose parents had been members of Christian Science until their son developed tonsilitis.

But Finn spurned him too. "Esther is the only book of the Bible that never mentions God," he said. "How can I boycott the first Jewmanist manifesto?"

Since Esther was memorable only for the bounce of Joan Collins' breasts in a sultry movie incarnation, I went to audit her book in a neighborhood synagogue, which resembled a child's version of M-G-M's back lot. Queens, kings, courtiers, harem girls, cowboys and Indians, pirates, Mickey Mouse, and several skeletons left over from Halloween. It took the rabbi twenty minutes to quiet them. Even then, the service was hard to follow with little kids crawling over the pews and scampering up and down the aisles.

Came time for the reading of the Megillah, wherein Esther marries King Ahasuerus after winning the fifth-century B.C.

Miss Persia contest. Cousin Mordecai reminds the Queen of her Jewish heritage after Haman casts *purim*, lots, for the date on which to destroy Persian Jewry. Every mention of the wicked prime minister's name was not merely booed and hissed, but blasted with metal noisemakers and New Year's Eve horns until the rabbi, holding up both his hands and jumping up and down, would shout, "Enough, already!" When in the final reel, Queen Esther bares Haman's machinations and King Ahasuerus allows the Jews to defend themselves, which results in the turnabout execution of Haman and cohorts . . . *pandemonium.*

The children's abandon delighted this uptightnik.

On my way out of the synagogue, I bumped into an adorable dark-haired child in a nightgown and crown. "You dare to step on Queen Esther's foot?" she said. "Who are you?"

"I wish I knew!" Being a half-and-half hadn't afforded me the best of both worlds, but of neither. Occasional anti-Semitic slurs, fewer Christmas presents, total confusion.

The next morning even those who regularly cut weekly chapel attended the Purim service, giving rise to suspicions that Stanford Price was in reality an agent provocateur. And when the reader of the Megillah substituted Price's name for Haman's, while he was being hanged, the congregation went wild.

Isaca was the preacher. With her long red hair braided atop her head like a crown, she replied to Price with a list of the most prominent pogroms since Haman's time. A list of cities and dates and the numbers of Jews murdered. All very impersonal, like a police blotter. As her voice droned on, citing number after number, a feeling of numbness set in. Then, annoyance. Strange. But tuning Isaca out proved impossible. Now I no longer thought it bizarre for the eighteenth-century Newport, Rhode Island, synagogue to construct a pulpit with a secret trap door and tunnel leading outside. An escape route in case of attack.

When the bell rang, everyone stayed put, as if

transfixed by a creeping terror that Isaca's list might grow to include him too. Finally, she concluded with a wistful "So many Hamans, and only one Purim."

By then, feeling indicted for crimes at least half of me was innocent of, I had begun to resent Isaca's numbers game. Where there was so much persecution, perhaps there was reason, too. Paradoxically, my compassion had given way to repugnance bordering on hostility.

Others were nearly as perverse as I, however. Only hours after Isaca's catalogue everyone was laughing like crazy at the Purim *spiel*. Later, several students went home with a senior who was getting married that weekend, tied him to his bed, and shaved a cross on his chest. To serve as a conversation piece, they explained solicitously.

One morning Bernie came to school distraught and asked me to cut the first period. He had something vital to discuss. It was, he said, Margarita. She was in terrible trouble, so was Bernie. And neither knew what to do.

"She's pregnant?"

Bernie was amazed. "How did you know?"

"Abortion is legal now," I pointed out. "Not exactly immoral either."

"Abortion is murder legalized, Margarita says."

I had forgotten about Catholic law. "Then adoption."

"That, Margarita calls abortion life-long."

"What *does* she want?"

"To marry me."

"And you?" As if I didn't know that either.

But Bernie surprised me. "Same thing, marriage. Margarita is so good and giving and beautiful."

Then what on earth was the problem? "Her engagement?"

"She never *loved* Carlos. And nobody wants to marry a girl who doesn't love him."

"True, Margarita is too young for marriage."

Bernie turned on me. "She's older than Ariel when Will Durant married her. And together they went on to write *The Story of Civilization*."

I had run out of questions. "Then why so upset? If you both want to get married—"

"Andrew!"

"You mean, Margarita is Puerto Rican."

"So what? My mother is Hungarian." He burst out, "It's my children. I'd lose them and *their* children forever. The mother's religion determines theirs."

"But with their father a *rabbi*—"

"What difference does that make? There's no such thing as a half-Jew."

"*What?*" Terri had been a lot of things, but never Jewish. Was I to be deprived of even half a loaf? "But Barry Goldwater—"

Bernie stared at me. "That's Jewish law. All or nothing."

No choice in the matter? I was struck dumb. An out-and-out Gentile. Machiavellian indeed for such a one to be attending rabbinical school. A total non-Jew. God forgive me!

". . . And I didn't ask Margarita to convert," Bernie was saying. "How could I, knowing what my own religion means to me."

I turned nasty, projecting a sudden attack of self-hatred at him. "Well, if your unborn children mattered that much, why didn't you take precautions?"

He affected innocence. "But I did, I always have. That's why I never date Gentiles."

"Never?"

Bernie shook his head emphatically.

The question slipped out, crudely. "How do you knock up someone you never dated?"

He grabbed hold of my jacket. "What are you talking about! I don't have enough problems? *Carlos* is the father."

"*Carlos?* But I thought. . . . Never mind. Then why are *you* in trouble?"

Bernie turned away. "It's all my fault, don't you see? Making Margarita dissatisfied with Carlos. I didn't do it to get her for myself. Honest."

"What you did, Bernie, was to speed up the process of disenchantment."

"If only that were true!" he said. "All the same, Margarita is pregnant and miserable, and I'd marry her in a minute if not for the damned difference in religion."

"Look. Suppose *I* talk to her."

"No, Andrew! Promise you won't."

I gave my word and kept it for a good ten hours. Bernie must have expected the renege, else why confide in me? Certainly, it was foolish for the two of them to be separated forever by a misunderstanding. Hadn't Romeo and Juliet already died for that sin?

In the hospital that evening, I took Margarita into an empty office and put it to her. Would she convert in order to marry Bernie? A convert was considered as much a Jew as Isaiah or Bella Abzug. That much I had learned.

She praised Bernie's stability, goodness, maturity, forcefulness. Then: "But to me the Church is everything. Ever since my father left, the Church is all I've had. 'Without Me,' said our Blessed Savior, 'ye can do nothing.' Without the Church, I *am* nothing."

And without Bernie?

Tears welled in the girl's eyes. "Outside the Church there is no salvation. I don't want to end up in hell. *This* life is horrible enough."

At that point Bernie entered. One look at Margarita told him of failure.

The girl turned toward him. "You said Judaism doesn't care about individual salvation. So let's go on this way, me being saved and you observing commandments."

"But our children."

"That can wait, can't it? Let them make their *own* choice."

"How fair is that? Kids have a right to know who they are from the start."

I found myself nodding in agreement.

She burst out, "You'd let religion change everything between us?"

"It doesn't change *everything*," he said. "You're still the same girl I want to marry."

Margarita darted into his arms.

He stroked her long black hair. "Only . . . I *can't* marry you. God! That *is* everything, isn't it?"

The girl pulled away. "Margarita loves Bernie without his converting. But Bernie can't love Margarita—"

"He does, Margarita, he does. Believe me—"

"Then why—"

Bernie took both her hands in his. "Bernie also loves his people. He identifies with their four thousand years of history. And with their future, too. I can't help feeling a mystical relationship between America's six million Jews and those destroyed in the Holocaust. We are their living memorials. . . . Margarita, please don't ask me to grant Hitler a posthumous victory."

The girl looked as if she had been struck. "What does the end of the Jews and—did you say *Hitler?*—have to do with *me?*" She sobbed.

Unfortunately, the singing nurse, who had come looking for Margarita to take charge of the emergency room while she gave another concert, happened on the scene. Finding the girl in tears and Bernie drying them manually, she felt duty-bound to snitch to Father Joyce. He reported to R.I. that one of its seminarians seemed to be practicing marriage without a license.

Summoned to the dean's office, Bernie told all. Dr. Diamond was sympathetic but stern. While he couldn't prevent anyone from marrying out, he would bar him from ordination. With the intermarriage rate soaring, it wouldn't take long for love to accomplish what millennia of hatred could not. So a rabbi's job was, at the very least, to set an example. "The man himself is the message."

Since Bernie concurred, that would have been the end of the affair if Dr. Furth hadn't gotten wind of it. He whose lightest touch would stun a stallion spoke to the class about mixed marriage. To accommodate the rising number, Dr. Furth said with side glances at Bernie, two out of five Reform rabbis now officiate without prior conversion of the non-Jew.

"Are you proselytizing for mixed marriage?" asked Isaca Zion.

"For reality. To give emotional support to a member of this class who shall be nameless." Now Dr. Furth looked at everyone but Bernie.

The poor guy was soon flooded with conflicting advice. Seth Astrachan said that refusing to officiate at a mixed marriage would only drive the couple away from Judaism. And Samson Finn declared mixed couples entitled to a Jewish wedding ceremony, being children of Adam and Eve, same as every rabbi.

But, Perry Davis argued, how can a rabbi solemnize a ceremony that has no traditional sanction?

Dr. Furth cited the absence of criticism in the Bible of Esther's marriage to the King of Persia, which had benefited all of Persian Jewry. When Gary Himmel mentioned Ezra the Scribe's order to disband all mixed marriages, Dr. Furth countered with the Book of Ruth, written afterward. To demonstrate, many scholars contend, that King David's great-grandmother was a non-Jew.

"The law bans mixed marriage," Isaca Zion stated. "Only two Jews can contract a Jewish mar—"

Stanford Price cut her short. "We missed the boat two thousand years ago because of such legalism. It drove all the pagans to Christianity. If Judaism had been flexible about marriage and circumcision and bacon and eggs, who knows? Maybe today the Pope would have been a Jew."

So it went, back and forth, with only Bernie and myself abstaining. Which soon made it all too obvious that one of us was the guilty party.

"Let's vote on it," said Dr. Furth, and Bernie's face turned pale and clammy.

The class divided two to one against, with most of those in favor insisting on special conditions, such as raising the children as Jews. Only Stanford Price recommended having a mixed couple prove their allegiance to Judaism by paying the officiating rabbi twice his usual fee. "To eliminate the insincere," he said.

Dr. Furth offered his own advice. "Let your classmate's conscience be his guide."

Everyone turned to look at Bernie and me.

There was no other way. I stood up. "Thank you all for your help," I said and left the room.

Isaca Zion was no judge of character. She stopped me to say, "That was very selfless. Diverting attention from Bernie."

"Selfless? Nobody's ever accused me of that before."

"Modest, too."

I made a face.

"Why do some people find it hard to take a compliment?"

Some people, Isaca didn't realize, had little experience.

Margarita for one. Abuse was what she knew. Less than a month after the wedding, which Bernie had observed from across the street from the church, she showed up at R.I. It was hard to recognize the lovely girl who now looked like her own ghost. I took her to where Bernie was studying.

Oblivious to the library surroundings, Margarita blurted, "Carlos is after you! I'm so afraid!"

We led her to an empty classroom. After calming down she said that at first Carlos was elated to hear about the baby. He felt *muy macho*. But Carlos was too young to be saddled with a child at this time, when he had just made a down payment on his first car. Soon he decided on an abortion and tormented Margarita to go for one. At the last moment, however, she left the clinic without undergoing the procedure. It didn't take Carlos long to realize that what was being passed off as the abortion's side effect was morning sickness. He became enraged.

Bernie reached for the girl.

She drew away. "I didn't come for sympathy." Her husband

got the crazy idea that the baby was Bernie's. Vowing to abort the child himself and afterward its "real" father, Carlos beat her up. The following morning she fled. "Carlos taught me to make love, now he's taught me to hate. I wish one of us was dead," she cried. "I don't care anymore which."

It would have made another bad movie for my actress mother. Yet Margarita was trapped in it.

Bernie discounted the possibility of danger, disregarding Job's teaching that the good often suffer for no good reason. Indeed, Job's complaints were a good deal more to the point than God's answer.

Sure enough, no sooner did the three of us set foot outside R.I. than we were confronted by Carlos himself. He struck Bernie to the ground. Margarita screamed something about a gun. That set me screaming too, while people on the street ran in every direction but toward us.

I grabbed Carlos too late to prevent his kicking Bernie in the side. When Margarita jumped between them, Carlos' kick came inches short of rendering the question of abortion academic.

Two classmates fell upon Carlos. Together we pulled him off Bernie. It took the three of us to hold Carlos down. Even though no gun was found, I wanted him handed over to the police. But Bernie feared that would make matters worse. So we shoved Carlos into my car and, with Margarita, drove to Father Joyce's church.

The result? Margarita and Carlos were to separate for the time being. Father Joyce would find her an apartment, to be managed on her allotment and welfare, while she returned to high school. After the baby was born, perhaps the young couple would get together again. Meanwhile, Bernie had to promise to stay away from the girl. Not the happiest arrangement, but it beat killing.

Margarita didn't entirely agree. "Eighteen years old and my life is over. For sleeping with one boy in my life. Sweet Jesus! Where is God's mercy?" She turned on Bernie. "Where was *your* mercy? If we had gotten married—"

A tear trickled down Bernie's cheek.

At the next session of pastoral psychiatry, Dr. Kohler spoke uncoincidentally on transference, whereby a counselee transfers his affection from an inaccessible love object, like a parent, to an acceptable substitute with whom he seeks to establish a childhood relationship. The counselee who becomes too dependent on the counselor will not be able to establish new emotional relations. For his part, the counselor, in assuming the role of temporary love object, runs the risk of countertransference, falling victim to his own unconscious need to help someone in trouble.

"There are two rules," said Dr. Kohler. "Know thyself. And always doubt thy motivation."

At lunch afterward, I asked about Bernie's ribs, cracked by Carlos' assault.

My friend stirred his coffee with a knife. "Very illuminating. Seems I wasn't Margarita's true love, but merely a love object, and our relationship a substitute for her abortive relation with her father. What a relief to learn that my feelings for her resulted from unconscious needs to respond to someone in need. Yes, it's all so clear now. Bernie never loved beautiful, good-hearted Margarita. I . . . countertransferred her." He stared bleakly into his coffee cup. "My ribs, Andrew? . . . Oh, *they'll* heal."

SIX

A phone call from Levi, on leave, aroused warring emotions.

I insisted on the Simons being my guests at a kosher restaurant, since most Reform Jews don't keep kosher. A plan plagiarized from an adulterous neighbor of mine who always rendezvoused in pews—nobody he knew attended church.

Levi and I met in front of the Metropolitan. But all desire to enter fled when Levi mumbled that he wasn't being sent to

England, as his parents believed. A mutual friend of ours at Oxford would route Levi's letters home. They would originate in Vietnam.

My stomach did a somersault. "You're a chaplain's assistant, aren't you?"

Alas, his duties included serving as bodyguard for chaplains, who go unarmed.

Immediately, I envisioned my friend caught between advancing Vietcong troops and his chaplains. "But you're a conscientious objector!"

To qualify as a C.O. one must oppose *all* wars. Levi didn't. The Sixth Commandment, often mistranslated as "Thou shalt not kill," read in the Hebrew original, "Thou shalt not murder."

My nightmare wouldn't depart. Levi, surrounded by enemy soldiers, forced to kill or be killed. "What if—" I checked myself.

He answered the question, nevertheless. "That's where faith comes in."

"And if God is out to lunch?"

Levi gave a wry chuckle. "Not so far. The people I've met couldn't be nicer. They do have peculiar notions, though." One soldier asked if Levi was a Protestant Jew or a Catholic Jew. Several thought synagogues had chimneys to let out the smoke from animal sacrifices. "I had mentioned I'm a *kohen*. A descendant of the priests who served in the ancient Temple."

And now, would Levi be offering up himself? I had a terrible premonition.

"Your father, judging from Baron, may be a *kohen*, too."

Dad—not I, being Gentile. (Though if my name was Gallagher and my mother's Cohen, I'd be a full-fledged Jew. But, because Jews' lineage follows the father, not a *kohen!*)

We were approaching our destination when my friend did a sudden about-face and hurried in the opposite direction. I ran after him.

"Rabbi Zion," he said, walking very fast. "He was coming out of the restaurant with his daughter—"

I beat Levi to the corner. After he caught up with me, I asked why *he* wanted to avoid the Zions.

"Rabbi Zion is a leader of the antiwar movement. I can lie to my parents. To spare their feelings. But not to Rabbi Zion to spare my own."

When we finally reached the restaurant, the Simons greeted me with such warmth, I felt myself an ex post facto victim of emotional malnutrition. Whereas I had always regarded myself as something the stork dragged in, the Simons treated Levi as an extension. Whatever happened to him—from eggshell in the chopped liver to a toothache—seemed to happen to them, too. Such oversolicitousness probably had spoiled Columbia radicals like Mark Rudd, whose mother called him "my revolutionary . . . my rebel." Yet the demands of Levi were always upon himself. Did religion make the difference?

Just before our leave-taking, Mr. Simon raised his glass of wine high. "Never thought I'd be toasting England, which barred all refugees from Palestine during World War II," he said. "But here's to England. For not being Vietnam."

Levi and I exchanged looks.

Mrs. Simon didn't touch her wine. "It occurred to me," she noted sadly. "If our Levi isn't going to Vietnam, another innocent boy is going in his place."

"Create an original Haggadah for the Passover Seder."

That group assignment delighted the majority, who rhapsodized over the opportunity to be creative at the meal celebrated by Jesus and the apostles at the Last Supper. Me, I had never met anyone who used the word *creative* who was.

Curious book, the Haggadah. Its account of the Exodus made it an event better forgotten than commemorated. Whereas the ancient Greeks and Romans traced their ancestry to gods and goddesses, the Jews insist on reminding themselves of slaves escaped from Egypt. It's as if the Daughters of the Australian Settlers would throw a ball each year to honor their jailbird forefathers.

The first few minutes of our after-class meeting set me wondering whether the exercise's real purpose was to determine how long thirteen pre-people of God could work together without coming to blows.

Ezra Farber shouted down a proposal to include a quotation from *Soul on Ice* in our Haggadah. "At this very moment Eldridge Cleaver is living in Arab Algeria—"

"Like Moses, a fugitive in Midian," interjected Stanford Price lyrically.

"—urging the destruction of the State of Israel."

"Oh, well. A man that persecuted is entitled to let off a little steam."

Quote Cleaver, Bernie List asked, when the original Haggadah never mentions the name of Moses? Moses was deliberately omitted to keep the Jews from deifying him, Stanford Price replied, then offered to compromise with a quotation from LeRoi Jones.

Strange, the attraction of black extremists for elite white liberals, many of whom disdain lower-middle-class white ethnics. Hank Brenner attributed it to the underlying kinship of lower-class morality to upper-class uptightness, the strait jacket we all yearn to escape.

Harvard's Perry Davis took charge as bickering broke out. He assigned each of us a number, like at the bakery, for speaking in turn.

Número uno wanted the Seder to have a theme. Since the holiday commemorates the birth of the Jews as a people, he suggested celebrating Passover as a big birthday party.

The Seder already *had* a theme, several men asserted. Liberation. The redemption of the Israelites from Egyptian slavery.

Donald Stein vented his disappointment. "That's so *cliché*."

The birthday-party idea was voted down as perhaps too innovative. "No birthday cake," said Ezra Farber, "has over three thousand candles."

Then a proposal from Isaca Zion. Since the *Union Haggadah* bowdlerized the traditional one, wouldn't it be creative simply to revert to the original?

That brought down the wrath of Stanford Price. "You mean, restore the recitation of those ten revolting plagues?"

While recalling the plagues, Isaca reminded him, traditional Jews always spill ten drops of wine to signify that their cup of joy cannot be filled to the brim when even enemies are smitten.

"You call that compassion—ten measly drops?"

Isaca seethed. "What would you have us do at the Seder? Hold memorial services for the Egyptians?"

Stanford Price strode to the front of the room. "As for me—whoever's the underdog, that's *my* people."

Perry Davis called for order. "Let's get on with this. Look at the time."

Relevance got a big push from Seth Astrachan. Until Perry Davis finally interrupted to ask, "Relevant to what?"

"Vietnam."

"Racism."

"Ecology."

"Overpopulation."

"The Third World."

"*People.*"

"Terrific," said Perry Davis. "Now how about making our Haggadah also relevant to Jews?"

"Let's include a poem by the man who inspired me to enter the rabbinate," said Donald Stein. "Father Daniel Berrigan."

A prayer for peace in Vietnam also won unanimous approval, though the wording almost became a *causus belli* between the dovish majority and a few hawks.

"Suppose we leave one chair empty at the Seder table," Ezra Farber said. "To remind us of those unable to celebrate our Festival of Freedom. Soviet Jewry and others."

Levi came to mind at once. Perhaps I'd read too much Ibsen. A gun mentioned in any first act of his was sure to be fired by play's end. Would Levi's gun rust peacefully in its holster?

"Speaking of relevance," said Bernie List. "Each of us should bring one of New York's three hundred and fifty thousand poor Jews to our class Seder and to his family's, then adopt him or her afterward."

Everyone thought that a great idea. "Where can we find poor Jews?" several asked.

Bernie List produced the list of members of Connect & Sustain.

When my number came up, I put in a word for timelessness, for allusions as well as specifics, for something in addition to the daily headlines. "In one way or another, everyone is enslaved," I projected. Levi, too, fettered by scruples. "The liberation of the Israelites offers the hope that maybe next time around the beneficiary will be one of us."

Samson Finn hailed my words as a call to suffuse our Haggadah with poetry. "So let's include stanzas from that great poem, *Hallel*." Apprised that every Haggadah contains the Hallel prayer, the Jewmanist referred us to the *Hallel* of poet Allen Ginsberg, then quoted from it:

> Everything is holy! everybody's holy!
> everywhere is holy! everyday is in eternity!
> Everyman's an angel! . . .
> The world is holy! The soul is holy! The
> nose is holy! The tongue and cock and hand and
> asshole holy!

With noise nearly drowning out the three o'clock bell, Perry Davis shoulted, *"Quiet!"* And when the recital continued over everyone's objections, the Harvard man raised his *Union Haggadah* high in the air and brought it down on Finn's head. Whereupon the Jewmanist enacted the title of another Ginsberg poem, *Howl.*

Uh-oh. All it would take to make me a rabbi, I suddenly suspected, was three more years. Heaven help the Jews!

1971-2

SEVEN

After piling up enough credits during Columbia's summer session to bring myself up to date, I flew to San Francisco. The divorce decree granted Dad full visitation rights, but Terri having gone off to Hollywood, me in tow, I was the one who did all the visiting. Always between the end of summer camp and the start of school. Some basis for a relationship. It was like trying to learn a foreign language in two weeks per year.

To compound the distance between us, Dad was a reserved man of few words, and those mainly about sports. I was always desperately hurling remarks and queries into the long silences, as someone frostbitten might throw anything at hand into a fire to keep it from dying.

Truth to tell, Dad and I were something of a disappointment to each other, me wanting Gregory Peck of *To Kill a Mockingbird* for a father, him hoping for Charles Bronson for an only son. Dad still got nostalgic over the good old days of the Normandy Invasion and the Battle of the Bulge. An athletic outdoorsman, tall, prematurely white-haired, and trim, Dad's idea of fun and games was hunting. I'll never forget the first deer I saw him shoot. Dying, it looked up accusingly, as if to say, "How *could* you?" I threw up all over myself and burst into tears. Dad reprimanded me. "Only girls cry." I never cried again after that. Did throw up from time to time, though.

This year I had something novel to report. Did Dad know of his probable priestly lineage? Ridiculous—priests couldn't have children. *Jewish* priests. Dad never heard of such a thing. What in hell did they do? Offered animal sacrifices in the ancient Temple.

"Disgusting," said Dad.

I pointed out that his sporting-goods stores sold tons of rifles to people who never went after anything that could shoot back, adding, "Why on earth are such people called sportsmen?"

Dad and friends revered wildlife, their biggest regret being the inability to toss back alive what was downed. When he went on to hymn hunting as a primal way of communing with nature, I cut him short with the Talmudic ruling that overloading a beast of burden is a sin. How much more so, then, murdering.

Dad gaped. "*Sin?*"

On to Beverly Hills. Some of you may recall my mother, one-time starlet Terri Dare, nicknamed Derri Aire after showing up at a fifties' movie premiere in a turtlenecked, long-sleeved evening gown with a plunging backline. That, after having undergone plastic surgery at both ends. "You think," she often said, "Raquel Welch was built in a day?"

As pert as a doll—big, blue eyes, blond hair, upturned nose, dimpled chin—and with Barbie's acting range, Terri always yearned for celebrity. "Lucky woman," she exclaimed on seeing *I Want to Live!* Only, it wasn't Susan Hayward whom she envied for her Academy Award-winning portrayal of Barbara Graham, who ended up in California's gas chamber. "Imagine having a movie made of your life!"

After the breakup with Dad, Terri worked in movies off and on, but she did better at matrimony. Would have done better yet without me for an encumbrance. Yet when I asked why she hadn't refused delivery, she waxed indignant. "How can you suggest such a thing! Lana Turner and Doris Day have a child apiece."

Now, unexpectedly, she had become a household word with the release of her T.V. commercials as Suzie the drudge, who goes around sniffing tiles, tubs, and toilet bowls, then scours them with a disinfectant.

Was Terri happy now? No, and that depressed her. "There's more to life than public acclaim and influencing the buying habits of an entire nation."

In search of the more, Terri restlessly explored Los Angeles' flea market of religious off-brands. So perhaps it was no accident, attending R.I. The religious inclination may have been lying dormant in my genes all along, awaiting fertilization by the draft.

What about the Church?

"She blew it." Terri tossed her thick streaked blond lion's mane. "Imagine letting someone marry again after murdering a husband, but not after divorcing him."

A new addition to Terri's home was a meditation room with Oriental *objets d'art* and an open roof, where she meditated morning and evening in the lotus position. What, I asked, did she meditate about?

"Nothing," she said.

"Is nothing . . . enough?"

"Yes, when one has purged the self of all earthly cravings. Inner peace is the best that life or death can offer."

"Have you achieved it?"

"No, goddamnit! But one of these days. I'm up for a new film, *No Greater Love Story.*"

The film's director was Terri's new boy friend, whose previous movies might as well have been directed by a blunt instrument. They stopped just short of Tertullian, who had actors burned alive at the Colosseum. Dirk Taylor's films only reflected reality, he asserted. In New York a juvenile had set a drunken derelict afire, as happened in Taylor's latest. He disclaimed all responsibility, however, with: "What movie did Jack the Ripper see?" Taylor was now working on a screenplay based on a true incident of honeymooners who got lost at sea. Running out of food, they tossed a coin to determine who would dine off whom. The bride lost, and after being rescued, the broken-hearted if well-fed groom auctioned off the book and movie rights.

"I've heard of show-and-tell and kiss-and-tell," I remarked. "But *eat*-and-tell?"

Dirk Taylor took a swing at me. I ducked. Terri apologized.

I myself wondered about my recent sporadic attacks of virtue. One morning at R.I. someone circulated a brief note: "If you got laid last night, smile." I didn't pass it on. Good thing I wasn't studying for the priesthood. I'd be more celibate than the Pope.

Funny, the parting words of Terri and Dad, at either end of California, were identical. "Keep in touch." But how do you keep something you've never been in? Like previous visits home, this one was memorable for what never happened. If my family were a car, one would describe our clutch as being disengaged.

That sounds harsh, I know. Unhappily, the child in me never recovered from the divorce and the rounds of step-parents, step- and half-siblings. Or outgrew the fanciful hope of seeing Terri and Dad reunited and love reborn. Yes, just like in the movies that are no longer produced.

The airport spurred another of my acts—reporter—when the overbooked airline bumped me. A clerk escorted me into the plane's first-class section, however, after I flashed a *New York Times* stringer calling card, which had expired on my graduation from Columbia.

At Kennedy Airport, a very warm welcome was tendered me by a luscious blond, built like a trio of cookie jars, who had also flown from L.A. and, after sharing a cab to the city, invited me up for a nightcap, following which she volunteered herself till Monday morning. The first thought to pop into my mind was, Tomorrow I'll be smiling. Yet I had never stayed the night with a girl without exchanging a minimum of ten thousand words first. To me, a meaningful relationship is a banquet, sex the dessert and after-dinner smoke. Would a gourmet start a meal by pulling out a cigar and downing a brown betty?

"This," I noted, "is Friday."

"Don't worry. I'll pace you." She refilled my glass of scotch. "Why the hesitation? I won't think you a pushover." She placed a hand over a perfectly rounded heart.

"Well, you see . . . I don't believe in sex before names."

She uncupped her hand and stuck it out. "Lorna. And you?"

How soft the hand, and still warm. "Baron, Andrew."

"Oh, royalty. Well, your highness, what now? My social security number?" She looked me up and down.

"Lorna? Ever read Martin Buber's *I and Thou*?"

Both hands flew to her curly blond head. "I guess you can lead an intellectual to bed, but you can't make him!"

"Oh," I riposted, "is that so?"

Afterward, I discovered Terri was right about one thing. Actually, something Orson Welles had told her. It's impossible to make a great movie in Technicolor. With color overloading the visual senses, viewers can't concentrate on character development and personality interplay. Had we gotten to know each other before knowing each other, surely Lorna wouldn't have declared the next morning, "I believe in total honesty, don't you?" before presenting a critique like one that faults an author for the book he didn't write. Evidently, whatever happened in Lorna's bed was mere curtain raiser to her review, the genuine climax.

When I asked, testily, if my performance was being graded, she shrugged. "If you're that sensitive, I'll mark you on a curve."

A kidder myself, I often assume people are putting me on. Take Nixon at his inauguration swearing on the Bible to uphold the Constitution.

"Fix breakfast, will you? I find it degrading to make men meals." Lorna also deplored, endlessly, husbands, children, and the family, which also kept women in bondage.

Finally, I interrupted to note that the exodus from Egypt would have meant nothing without the Israelites' accepting the responsibility of the Ten Commandments seven weeks later.

Three blinks in rapid succession. "Why, you're not even—" She threw back the blanket and took another look. "You a religion reporter?"

"No, a grad student in sociology."

Lorna jumped out of bed. "Of all the piggy tricks! Just to get me into the sack. You knew I'd give my right arm for a job on the *Times*. Passing yourself off in the L.A. airport as a reporter—"

Alas, idyll's end. I suppose that's what you call it when a woman drops your suitcase out of her window.

Dear Drew,
Sometimes I think I'm back in New York's Lower East Side or Brighton Beach. Saigon's streets teem with the same perpetual motion of shoppers and strollers, fruit and vegetable stands, vendors with their singsong cries, kids playing on the sidewalks.

Other times nothing seems real. The human turkey shoots called search-and-destroy missions in free-fire zones. Notches on rifles. Daily announcements of body counts, like box scores at a ball game. Few condemnations of Lt. Calley. "Who am I to judge him?" soldiers say. "It could have been any of us."

I wonder how many other My Lais there were. Last week, seeing American troop carriers drive by with a dozen or more figs attached to their antennas, I asked where to get some to supplement my kosher vegetarian diet. "Those aren't figs," I was told. "They're Vietcong ears."

The chaplain I've been assigned to has never mentioned Calley. He's too busy blessing bullets, a swift way of bringing souls to God. To hear him preach, you'd think God were bucking for His sixth star. At funerals this chaplain delivers pep talks calling for Revenge with Honor. After one, a mourner punched him in the mouth.

And I, Levi Simon, am his assistant.

A note from Rabbi Brownmiller brought an apology for not inviting me back for the High Holidays. He didn't want to antagonize Mr. Sheridan when a more serious battle loomed over his plan to open the annual temple bazaar on the Sabbath. "Everyone knows," maintained the president, correctly, "Saturday is the best business day."

Since R.I. required sophomores to teach Sunday school, I

phoned Rabbi Brownmiller. Would Mr. Sheridan object to my teaching at the temple?

"Not if you don't make him sit in the corner," said the rabbi.

When I picked up the syllabus and books, he showed me through the beautifully appointed classrooms, commenting, "The previous generation of rabbis was far too successful. They helped to turn hundreds of thousands of immigrant Jews into Americans. Today, it's up to us rabbis to turn millions of their grandchildren into Jews. Only, nobody knows for sure how to do that. Though Jews are America's most educated group, they know little about Judaism. A colleague suggested giving boys umbrellas instead of Bibles at their bar mitzvah. Umbrellas, they're sure to open." He held out his hands, palms upward. "Meanwhile, we rabbis wait like encyclopedias on a shelf for congregants to pick us up on occasion."

Yet Terri reported a disproportionate number of Jews in Zen, Vedanta, Subud, Bahai, and the Theosophic Society.

"We should make it easy for people to join temples, Andrew. But difficult to stay. Impose standards."

R.I. had done just that, mustering out Stanford Price. I was pleased the school had standards. Delighted they hadn't been applied against me.

"Only intensive Jewish education, day schools, can save us. At a recent wedding reception, a Nobel Prize winner quoted to me all he remembered from Hebrew school. 'Hatarn'gol korei kukuriku.'"

English translation: The rooster cries *Cockadoodledoo.*

Back in his office, the rabbi grew reflective. "Unfortunately, we've been so damn efficient at organizing temples— the bigger the better—they now alienate Jews and undermine Judaism. Many are too large, impersonal, cold. Andrew, know the cry most often heard by rabbis? 'Rabbi, I bet you don't know my name.'"

That had a familiar ring. A score of people had remarked that even to me. And they didn't even know *my* name.

Rabbi Brownmiller spoke of dividing the temple's eight

hundred families into *havuros*, small fellowships. Groupings of up to ten families would create a sense of belonging to each other, strengthen their ties to the synagogue and to Judaism. "Belonging precedes believing," he declared. "So does doing. *Havuros* meeting in homes for study and observing the Holy Days together. Celebrating the rites of passage as a single family. Supporting each other during adversity. That has to be the next phase in the development of the synagogue. We must restore the sense of community. The synagogue can't manufacture Jews or create Jewish life. It can only be the end product of living that goes on outside its walls." He smiled sheepishly. "Well, Andrew? What do you think of my Rosh Hashonah sermon?"

Ever find it difficult to crawl out of bed in the morning? Or catch yourself crawling back in the afternoon? And napping in between? I spent all the next day in the sack. The Vietnam War still raged, while ahead loomed another year at R.I. as phony-in-residence.

With neither of my schools in session during August, and nearly friendless on account of my dual work load during the rest of the year, I grew restive, sick of myself. How wonderful, then, to happen on Isaca Zion near Columbia, despite my having to reveal my moonlighting at the university when she detected my load of sociology books. The news pleased her.

"Everyone speculated about your daily disappearances at the stroke of twelve." She invited me over for later in the week.

Oddly enough, when I showed up at the Zions', Isaca reacted with surprise, and stared at the box in my hand.

"Strawberry shortcake."

"I take it you don't fast on Tisha B'Av, Andrew."

Another fast? Then I recalled: Tisha B'Av commemorated the destruction of the First and Second Temples. But Reform Jews, glad to be rid of the sacrificial cult, didn't observe the holiday.

Isaca handed me a skullcap. "You'll join us at shul tonight, won't you?"

"Us," gathered in the living room, were several of Dr. Zion's colleagues and students. Also an assistant dean from Union Theological Seminary.

My forgetting Tisha B'Av spurred Dr. Zion to comment on the result of the emancipation of the Jews in the wake of the French Revolution. Having been freed at last to participate in cultural and social Europe, Reform Jews sought to integrate themselves into Western society. "But the process eroded the identity of many. Then, Jews fought to be equal, modern. Now, our struggle is to be different. To be Jews."

Where did the Conservative Movement fit in? "It was the response to Reform's radical swing to the left," said Dr. Zion. "Reform abandoned *halacha*, Jewish law, whereas Orthodoxy, by refusing to allow any changes, allowed the law to abandon the Jews."

Isaca charged her father with selling Reform short. It had prepared the way for the rise of both the Conservative Movement and Modern Orthodoxy.

"True," Dr. Zion said. "And there's more." Reform's universalism balanced Orthodoxy's exclusivistic tendencies, just as Reform could fly away into abstractions and platitudes if not for traditional Judaism's insistence on performance of commandments. Also, Reform Jews had been the financial mainstays of the Jewish Theological Seminary.

Who could understand the love-snub relationship among the three branches of Judaism? God . . . Maybe.

Someone called attention to the time. The name of a latecomer, who was awaited, prompted a *"Father Chuck Jovak?"*

Dr. Zion misunderstood my gulp. "His *true* collaborator finally came forward. He had been mad at Father Chuck for mistaking another black for him."

"You don't say." I grabbed Isaca's hand and pulled her to the door. But it opened on Father Chuck. And me with no lampshade over my head. Fearing a reference to my Gentile mother, however lapsed, I congratulated him at once and at great length for having been cleared.

"It was a bum rap. Nobody can tell blacks apart better than this honky," the priest insisted. "The F.B.I. framed me." Then, alas, he thanked me for having sheltered him.

Isaca asked for details, but by then fourteen of us were cramming into two cars that took us to an imposing Orthodox synagogue on Central Park West, where an usher directed Isaca upstairs.

"Separate but equal praying," she muttered.

The sanctuary, set up like a theater in the round with the pulpit in the center, was illuminated only by candlelight. The male congregation sat in a circle on the floor and on low benches. Up front a black curtain hung over the Ark like a shroud, and the dirges and lamentations that ensued resembled a protracted funeral service. How odd that the Catholic Mass focused on the suffering of one Jew, Jesus, but the Six Million were neglected. "Why," I asked, "doesn't Judaism observe a holy day to memorialize the Holocaust?"

A look of pain creased Dr. Zion's brow. "All are guilty of that omission. It takes decades to transcend ineffable horror." An impatient wave of the hand. "No, that's a rationalization. We fear seeing ourselves for what we were and always shall be. 'A people dwelling apart, not reckoned among the nations.' Jews are like mice sent on ahead in mines. Their being overcome by coal gas alerts miners to danger. Mice save countless lives that way. At the cost of their own."

After the service there was a festive gathering outside the synagogue. From sad to glad so swiftly, it was a wonder nobody got emotional bends. Soon our party left for an antiwar rally in a church nearby whose many empty seats indicated that the peace movement would very likely end long before the war did. Especially since the Administration gave no evidence of wishing to tamper with failure.

"Hiding Father Chuck at your place," Isaca said. "I suppose that wasn't selfless either."

I shook my head. *"Roué oblige."*

"Andrew, why do you always put yourself down?"

"Do I? I wasn't aware of that. Sorry."

"No need to apologize to *me*," she said.

Father Chuck, a powerful speaker, excited the crowd to whose responses he reacted like a motor to fuel injections. In referring to a number of clergymen who had organized groups urging Nixon "to use the sword as God intended," the priest remarked, "It's a good thing for God I don't believe in guilt by association." He called for open warfare against the war. If need be, shutting down the U.S. Government.

Subsequent speeches set me to contemplating Isaca. It is good to look at the fair, Mrs. Simon once said, and live with the wise. Dr. Zion's self-possessed daughter was both. Her integrity and purposefulness made me feel inferior. Envious. Suddenly, it occurred to me how easy it would be to fall in love with her. Assuming I was capable of that emotion. Isaca *liked* me.

Now, if only I could like myself.

She caught me staring. "Anything the matter?"

"I was just thinking . . ." Lornas were transient, Isacas enduring; Lorna junk food, Isaca a feast.

"Yes?"

"You'll make one hell of a rabbi."

"Think so?" She sighed. "My father worries about me."

"What on earth for?"

She averted her eyes.

"Isaca?"

"Yes?"

But Dr. Zion was now at the lectern. "After he finishes."

The rabbi read a selection from the prophet Amos with several slight emendations that electrified the crowd.

> Woe to them that are at ease in Washington,
> And to them that are secure in the White House,
> The notable men of the first of nations
> To whom the people of America look.

Thus saith the Lord:
Because they have threshed Vietnam with sledges of iron,
So will I send a fire into the White House,
And it shall devour this Administration.
Because they send soldiers to pursue their brothers
    with the sword,
And did cast off all pity,
Because they have ripped up the women with child
    of Cambodia
That they might enlarge their war,
So will I kindle a fire in the White House,
And it shall devour the Administration thereof.
And their President shall go into exile,
He and his officers together.
Because he burned the bones of Vietnamese with napalm,
So will I send upheaval upon the United States,
Because its leaders have rejected the law of the land
And have not kept its statutes,
And their lies have caused their people to err,
To stray from teachings of the Founding Fathers.
Those that cause violence while lying far away upon
    beds of ivory—
They are not grieved for the hurt of others—
Therefore, now they shall go to prison.
Take away from Me the noise of speeches,
And let Me not hear melodious verbiage anymore.
But let justice well up as waters,
And righteousness as a mighty stream.
Are ye not as the children of the Vietnamese unto Me,
O children of America? saith the Lord.

During the standing ovation that followed, Isaca turned to
me, eyes shining. "You once asked why I wanted to become a
rabbi, Andrew. Well, now you know."

"The acclaim?"

She was taken aback. "The *continuity*. Look how words
three thousand years old can still affect people."

Continuity. Her reason for maintaining the unbroken chain
of Zion rabbis. Continuity. What I could never offer Isaca. It

was one thing to deceive a girl, but quite another to do so in perpetuity.

". . . Andrew. You were about to say?"

"Tisha B'Av," I said. "Such a sad holiday." Who would have thought one could lose a woman not to another man but to the ages?

EIGHT

It threw me, two o'clock in the morning a voice identifying itself as Rabbi Brownmiller's commanding, "Come right over. Fourteen Ash Avenue. Hurry!"

Had that really been the rabbi? What could he want at that hour? And the night without moon or stars or traffic. Nothing eerier than no cars on Manhattan streets and the Long Island Expressway. Were muggers now picking off automobiles?

At Ash Avenue, who should open the door to its Beverly Hills-type mansion but President Sheridan, pale and haggard. "What are you doing here?" he said.

"Andrew!" The rabbi materialized in the foyer. He looked completely drained. "Thanks for coming."

Sheridan gestured in my direction. "Why call *him*?"

Mrs. Sheridan dragged herself into view. Two buttons were missing from her housecoat. "I thought it was the police," she said. "All that screaming in the attic—"

Rabbi Brownmiller grabbed me by the arm. "Stay!" What was going on here? The Sheridan's teen-age son had been locked away, to save him from the Messiah.

"You did say the *Messiah*?"

The rabbi nodded wearily and pointed to an oil painting. Lloyd, a freshman at an Ivy League college, had been lured away by a self-proclaimed descendant of the Virgin Jesus and Mary Magdalene. Now Lloyd denounced his parents as emissaries of Satan.

"We're Reform Jews," Mrs. Sheridan interjected, bewildered. "We don't believe in Satan *or* the Messiah. Do we, Rabbi?"

Sheridan continued the story. His son had quit college to go begging in the streets of New York for fictitious drug programs and to sell novelty items to aid nonexistent poor children. When he demanded the money in his bar mitzvah gifts bank account, Sheridan had taken along two of his employees, and together they had spirited Lloyd off.

"You kidnaped him?"

Mrs. Sheridan bristled. "We can't kidnap what's *ours*."

I turned to Rabbi Brownmiller. "What did you expect of me?"

"Get Lloyd to talk. In four days he hasn't said any word to anyone but *love*. Maybe you can get through to the boy, Andrew."

"Convince Lloyd we're not devils," pleaded the mother.

"What did God's Grandson ever do for Lloyd?" cried the father.

"Lloyd is a Jew," said the rabbi. "He doesn't need to be saved."

Of all people to turn an apostate back into a Jew, and a parent-hater into a son and lover. "This requires a Jew . . . ish psychiatrist."

Mrs. Sheridan burst out, "Today's men of God! Pose a religious problem, and they lay you on the couch."

Two psychiatrists had been consulted, Sheridan volunteered, but they wouldn't come. And Lloyd only chanted at a third psychiatrist, who advised against a deprogrammer. "He said it was too risky. Might drive Lloyd over the edge."

"But why would your son talk to *me*?"

With a side glance at Sheridan, the rabbi replied, "Lloyd has to speak to *somebody*." He asked me to walk him to his car.

Outside, he remarked that if the temple had been *havura*ized, the other families could have helped the Sheridans now, might even have prevented Lloyd's defection. An extended family was a counterweight to peer group pressure that can drag kids into uncharted whirlpools.

"How you can be so nice after his open letter to the congregation." Sheridan had called the *havura* a concept that was ass-backwards, though not of course in that word.

"He's not at all unique, Andrew. Any clergyman will tell you that parishioners want to be inspired and uplifted, but not changed." Rabbi Brownmiller got into his car and slumped behind the steering wheel. "And remember. One of the six hundred and thirteen commandments obliges us to return a lost animal that belongs even to an enemy."

"Isn't turning the other cheek a Christian teaching?"

The rabbi nodded. "But justice and compassion are owed not only to those we like. Andrew, next time in my office let me show you the contents of a desk drawer. A dozen trulogies. A membership of almost one thousand families just by the law of averages has to include a certain percentage of nudniks. After tangling with some, I write out their eulogies. With this difference. These never-to-be-delivered talks tell the absolute truth. Later, I can again serve them with equanimity," he said. "Andrew, one mustn't visit the sins of the fathers on the children. Poor Lloyd is hurting. His parents too."

"All unearned?"

Rabbi Brownmiller shook his head emphatically. "Hatred they don't deserve."

I must have looked unconvinced. "You resent Sheridan's keeping you from assisting me again during the High Holidays." The rabbi averted his eyes. "Well, here's another truth. Sheridan would have given in if I had really insisted. But . . . the great disparity in our height. I thought it made me look foolish."

I was touched by his confession. "About Lloyd. Anyone warn him that staying out of school will end his student deferment?"

Rabbi Brownmiller beamed. "None of us thought of that."

Back inside the house, the Sheridans sat me down and

pleaded their case to convince each other of their innocence. "Episcopalian, at least I could understand. But a crackpot!" Sheridan exclaimed. "After the best private schools. Summer camps in Switzerland. A large allowance. Sports car. Everything I was denied as a kid. All the opportunities. And what did we ask in return? Just that Lloyd work up to his potential."

"And don't think he was one of those latchkey children," Mrs. Sheridan put in. "I was always home when Lloyd returned from school. Always in contact with his teachers. Constant heart-to-heart dialogues. Why, my husband and I focused our lives on Lloyd. All we wanted was for him to be happy."

Everything I resented Terri and Dad for neglecting to do. What, then, had gone wrong? "There must be *some* reason," I said.

The coffee cup rattled in Sheridan's hand. He placed it on the table and said bitterly, "To be a parent today is to be guilty."

Mrs. Sheridan nodded. "It isn't just us. These days, if you want to make people cry, just inquire about their children." Wistfully, she added, "How I envy your parents, Mr. Baron. They must be so proud."

I winced. "Come. Let's go."

On our way upstairs, she urged me to remind Lloyd to put antibiotic ointment on his foot, while Sheridan expressed fears of his son's doing himself harm. He opened the attic, padlocked from the outside, after promising me a stereo. "Eighteen speakers."

I'd have swapped all eighteen for one match. For no sooner was the door locked behind me than the light went out. The sudden darkness had me reeling. "Lloyd!" I cried. "Turn on the damn light."

There was no response.

"*Please* turn on the damn light."

Not a sound.

And my father wanted me to be a hunter. I banged on the

door. When nobody responded to that either, dozens of old horror films flashed through my mind. "*Lloyd!*"

Not so much as an echo.

If the kid didn't want to talk, that was all right with me. I wouldn't know anyway how to respond. So making for a studio couch glimpsed just before the onset of blackness, I stretched out in what felt like a grave filled in.

All of a sudden, "For God so loved the world that He gave His only begotten Son . . ." It was Lloyd, I presumed, who chanted in singsong fashion half a dozen verses that proceeded in sixty seconds from God's love to man's estrangement to the Messiah's saving power to Christ's invitation to receiving the Son of God. This formula Lloyd repeated endlessly like a robot. Whenever the kid got stuck, he had to start all over again, for he spurned my prompting. Over and over again, the same verses in the same monotone. . . .

Someone was standing over me. The light being on, I could see two glassy eyes shining down.

"You were snoring."

I rolled off the couch and scrambled to my feet. A second glance revealed a dark, scrawny kid in a bathrobe with a crew cut, acne, and a spaced-out smile.

"Aren't you the guy who put my father in his place?"

Clever Rabbi Brownmiller. He was banking on Lloyd's taking the enemy of his father for a friend.

"You should have heard the names he called you."

"Tell me, Lloyd."

When he did, I regretted having asked. Seeing my reaction, the kid said, "Help me get back to my *true* family."

"If you give me good enough reason, Lloyd."

"That's easy." As a child titles his recitation before delivering it, "My bar mitzvah reception." He described the Plaza ballroom transformed into a medieval palace and a crown of semiprecious stones and a big Star of David set on his head. Sheridan didn't wear a suit of armor, but Mrs. Sheridan's beaded gown weighed forty-five pounds. Took four months to make and two women to help her into it. There were seven hundred and ninety-six guests. Only the Sheridans' nearest and dearest, plus a few business associates.

Giant skateboards ferried them across an artificial moat to roundtables with centerpieces of paper maché stags amid miniature fields of flowers. Shields bedecked the walls and a group portrait of King Arthur and the Knights of the Roundtable hung over the dais. After Lloyd was toasted with mead in metal beakers, an orchestra playing only the entire score of *Camelot* alternated with a rock band. There was a floor show, too: a trained seal, a magician who sawed Lloyd in half, and a hypnotist whose post-hypnotic suggestions had a surprising number of people taking off their clothes. "Are you listening, Baron?"

"I'm listening, Lloyd."

"Fit for a king, my reception. But not for a teen-ager. How could anyone live up to it? And why did the rabbi allow it? I mean, a bar mitzvah is a *religious* occasion, isn't it?"

"Yes, Lloyd."

"A small sign of my parents' expectations. They wanted me to make a name for them. Even though Dad changed his from Shapiro."

Now there was no stopping Lloyd.

". . . So we moved into this neighborhood, because it's restricted. You should see it at Christmas, ours the only home on the block without lights. Inside, of course, we always exchange gifts, and we have a tree. Yet Dad sued to have a manger removed from the town mall."

I limited myself to noncommittal responses.

"My search for leaven before Passover with a wooden spoon and a feather. It embarrassed Dad. We had company at the time. So he stuck the feather in my hair and called me Yankee Doodle."

Funny. Lloyd was describing the culturally deprived child.

"Baron, you know the only two commandments my parents ever taught me. *Be Happy* and *Excel.* As if I could know what would make me happy. Then going away to college. I had no idea what to excel *in*. And the moral degradation there. But now I've found a religious community whose welfare means more to me than just my own."

"What about Judaism?"

He scoffed. "Ask Jews what's a good Jew, they'll come up with the definition of a good person. So why stay Jewish? Judaism never *claimed* my soul, the Grandson of God does. Do you have any idea what it means to belong nowhere?"

At last a question I could answer. A sudden, chilling thought. What would happen when I wouldn't have the Vietnam War to kick me around anymore?

Lloyd went on like the mills at the bottom of Davy Jones' locker. "I could never feel at home with myself before. Always the fear of falling short. Always another hurdle ahead. St. Luke was right. 'If any man come to me and hate not his father and mother, he cannot be a disciple of mine.' Thank God for the Grandson of God! He loves me *unconditionally*. . . . Help me escape, Baron, and you can have my sports car."

Morning, finally.

The attic door opened. Sheridan hurried over. "Well? Well? Did he talk?"

Too exhausted to speak, I nodded.

Over breakfast, Mrs. Sheridan pressed for details. "And how's Lloyd's foot?" Had the Sheridans consulted parents with a similar problem? "No," she said. "My husband would never associate with the sort of people whose children go bad."

Sheridan had another idea. Might Lloyd's problem not be basically hormonal? Suppose he sent a girl up into the attic. When I expressed reservations, Sheridan said, defensively, "That's what the family of St. Thomas Aquinas did. To deter him from joining the Dominican order, they locked him in a room with a whore."

To my surprise, Rabbi Brownmiller wouldn't pin the blame entirely on the Sheridans. "Sometimes the fault lies within the child. His personality, misinterpretation. Take the regal reception, Andrew. It never happened."

I couldn't believe that.

"A friend of his had that affair. King Cohn. Lloyd's was lavish, but not as extreme as that of the heir to the Frankfurter King chain. The boy's confused."

The Sheridan's then, weren't responsible for their son's freaking out?

Rabbi Brownmiller weighed his words before replying. "Responsible in part for his over-dependence. The family relationship is too intense. Lloyd was a sickly child. Asthmatic. That threw them together too much. But who knows? Maybe the fault is mine. Long before this I should have done something about the bar mitzvah. Postponed it till eighteen. Many families quit the temple on the way home from the reception. Jewish education they regard like bed-wetting— something to outgrow."

Dr. Diamond claimed to have discovered what happened to the Ten Lost Tribes of Israel. They weren't lost, he announced one day. They just got bar mitzvahed. "Rabbi, I don't understand Lloyd. The Sheridans are genuinely concerned about him, and they've given him so *much*."

"*Too* much," said Rabbi Brownmiller. "Raised permissively, on relativism, many kids now demand absolutes. And too many parents are fresh out. Sophisticates don't understand that the religious impulse is a constant, that someone who doesn't stand for something is liable to fall for anything."

"Have you explained that . . .?"

"To whom? Too late to tell the Sheridans, and Lloyd won't let me near him." He looked crushed.

They tell us the war is winding down. Closer to the truth is that our troops are cracking up. Nobody hankers to be the last American killed in Vietnam for a mistake. The thrill has even gone out of the kill, with search-and-destroy missions turning into search-and-evade. Now the reigning acronym is CYA & GIH. ("Cover your ass and get it home.")

Drugs are everywhere. Men refuse to go out to fight. Officers are fragged, sometimes killed, by grenades rolled under their beds by their own men. Morale is so bad that Bob Hope, come to entertain us troops, was booed. *Bob Hope!*

The remedy has been to step up the air war, to substitute machines that will fight for men that won't. Salvation through technology. Death sanitized. Few air force personnel have conflicts about a war 40,000 feet down from them. The ones I've met never question why, they merely fly, fly, fly. For all they know, or care, their aircraft could be dropping dew.

Please know, Drew, I've been true to my word. I've never harmed a soul here. All I am is a glorified clerk-typist. So why do I feel as if my typewriter were a machine gun, and every form I fill out a death sentence?

Most nights its difficult for me to fall asleep, even after smoking a joint or two. The hard stuff I avoid, of course. So far.

The night after I returned the Sheridans' stereo, they phoned to invite me back to the attic. Worn-out people, at their wits' end. He could hardly form sentences and she broke down. My heart went out to them. I said I'd come on one condition.

"You'll have a color T.V. first thing Monday morning," said Sheridan.

"Make that *two* conditions. No gifts. And you both go to a motel tonight and get some rest."

"We can't leave Lloyd alone," Mrs. Sheridan said. "What if there's a fire?"

I volunteered to house-sit. Another night-long session in the attic being too much to bear, I'd see Lloyd the following afternoon, after my teaching stint at Sunday school.

I didn't know who to feel sorrier for, parents or child. Three wrecks. Sheridan had to drag his wife away from the house, and Lloyd, upstairs, could be heard through the night chanting about love. Sleep didn't come easy.

Neither did conversation. At our reunion Lloyd would talk of nothing but a ride he wanted me to take him for. A trick,

Sheridan declared. After Lloyd went on a hunger strike, Mrs. Sheridan changed her husband's mind. He then gave me his Bentley, all its windows jammed shut and only one door that opened.

"Take care of your foot," Mrs. Sheridan called as Lloyd, in a bathrobe, padded shoeless and wordless past her into the car. "You only have two."

I followed into the driver's seat, and, heeding Sheridan's instructions, drove away from town with its traffic cops. No sense in risking the boy's banging on the window and crying kidnaped.

After a replay of the other night's monologue, Lloyd launched into a discourse on touching. Apparently Jesus, who regularly practiced the laying on of hands to heal people or forgive them, had instructed his followers to do likewise. "Touch transmits energy and grace from one to the other like currents of electricity," the kid said, then asked, "What's the most intimate form of touching?"

Terrific. Now we'd get into, after religion, my second greatest area of nonexpertise.

"No, not sex. Communion, ingesting the flesh and blood of Christ by eating the host and drinking the wine." Even prior to the Last Supper, Jesus ordered his disciples: "If I then, your Lord and Master, have washed your feet, ye also ought to wash one another's feet." Hardly were the words out of Lloyd's mouth than the kid offered me a footwash.

Evidently a family with a foot problem. "No, thanks. I took a shower this morning."

"I *mean* it." Foot-washing, which involved touch, took precedence even over Communion. Bowing to Jesus' command, the Pope washed lots of feet on T.V. once a year. Only, he merely dabbed one big toe with a wet rag as if applying nail polish. "Come, let me show you how we do it."

The kid was really into feet, calling them the spiritual litmus paper of our being in touch with our own bodies and accepting others' in all their extremities. Was anything so nutty anymore that it couldn't pull a following plus a segment on *Eyewitness News?*

Lloyd persisted. "Quick! The first thing to come to mind when I say foot."

"Mouth," I said, "in the."

That stopped him, but only for a moment. "Feet."

"Pretty."

"*Pretty?* Feet?"

"A recent ad for a product called Pretty Feet. It said that feet, being the ugliest part of the body, yearned for it."

"Exactly. Ugly." Lloyd beamed. "That's what Jesus thought. Ugly, ugly, ugly. So he had people connect and interrelate by affirming each other's ugliest parts."

"As it happens, my feet are my best features," I joked. "Better proportioned than my face, whose nose looks like a toe."

"I'm serious, Baron. Stop at the pond ahead and I'll prove it." Lloyd jammed his bare foot on the brake. "Let's go," he said.

I hesitated. Suppose someone saw us playing footsies in the grass. Who'd believe we were only doing Jesus' bidding?

"Come, Baron. Nobody here to watch."

We got out of the car and entered the park. He had me sit on the grass, then removed both my shoes and socks and rolled up my pants legs. That revived memories of pail and shovel.

"Be right back." Lloyd ran to a pond and pulled from his pocket a shower cap, which he filled with water. Returning, he doused my feet, again quoting St. John.

"Close your eyes now while I dry you. Experience this spiritually." He pulled off the towel worn around his neck like a muffler.

Close my eyes and have him smother me? Nothing doing.

The kid toweled my toes one by one. "What do you feel? No, don't tell me. Tell yourself."

Something was missing. What? Soon I realized. Nobody

was chanting, "This little piggy went to market, this little piggy stayed home."

"Shut your eyes, Baron. For maximum spiritual sensation. Come on, shut them."

I lowered my eyelids to half-mast.

"All the way. That's right. . . . Now do you feel our interrelationship?"

What I felt was something affirming my thigh and inter-creeping into my pocket. A moment later, the car keys were jangling in the foot lover's hand. Infuriated, I grabbed his fist and enclosed it in mine, then squeezed until he howled. "That's right, Lloyd, close all five fingers. Closed now? Good boy." When at last I relaxed my grip, the keys slid into the grass.

Even before I retrieved them, Lloyd took off. I started after him, only to fall on my face. The *momzer* had tied my feet together with the towel, knotting it tightly enough to invite gangrene. Happily, the thickness of the towel made it easy to untie. But now Lloyd was nowhere to be seen. When I ran back to the car, instead of driving up and down the road we had come on, I turned onto a pedestrian walk and drove across the park to the road on the other side.

And there was Lloyd in bare feet and flapping bathrobe, trying to flag down a car. Seeing the Bentley, he took off again.

Fine, for I felt like subduing the cheat after a brutal battle. Jumping out of the car, I chased Lloyd across the grass and felled him with a flying tackle. The kid struggled.

"You can't take me back. Something terrible will happen to me!"

That shook me. "You broke your promise, Lloyd."

"Of course I lied. I had to. To survive."

My own defense for being at R.I. I released the kid.

He rolled away. "It wasn't *all* a lie. The foot-washing rite I meant. But you don't want my fate on your conscience, do you?"

"Look, Lloyd—" It was then that I saw the blood on the kid's foot. Had my tackle broken his leg?

Following my shocked gaze, he said, "It'll heal. The other one did." He wiped away the blood with his bathrobe.

On the right foot was an ugly wound, its scab ripped off. It resembled an infection I once contracted after stepping on a nail. Only, this was on *top* of the foot. No wonder Mrs. Sheridan had nagged. Oddly enough, Lloyd's other foot bore a scar in the same place.

The kid drew his knees up to his chest and hid his feet under the bathrobe. "It's nothing." Not another word about his feet, despite all the liberties I had allowed him with mine.

"Compromise?" I would try to persuade the Sheridans to free him if he could hold his own against them. "Nothing to lose by one chat. Besides, how far can you get in a bloody bathrobe?"

He considered the proposal for a few minutes. "Okay."

Late supper was a contest of how much food Mrs. Sheridan could pile on Lloyd's plate—"It makes me feel good," she kept saying, "when you eat"—and how much he left over to deny her satisfaction. Yet when he thought himself unobserved, the kid sneaked brownies into his pocket.

Afterward, we gathered in the living room. At my suggestion, for the bathrobe made him look like a hospital patient, Lloyd had donned blue jeans and a shirt and one shoe. A bandage covered his freshly anointed right foot.

Having yearned for just this encounter, nobody knew where to start. Sheridan sat stiffly in a wing chair, clearing his throat time after time. At one end of the couch his wife kept brushing imaginary dust from her immaculate skirt. At the other end the rabbi crossed and uncrossed his arms. Lloyd sat on the floor, legs tucked under him, as if to convey, Nobody here will touch *my* feet. They belong to the Grandson of God.

Finally, Rabbi Brownmiller opened. This was no debate, he said. "Let's start with something all of us can agree on."

"Right." Lloyd nodded. "Let's talk about God."

Mrs. Sheridan looked at her husband in dismay. He said, "What?"

"God Almighty," said the kid, as if naming Him in full. "You never think of Him, do you? This house never heard God mentioned except before damn."

Sheridan replied, "I'm a busy man—"

"Of course you are," said Lloyd. "Making money."

Sheridan retorted, "So you discovered a new crime. Upward mobility."

Lloyd's head swung like a gun turret in the rabbi's direction. "Come to think of it, I never heard much God-talk from the pulpit. Social action, Vietnam, psychiatry, best sellers, blacks, sex. The 'David Susskind Show' without commercials. Rabbi, you must be a busy man, too."

The color rose in Rabbi Brownmiller's cheeks.

"I never *felt* anything in temple. Only abstractions there. Head without heart. No music. Tell me, Rabbi, do *you* believe?"

"Of course, certainly."

"*What*, Rabbi?"

"I believe, as the Talmud states, on Judgment Day the *first* question asked will be 'Have you acted honorably toward your fellow men?'"

Lloyd rubbed his thighs, as wrestlers often do before an assault. "You certainly have a way with evasions, Rabbi. And you call yourself a man of God?"

Rabbi Brownmiller heaved a sigh. "I don't *know* God, never having double-dated with Him. Which is the impression some people like to give. As for religion, that word never appears in the Bible. Whatever we do that affects others is religious."

Lloyd applauded. "Beautiful, just beautiful, your generalizations." He went to the bookcase and took out a copy of the *Union Prayer Book*, opening it at random. "You subscribe to this?"

Rabbi Brownmiller scanned the page. "I do."

Greater care went into the selection of a second passage.

The rabbi looked it over. "Not in its entirety."

The kid pointed out a verse. "And this?"

The rabbi's lips moved soundlessly while he reread the words. "No."

"One more." Lloyd pointed it out. "Believe?"

The rabbi flared. "You're so young, so positive. So corrupted by certitude. Lloyd, I pray every time I stand on the pulpit, I pray every day at home, I pray with all my heart that I *may* believe. Can you understand that?"

A smirk. "You also believe in Temple Shalom's annual dinner dance? Like the one in honor of the Year of the Monkey, complete with costumes and Chinese cuisine. My parents, I recall, went as Mr. and Mrs. Mao Tse-tung."

Mrs. Sheridan spoke up for the first time. "Your father and I never *forced* beliefs on you, Lloyd. We always gave you the freedom to choose, make up your own mind. Why, we treated you as an equal. So what on earth are you rebelling *against*?"

Was *this* the key to the mystery? Teaching confirmation class, I had noted that for every teen-ager who reveled in making up his own values, there were half a dozen others who felt threatened by the overabundance of options and choices. Yielding to class rebels often earned me not appreciation, but surliness. As if I had abandoned them to chaos. They seemed to need the law to be laid down. Any law.

"Against meaninglessness," Lloyd said. "Otherwise, I'm all for. For God, who is love. Only devils would try to keep us apart."

Mrs. Sheridan clapped a hand to her mouth, while her husband did a fast burn.

"Not that I hate you two, understand. My concern is a matter of record. You can get Xerox copies. I've had the Grandson of God baptize both sets of your parents. Would I do that for people I hate?"

"But, Lloyd," Mrs. Sheridan said nervously. "Your grandparents are all *dead*."

The kid nodded. "Proves my point. You have any idea how hard it is to dig up their birth dates for the baptism by proxy?"

"But *why*?" That was me.

"The unbaptized can never gain eternal salvation. So once a week the Grandson of God conducts baptism for those in the hereafter. Of course, they're free to reject it."

"Sounds to me," Rabbi Brownmiller remarked, "the Grandson of God thinks the only good Jew is a dead Christian."

Lloyd said, "I didn't expect you to understand. Performing a public service that those in the spirit world can't perform for themselves. Is there a greater *mitzvah*? One day I'll have my parents baptized too."

Sheridan jumped up. "Over my dead body!"

"Yes," said Lloyd calmly. He went on to describe his new life, boasting like a spiritual stud. "Now I have *multiple* mystical experiences. What about you, Rabbi?"

A wistful look appeared in the rabbi's eyes. He rubbed his jaw and looked away. "Mystical experiences? I can count them on my fingers—and have several left over. The day my father died. My son's *bris*. The March on Washington in '63. The Six-Day War. A few others. I wish there'd been more. But I've never forced any." He turned his gaze on Lloyd and a note of iron crept into his voice. "Still and all, mountaintops were made for billy goats, not for people. Life is lived on the plains, with only occasional side trips up to the peaks or down into the valleys. Religion is not for extraordinary occasions, any more than marriage is. It's for summoning us to do our duty by others."

"You forgot love! What of love? It's. . . ." The more Lloyd lectured us on the Messiah's redeeming love, the more it sounded like gratitude for being loved *for* his sins, the fate of all men. Enter the Grandson of God. Not to dispute feelings of worthlessness, but to confirm them. To get losers to lie back and relax and let life happen to them. Love? More like rape.

Growing circles of red on the kid's bandage caught my eye. "Lloyd? What are they? You never did say. Those things that look like stigmata."

"Stigmata?" Mrs. Sheridan turned on her husband. "I *told* you to call the doctor for penicillin."

"*All right.* All right all right all right! Let them know about the initiation rites." Lloyd's eyes went wild and his speech frenzied. "When the Grandson of God had me identify with Christ by driving in the nails"—gasps from the Sheridans—"I did doubt his love. But Jesus also felt betrayed, remember. . . ."

Intoxicating! I wish it were mine, such exaltation, though one had to concede, eventually, that not even Sir Laurence Olivier's declaiming the telephone directory could enhance its meaning. The kid had showed me up. Since I was forever looking before I leaped, my feet never left the ground. True, Lloyd had landed in quicksand. But no leaps, no stars.

Rabbi Brownmiller exclaimed in a choking voice, "You allowed yourself to be *crucified?*"

The kid corrected him. "Vivified." He pointed to the rabbi's shoes. "You don't find *me* wearing high heels."

"Sick, sick, sick," cried Sheridan.

Lloyd confronted his father. "Know the real issue here? You're jealous of me. Every single one of you. Because I believe in something, and all of you believe in nothing."

"That's not true! Not true at all!" Mrs. Sheridan said, in tears. "We believed in *you*, Lloyd. We *worshiped* you."

The gathering broke up soon afterward. Only a resurrection could top a crucifixion.

Rabbi Brownmiller despaired of Lloyd's recovery. "That Grandson of God is a *devil*," he said. "Involving his followers in something so shameful. Now the boy will have to spend years rationalizing it. Maybe, God forbid, forever."

The Mr. Sheridan I saw in Sunday school was not the same man of the year or even the week before. Ashen, as if he had been gutted by a fire. "I did it. . . . Had to. . . . No other way." He made no sense until: "I called Lloyd's draft board."

"They'll send him to Vietnam!"

"You think me a terrible father, don't you?"

"Lloyd will hate you for the rest of his life."

"I'm prepared for that." A wince belied his words. "So long as Lloyd *has* a life. Something he'd lose programed by that soulsucker. Worse than a jailed son or a dead one is a living corpse. I turned Lloyd in out of love."

"*Love?*"

"It's true, I swear it! I told on Lloyd for his own sake. To save him. My God! If you don't believe me, Baron, how will my wife?"

NINE

Many couples have a song they heard while courting or falling in love that remains forever theirs. Isaca and I will always have strawberry shortcake.

Invited with several other classmates for dinner before work on a group project, I was first to arrive. With me, another strawberry shortcake.

Isaca opened the box and said, "You should have. Tisha B'Av's was delicious."

Just then, the phone rang. Starting toward it, she twisted her ankle and fell sideways. On me. "Oh!"

The delicious cake slid from Adam's apple to crotch. Knocked off balance, I dropped to the floor, squishy with the cake that had preceded me.

Isaca stared in disbelief, then howled. She could barely get the words out between whoops. "You—look—like—a—Charlotte—Russe."

It took half a roll of paper towels to clean up. And then I still felt like a greased pig.

"How awful! I've ruined your clothes." A giggle as she removed a strawberry from my hair.

"I don't understand it, Isaca. In the movies it's always the woman who gets soaked in order to be slipped into something comfortable."

Quickly, she said, "I don't think my robe would fit you."

"I know for sure your father's doesn't." I headed for the door. The sight in the hall mirror, coupled with the thought of my car upholstery, stopped me. "Do you have a large Baggie?"

Isaca went to a closet and took out a roll of Saran Wrap. "How's this?" She tore off several yards.

"The last time I put on Saran—" I checked myself.

"You *wear* Saran? What on earth for?"

Blushing is why I made do with Saran. To avoid drugstore proprietors. "See you later, Isaca." I went to the door and opened it.

Dr. Zion was standing on the threshold. His eyes widened as they traveled the length of my body, gleaming in Saran. For several moments he said nothing. Finally: "You find you keep fresh this way?"

The next move, Isaca's came via parcel post. A gift package containing a can of Reddi-Whip and a jar of strawberries, plus a thin plastic raincoat "to be used"—said the note—"instead of Saran Wrap." (Well, to each his own.)

Naturally, I called. One word led to another, then to a date. But not with the Isaca who laughed herself silly. This was my beauty with the unempty head. To discuss with, if the world is your cup of tea.

After a lengthy preview of Dr. Zion's latest book, I wondered aloud. "Whatever happened to that girl with the attractive giggle? You sound like an editorial."

"And men prefer sports and amusements."

"See what I mean?"

"I want to be taken seriously as a rabbi, Andrew. So I can be effective," she said. "Fun-loving females are written off as weak sisters. Would *you* respect a woman who—" She jabbed her fingers into my midriff and tickled me.

"Golly," I said, "you're beautiful when you're angry."

"I'm *not* angry!"

"What about beautiful? You challenge that, too?"

Isaca couldn't suppress a smile.

A few more dates turned us into friends. I made her laugh, she made me think better of myself. And on a visit to her student pulpit, feel deeply. The service was held in a Jewish center on the Lower West Side. When I dropped in, unexpected, Isaca was saying, "Let us pray together."

Only her voice sounded, while she motioned with arms and hands. Everyone followed suit silently, for Isaca's was a congregation of the deaf. None of the prayers, having been revised for signing, was bloodlessly abstract, all were as concrete as the human body itself. An exquisite ballet. Isaca didn't merely lead the group. She became prayer. Prayer in motion. A person who was what she said. Flesh made spirit.

While the congregation exchanged Sabbath greetings afterward, she approached with a *Shabbas shalom.* Too moved to speak, I took her in my arms and kissed her.

"Andrew!"

I disengaged. "Sorry."

"Apologizing again?" she said. "Stand up for yourself, Andrew."

Did Isaca feel something more for me than friendship? Not a chance. Levi was her type. She was much too close to her famous father to be attracted to anyone vastly unlike him. Twice she had asked if I was avoiding Dr. Zion. Her other dates spent almost as much time with him as with her, whereas I always double-parked, calling.

"Come, Isaca. I'll drive you home."

She shook her head. "I don't ride on *Shabbas.*"

"It's drizzling."

"I won't melt."

I caught myself thinking, My heart has. But said, "I'll walk you."

"It's drizzling, Andrew."

"It's *ridiculous.*" More so since Isaca would neither carry an umbrella on the Sabbath nor let me. No, walking five miles in the rain is not my idea of religion *or* fun.

Yet being together made it as romantic as two in a shower. Isaca's face still glowed, or perhaps was just wet. Slyly, I asked for lessons in sign language, finger spelling, and lip reading. A subterfuge, of course.

After four miles of my drinking her in with my eyes, Isaca put me to the test. "You rarely talk about yourself"— signing. "About your family, never."

I replied orally, "Not much to tell."

"You a foundling?" she finger-spelled.

I hesitated.

"Don't you know?" When I couldn't lip-read what followed, she spoke. "You must be very attached to your mother and father."

A laugh so discordant, I topped it off with a big smile. "What makes you say that?"

"You never mention them."

Feminine logic! "So you're *un*attached to your father?"

Isaca considered thoughtfully. "Maybe I'm trying to talk him out of me. I don't want to spend my life being Dr. Zion's daughter."

"You'd *break* with him?"

She stopped short. "No, never! I idolize my father. But I have to be my own person. Separate myself."

At which she'd probably succeed far sooner than I. Far easier to rebel against love than indifference. A person needs his departure noticed.

Once inside Isaca's apartment, I understood the sudden interest in my family. It was Dr. Zion's. While she changed, he inquired about my background with the concern of an admissions committee that had only one opening. And he seemed less than thrilled with the prospect of an alliance with the son of the star of *Curse of the Bat Woman*.

Strangely enough, when I exclaimed over Isaca's performance at the congregation of the deaf, his reaction was more that of a troubled father than a proud one. I voiced a sudden thought: "You're not happy about her becoming a rabbi, are you?"

"It's a boon to Judaism and the Jewish community, of that I'm sure. But as for Isaca herself . . ." Dr. Zion stroked his reddish beard. "There's the isolation of the congregational rabbinate, the loneliness. Clergymen are a group set apart, living symbols. Like policemen and nuns, their closest friends are colleagues. But Isaca won't have even that. She can never be one of the boys. Or, now, one of the girls."

"But once Isaca is married—"

"Hal'vai!" exclaimed her father.

"She must have a dozen men after her. A girl like that."

"The choice is limited," Dr. Zion pointed out. "By her superior intellect, religiosity, yes, even her height. Now. rabbinical school."

After ordination, I realized, it would be harder yet for Isaca to get married, most of her evenings and weekends being taken. She couldn't very well ask to be excused from meetings and services every time someone asked for a date. And if it wasn't easy being Dr. Zion's daughter, how many eligible Mr. Rights would care to become Rabbi Zion's husband? Always a rabbi, her father feared, never a bride.

"Pioneers command my utmost respect and admiration," said Dr. Zion. "Where would the world be without them? But as for a daughter of mine . . ."

"Papa!" Isaca had returned.

Laboriously, I signed. "He is your father. Your father loves you."

She brightened. "Thank you," she finger-spelled.

"No fair," said Dr. Zion with a smile. "Talking in front of my back."

What was truly unfair was to take up more of Isaca's time. I was unworthy to be her husband, and she wasn't the sort for an affair. Happily, the flu struck two days later and kept me in bed for a week. Afterward, I used my dual program of studies to cut down on my social life.

Didn't bother Isaca in the least. Or so she led me to believe with an airy "I'll keep next Tisha B'Av open."

Baron—

Lloyd did get drafted. He could have elected Canada or jail, but neither would have aggravated us as much as the possibility of being shipped to Vietnam and killed.

Of course, I told on Lloyd for the same reason other parents have turned in children who are addicted to drugs. But my wife won't accept that. She's suing for divorce. . . .

R. Sheridan

Dr. Vilno's job was to introduce the class to those commandments not as heavily publicized as the Big Ten, our job to follow the roly-poly rabbi without the benefit of subtitles. His accent was so Lithuanian that nobody understood his advice, "Be svob," until he wrote it out on the blackboard. "Be suave."

A devotee of visual aids, of necessity, Dr. Vilno brought in a two-by-four of pinewood, the inexpensive material from which all Jewish coffins should, out of consideration for the poor, be made. He further taught that in respect to the dead, Judaism bars public viewing of the corpse. "No buddy vants to be seen vhen he's not looking his best."

Samson Finn interrupted. "Know what I find tremendously effective? After the coffin is covered with dirt, I lay a single rose on the grave."

"On *my* graves," said Hank Brenner dryly, "I place daisies."

Dr. Vilno introduced marriage with the Talmudic tale of a Roman matron's inquiring what God had been doing since the Creation. The reply: "Making matches between men and women." For the ceremony Dr. Vilno produced a wedding canopy made of a prayer shawl attached to four rods.

That day Perry Davis came to class in a tuxedo, confident

that nobody resembling Robert Redford can ever look foolish. He had wanted Isaca to wear a wedding gown. She refused, but brought in a home-baked cake topped with a bride and groom and strawberries.

Why a strawberry short wedding cake? Isaca just smiled.

Dr. Vilno recited the opening prayers. Instead of making use of the available woman, however, he took a ring from his left hand and put it on the forefinger of the right, which, according to legend, leads straight to the heart.

To contribute to verisimilitude, I took my Columbia ring and slipped it on Isaca's finger, while reading aloud the ancient formula from the *Rabbi's Manual*: "*Harei at m'kudeshet li b'tabaat zu k'dat Moshe v'Yisroel.*"

Before I could read the translation, as was indicated, she jerked her hand away. "*Andrew!*"

"Don't worry," I said. "That's not the poisoned ring the wicked stepmother gave Snow White."

"*What have you done!*" Isaca jumped up and bolted from the room.

"Efterer, efterer!" shouted Dr. Vilno. "Before it's too late."

The class picked up the cry. "After her! Kiss the bride!" Everyone laughed.

Except Bernie List, who kicked me. "Go on! What are you waiting for!"

"*Oy* oy oy oy oy." Dr. Vilno collapsed in a chair, head in hands. "You did it, Baron! You murderer!"

"What did I do?"

"Merry her."

"What?"

On the blackboard he wrote, "Mr. & Mrs. Baron."

"Mazel tov," everyone shouted. Until Bernie List silenced them with "It's for real."

"Yes," Dr. Vilno said faintly, "a velid merriage."

"But no rabbi pronounced us husband and wife."

"No need. *Oy* oy oy oy oy."

I was out of the room like a shot. But Isaca was nowhere to

be found. Downstairs, the receptionist said she had run from the building. I left, thinking to follow Isaca home, but stopped off at my apartment. No doubt Dr. Zion would soon set things aright. I waited for her call, bemused but not upset. Jews are noted for their sense of humor—they could take a joke.

An hour later the phone rang. "Please come right over," said Dr. Zion.

Isaca would probably return my ring while reciting another ancient formula equivalent to "Nuts to you."

As soon as he opened the door, Dr. Zion demanded to know precisely what had happened.

"Nothing. Ever," I said at once. "As for today. I merely slipped my Columbia ring on her and recited *Harei*—"

"Why?"

"Just kidding."

"You had no intention of marrying my daughter?"

I hesitated.

"You *wanted* to marry her?"

"Yes. No. I mean. . . . What's going on?"

The rabbi motioned me into the living room. Till then we had been standing in the hallway.

"Well, Dr. Zion?"

He looked unkempt, as if his reddish hair and beard had been combed by hand. "According to the law, you and Isaca are married. It's as simple as that. And as terrible. Unless . . ."

"*You* must be kidding! Isaca doesn't have a say whether or not she married?"

Isaca entered the room. She twisted the ring on her forefinger. "The groom *acquires* the bride. By giving her a ring or a coin in front of two witnesses."

The rabbi looked at Isaca. She glanced at me, then dropped her eyes. Neither spoke.

"Unless *what*?"

Dr. Zion said, "A *beth din*, the Jewish law court. I'll consult it tomorrow."

I recalled the translation. *You are consecrated to me according to the laws of Moses and of Israel.* "And if a Gentile said the *Harei*?" The marriage was invalid.

Dr. Zion ground his teeth. "Haven't we had enough kidding for one day!"

How many people have a chance to be a hero and villain at one and the same time? How many would seize it? Well, certainly the *beth din* would annul such a marriage anyway. Else no Jewish woman on earth was safe without mittens.

After a sleepless night, I set out for another opinion. But on my way to the synagogue we had attended on Tisha B'Av, I spotted an NBC-TV truck outside another imposing Orthodox shul. When the driver said that its rabbi was being taped, I decided to go with him.

The metal entrails of television equipment led to the temple office. Someone there was trying to get the bearded secretary to convince the rabbi to put on makeup.

The Bible prohibits men from dressing like women.

"But it isn't real makeup," said the T.V. man. "Would Kojak use makeup? It's pancake, for God's sake."

"Thou shalt not take the name of the Lord in vain," said the secretary.

When they reached an impasse, I asked to see the rabbi. The nature of my business? Suppose a man, as a gag, gave a woman a ring and said, "*Harei—*"

The secretary interrupted. "A very serious matter."

My heart sank.

Soon the rabbi appeared. A short, well-dressed man with a high forehead and a long gray beard. "Nu?" he said.

The T.V. man appealed to him. "The Conservative and Reform rabbis already taped their segments in pancake. You want to look like Nixon during his debate with Kennedy?"

"Well," said the rabbi, "maybe just a trifle."

My spirits soared.

A second man sat the rabbi down and placed a bib on him,

then opened a suitcase like an Avon lady's. While pancake was being applied, the rabbi pointed at me. "You have an appointment?"

"No. But . . ." I related what happened. To a very close friend.

"Hmmm. Serious matter. How old are they?"

"Over twenty-one."

The makeup man, having covered the rabbi's eyebrows, penciled them back in, longer and thicker and black.

"In possession of their mental faculties, both?"

"Yes."

"Hmmm. Were there two witnesses?"

I nodded.

With a distracted rabbi, the makeup man lowered his hairline.

"Sabbath observers? Two observant witnesses are required."

Elated, I grabbed the rabbi's hand. But then I remembered Dr. Vilno. Alas! Bernie List also. "Yes, two kosher witnesses."

"Hmmm. *Very* serious." To the makeup man: "What are you doing! *Lipstick*?" The rabbi stood up and pulled off his bib. To me: "I'm busy now, as you see. Bring in your two friends, and we'll discuss."

"I can't. They . . . live in California."

"California!" The rabbi tossed the bib aside. "Then this is not *our* problem." He pulled away from me and headed for the cameras.

So it came as no surprise that evening, the *beth din*'s ruling. There had to be a divorce.

"How can you agree?" I shouted over the phone. "You are Conservative."

Half a bottle of scotch threw a new light on the situation. What, after all, was terrible? I had married a super woman. One who'd make up for what was missing in my life. Tenderness, caring, someone to love. Now it was myself I was kidding. Under normal circumstances Isaca would never say yes.

How could she love me when those who knew me best never had?

I assumed the divorce would be handled stealthily. But Dr. Zion had invited three strangers. Two witnesses and another man dressed in pallbearer black.

Isaca, however, wore a dress the color of her hair. And my ring was returned with a breezy "Not my size anyway."

We all went into the dining room and sat around the table. The third man took out a piece of paper and a quill, then asked my father's name.

"Ben."

"Lineage. Priest, Levite, or Israelite?"

"Why?"

The man was writing a *get*, a bill of divorcement, for me to serve on Isaca.

"No way! Let Isaca divorce me."

"Might as well ask a cow to jump over the moon," she said. "A Jewish woman can't divorce her husband. That's the law."

"Can't go through with this." I stood up.

One of the witnesses asked, "What's the matter?"

All I had to do was confess to being Gentile. That would stop the proceedings. "What's the matter?" I sat down.

Handed the divorce paper, Dr. Zion read it aloud, then thrust it at me. When he whispered something to Isaca, she stood up and formed a cup with her palms.

I struggled to my feet. We stood there like two stalactites, staring at each other.

One witness nudged Isaca forward. The other pushed me from behind until I was close enough to breathe in the air she was expelling in shallow breaths.

"Now," said the scribe. "Give her the *get*."

Isaca's flushed cheeks looked slapped. Gone her earlier bravado. No! I wouldn't go through with it.

Another nudge made Isaca stumble forward. When I automatically reached out, the paper flew from my hand and struck her in the chest. She winced, as if cut open, but made no attempt to catch the bill of divorcement. It glided to the floor and came to rest on her foot.

"Good enough," said the scribe.

Cryptically, a witness added, "Not so bad. Isn't as if she were engaged to marry a *kohen*."

I fled, in my haste knocking over a chair and falling in a sprawl.

"Wait, Baron." Dr. Zion helped me to my feet, though he should have crippled them. "I don't want you to go through life hating Orthodoxy. Let me explain the *beth din*'s ruling."

Evidently, Isaca couldn't bear to hear the words spoken, for she silenced her father with a touch. Then, slowly, she waved her arms, hands, fingers. "My not throwing the ring back at you immediately. They interpreted that as acceptance," she signed. "I wanted, they said, to be your wife."

TEN

R.I. and I parted company too. I couldn't face Isaca again. She coated me with whipped cream, I spoiled her life.

For days the phone went unanswered, mail unopened. For the moment I didn't care.

When someone rang my doorbell, I switched off the T.V. and sat there in the dark. Several knocks. Then a note under the door.

> How about joining Roberta and me for dinner? You name the night. We even have a date for you. My mother-in-law.
>
> Ezra

Nice couple, the Farbers. So I tore up their invitation.

Hail Columbia for providing me with a haven. For the first time since enrollment there I attended all my classes. Got me a desk deep in the library stacks and buried myself between 327.48 and 341.27.

But every once in a while I'd turn a page, and there'd be Dr. Zion staring up at me, saying, "You and Isaca are married. It's as simple as that. And as terrible. Unless . . ." (Unless, he had meant, I'd have swept her up in my arms.)

Grieving, I felt as if sitting *shiva*.

Well into my second week of mourning the doorbell rang again. I turned off the T.V. and waited.

"Andrew, I know you're inside. Please. I have to see you."

See? Never! (It was Isaca.) I opened the door as far as the chain allowed and hid behind it. "I'm . . . not dressed."

"Andrew, have you quit R.I. on account of me?"

"No. On account of me."

"But why?"

To say I had humiliated her needlessly would only humiliate Isaca further. "A hit-and-run marriage."

"Nobody got killed, Andrew."

"Whiplash can be very painful."

"It can also clear one's head. Life is so easy for the Orthodox. They believe that without faith there are no answers, and with faith there are no questions. Well, from now on, Andrew, I am questioning."

"That's all this meant to you?" I felt worse.

"Why, Andrew? Did you want it to mean more?"

I leaned my head against the door.

"Andrew, you *must* return to R.I. You don't want me to feel guilty all my life for lov—for *ruining* you."

I was loved! *Me.* My lips pressed against the door. Something stung. If that wouldn't be poetic justice. A splinter in my forked tongue.

"Say you'll come back, Andrew. For *my* sake."

Sorrow canceled out joy. Now Isaca and I had a love song all our own. "This Nearly Was Mine." A solo.

It isn't tough to figure out why this war never ends. It has been assigned to America's losers. At least half of each rifle company is composed of blacks, Puerto Ricans, Chicanos, Nisei, Guamanians. Commanded for the most part by whites and Southerners. Nevertheless, few desert. Where would we go? On the town? . . . Before I forget, Drew. My heartfelt thanks for all the weekly letters, also the packages and books. It's a *mitzvah* to try to cheer someone up. Really cheering is the news that you're seeing this terrific girl. (Did you forget to mention her name, or did a letter get lost?) Sounds serious from the way you describe her. I wish *I* had a girl! To dream about. Make plans for. Come home to. Forget Vietnam with. Build a life on. See, Drew? Just the thought of one has me turned on! . . . But what's all this garbage about not being good enough for her? If you want to deprecate someone, pick on somebody your own size. My parents think you're great. Nobody like you in all the world, they write—your constant phone calls and visits. I've been remiss myself. Not that I haven't been writing home regularly via England. But I'm afraid to mail those letters until I can check them later for coherence. But by then sometimes I can't remember where I put them, or sometimes I think I've mailed them when I never did. Do you follow? No, I haven't become a pothead. Bad bad bad. Pot slows down the Enemy, stretches it out. After a joint you think, Isn't that wonderful, a whole day or week gone. But it's only hours. And then there's the rest of the night to get through. Fortunately, there are other things that do make Enemy Time zip right on by. . . . Hope I remember to mail this.

That the sermon is an art form goes unrecognized by two groups, parishioners and preachers. Which explains why I regard sermons the way nature does a vacuum. Quakers speak when the spirit moves them, clergy when the calendar and clock force them. Yes, I returned to R.I., and okay, you guessed it. I still hadn't gotten over my pulpit fright. Indeed, half my time was spent trading with classmates the date of my preaching debut.

Chapel each Friday, one student was assigned to lead the service and another to preach. The week a new French restaurant in the neighborhood ran a special on Châteaubriand, so many played hooky the faculty was, understandably, perturbed. Especially Dr. Vilno, who couldn't get a table. "Dis is how you pray? Vit knives and forks?" he exclaimed. "Vhat are you—kennibulls? God should see all of you here, He'd drop dead."

In a show of mortification, all upperclassmen canceled dessert, which was extra anyway. They then departed for their weekend pulpits to berate those present, as is the clergy's custom, for those absent.

On Monday, Dr. Tchernichovsky recounted the story of the Three Pillars of Judaism—Learning, Worship, and Kind Deeds—who bemoaned their inevitable fate after the dispersion of the Jews from the Land of Israel. The Lord assured the three they'd never be forgotten. "In the diaspora I shall have my people build synagogues," He said. "Rabbis will teach Torah, and cantors lead the worship." When Kind Deeds cried that he alone would be neglected, the Lord consoled him with "Not to worry. During services everyone will turn to a neighbor and offer him a pinch of snuff."

Dr. Tchernichovsky surveyed the class. "Last Friday I smelled no snuff, not a speck. Tell me, gentlemen—what's the problem?"

"Prayer," said Perry Davis. "That's the problem."

Bernie List took issue. "The problem is that word—prayer. To pray means to entreat, beg. We should call our service *worship*. Which means reverence."

"Call it what you will," said Hank Brenner, who thought there should be no more than twenty minutes of prayer, as a prologue to a lecture and discussion. "You see, it isn't only that prayers go unanswered—"

The professor rushed at Brenner. "Not so! Prayers are always answered. Provided they are *true*. That is, prayers implanted in us by God that we return to Him. Such prayers are rewarded with the gift of power from the godhead's vast storehouse of power."

"And in cases of"—Hank Brenner chose his words carefully to avoid giving offense—"a short circuit?"

"You mean defeat? Lord knows it happens often enough," Dr. Tchernichovsky thundered. "Yes, despite all that power, God does fail on occasion. Just as man does. How could they not?" He grabbed hold of the lapels on Brenner's jacket. "Yet no act of courage can be considered a failure when it illuminates our darkness, however briefly. Next time—and we live for those next times—the light shall last longer and the darkness retreat further. Then one day God Himself shall emerge fully."

"I can buy that," said Samson Finn the Jewmanist. "But why must we use other people's words? I'm a graduate of Yale."

"By all means pray from your heart," said the professor. "Just don't let yourself be overheard too often." As symphonies require Beethovens, public prayer demands genius. Chatty conversations with the Lord, gossip with the godhead are as inspiring as dialogue overheard on the bus. "Worthy additions, however, are welcome."

Ezra Farber remarked, "I think of prayer as an act of the imagination. We conduct ourselves *as if* carrying on a dialogue with God."

"So long as you remember," said Dr. Tchernichovsky, "God also needs good listeners."

Since nobody was being excommunicated for unbelief, I ventured a question myself. Why pray at all? An omniscient deity should know man's wishes. Why the need to keep tugging at His pants leg?

"Quite simply"—the professor heaved a great sigh—"because God can't do it all alone. He requires those reminders. Inspiration comes from God. But we are the ones who must focus His light and broaden its spectrum by adding our own colors, experiences, efforts—then return it, heightened, to God. The earth is the Lord's, but it's up to you to help make it divine. For the future is open, Creation still incomplete. And as the Midrash states, 'If not for me, Thou O God would not be sitting in the heavens.'"

Man and an assumed God joined together to battle the

forces of evil. A theological *High Noon*. Who wouldn't fancy being such a One's junior partner?

As a result of Friday's no-show, the administration threatened to make attendance at chapel compulsory. That, the student body denounced as a violation of their rights, if not of the separation of church and state. Finally, a compromise was hammered out in the spirit of the paradoxical Talmudic dictum "Everything is foreseen by God, yet man has free will." Chapel attendance remained voluntary, and on Friday everyone showed up.

Dr. Furth was overheard saying, "I like to pray only at sunrise. Before the world gets polluted with vanity and self-centeredness."

Ezra Farber, sitting beside me, observed, "Know what pollutes the world with vanity and self-centeredness at sunrise? Dr. Furth getting up."

The pulpit, too, was crowded. Across from the Stars and Stripes, in the place churches reserve for the Christian flag, stood a white flag with a blue Star of David. Gary Himmel led the congregation in singing his choice for the opening hymn, Psalm 137.

> By the rivers of Babylon,
> There we sat down, yea, we wept,
> When we remembered Zion. . . .

Dr. Furth, alone, did not join. His eyes were riveted on the Jewish flag, now fluttering in the breeze generated by one of the two chapel doors opening for latecomers. Probably fearing its tipping over, the professor rushed to the flag. But instead of securing it, he lifted it from the stand and carried it out of the chapel.

No sooner did Dr. Furth reappear than there was a large bang in the hall outside. The flag must have toppled over. Two Good Samaritans going to investigate soon returned with the flag and secured it in its stand. Oddly enough, these two now became the focus of Dr. Furth's glare. Moments later, he marched up to the pulpit, again seized the flag, and removed it from the chapel, then returned.

If I forget thee, O Jerusalem,
Let my right hand wither.
Let my tongue cleave to the roof of my mouth
If I remember thee not;
If I set not Jerusalem
Above my chiefest joy.

While I was still trying to make sense of the professor's behavior, another latecomer arrived. Yes, with the flag. To Dr. Furth's angry stage whisper, the student replied, "It was lying on the floor outside. What's the matter? You want me to kiss it?"

Dr. Furth grabbed the flag and carried it away once more, like a dog with a bone that refused to stay buried. What the hell was going on?

Ezra Farber explained. "Remember President Kennedy's *'Ich bin ein Berliner'*? Well, Furth is *ein Amerikaner*, two hundred percent. With him, Israeli flags are strictly *verboten.*"

Presently, both doors to the chapel swung open. Only the German-born rabbi entered, however. Either someone had left through the door opposite, or the Invisible Man had joined the congregation.

As Gary Himmel referred us to photo-offset pages of the proposed *New Union Prayer Book*, the pulpit darkened. Had a light burned out? Following his gaze upward, I saw the Star of David overhead. Someone had draped the flag over the chapel's skylight, where it hovered over the congregation like the wrath of God.

Wisely refraining from bringing down the flag with a poke of the American flag's staff, Dr. Furth sat out the service making a list of all those present. On the theory, no doubt, that only one of the absentees could have planted the Israeli flag on the skylight.

For his text Hank Brenner, preacher of the day, took the verse "His Majesty's Government view with favour the establishment in Palestine of a national home for the Jewish people, and will use their best endeavors to facilitate the achievement of this object." Opening sentence of the 1917 Balfour Declaration, which recognized the Jewish people as an entity in international law with a collective right to Palestine.

But in 1922 the British Government gave away eighty percent of the Palestine homeland to the artificially created Kingdom of Jordan. The U.N.'s 1947 Partition Resolution further truncated the Jewish state, and presently Jordan seized the West Bank for itself. So of the huge territories the Allies liberated from Turkey, ninety-nine percent went to form independent Arab states, one percent to Israel. Yet begrudging even that tiny sliver, the Arabs attacked Israel on May 14, 1948. Twenty states to one, 100 million people against 1.5 million. That war created not one, but two refugee problems. Six hundred thousand Arab refugees whom the fourteen Arab governments, with more land than all of Europe, refused to absorb, and a like number of Jewish refugees from Arab lands whom tiny Israel welcomed.

"Even so, the majority of Palestinian Arabs entered the Land of Israel *after* the Jews' arrival, because it afforded them jobs and higher living standards," Hank Brenner revealed. "So who can doubt that the rhetoric about converting Israel into a secular democratic state—which characterizes only Lebanon—is but a pretext for destroying the Jewish State?"

Suddenly, both chapel doors burst open, and in rushed two uniformed men, who stormed the pulpit and seized Hank Brenner, crying, "You're preaching Zionism! Zionism is racism!" Only when the pair, whose sleeves bore red hammers and sickles, dragged off Brenner did I recognize his captors as upperclassmen.

Himself startled by the sociodrama, Gary Himmel returned to the pulpit to announce "*Hatikvah*" as the closing hymn. As the congregation rose to sing the anthem, up jumped Dr. Furth. Swearing in German, he darted to the organ and slammed it shut.

"My God!" cried organist Perry Davis. "I'll never play again." Indeed, the two hands he held aloft numbered only eight fingers between them. When the congregation applauded his announcement, Perry returned his hands frontward and straightened the bent fingers. "Look! A miracle."

Usually, the homiletics instructor took first crack at the reader and preacher, but Dr. Furth couldn't contain himself. "Get up to the skylight! Take down that flag! *At once.*"

To the congregation he announced, "The existence of the State of Israel pleases nobody more than me and Dr. Kissinger. But fake police raids. Phony Russians. The Jewish national anthem. A political rally in a place of worship. A foreign flag. *Disgraceful!*"

Enter said flag with Perry Davis, who positioned himself behind the professor. "Go on, go on."

Dr. Furth darted across the pulpit to the American flag and raised it high. "*This* is ours." He aimed the staff like a giant blackboard pointer at the other one. "*That* is an intruder."

The former captain of Harvard's fencing team stuck out his staff and crossed flagpoles.

The professor exclaimed, horrified, "Dual allegiance!"

"*En garde!*" said Perry Davis, and banged his pole against the other.

Automatically, Dr. Furth parried. In a moment the two were engaged in a joust out of *Ivanhoe* with the congregation cheering them on. Gary Himmel, who resembled the beauteous Rebecca not at all, ducked inside the oak lectern, from where he waved a white handkerchief whenever his hiding place got thumped.

What stopped the match was Dr. Furth's "Davis, you're expelled!"

That brought Perry to a standstill. And an apology. "The Torah obliges one to grant forgiveness to those who ask for it, Dr. Furth. Isn't that so?"

"Shut up already!" The professor addressed the congregation, hampered at first by the American flag from which he disentangled himself. "Nationalism still being merely nationalism, Israel is only *one* of the possibilities for a Jew. Not the best one either. One can live just as authentic a religious life elsewhere. Why, even in the time of Jesus, most

Jews lived outside of Palestine." He restored the American flag to its stand, but did not salute it. "Holding Zionist rallies in the sanctuary, peddling a foreign ideology. These are intrusions on those wishing to be alone with their God."

Bernie List raised his hand and quoted Dr. Martin Luther King, Jr. At a dinner in Boston shortly before his assassination, he retorted to an anti-Zionist remark. "Don't talk like that! When people cricitize Zionists, they mean Jews. You're talking anti-Semitism."

The bell drowned out Dr. Furth's furious rejoinder.

Gary Himmel motioned the congregation to rise. "And now, the closing benediction. '. . . after the Lord opened the ass's mouth. Balak said to Balaam, what have you done to me? Here I brought you to damn my enemies, and instead you have blessed them! Balaam replied, I can only repeat faithfully what the Lord puts in my mouth. How goodly are your tents, O Jacob, your dwellings, O Israel! Blessed are they who bless you, accursed they who curse you.'"

Dr. Furth flushed. As unhappy as the classic jackass torn between two equidistant bales of hay, the professor couldn't seem to make up his mind who to bash first, Perry Davis or Gary Himmel. When he finally headed for the lectern, seven of the ten men in the first pew turned around.

They wore eye patches made of handkerchiefs à la Moshe Dayan.

ELEVEN

The marriage aborted my love life. I never dated another Jewish woman after that, and a relationship with a Gentile could get back to R.I. and Isaca. But don't feel sorry for me. I discovered during a succession of one-night stands that it's far easier to be a lover than a mate (just as it's less difficult to tell a joke or two than to be a witty conversationalist). But so lonely.

Isaca, that princess, did her best to ease my guilt. "Accidents do happen," she said. "Can't we continue to be friends, Andrew?"

Mere friendship. How sad. And yet . . . "Even that is more than I deserve."

"Andrew, someday you'll realize you're a lot nicer than you think," she said. "Hope I'm around to see it."

Could Isaca know something about me that I didn't? "Me, too," I said.

I don't know what I'd have done without the Farbers. Their invitations cheered me up. And Ezra and I had something in common, his turn toward Judaism coming almost as late as mine.

In vivid detail he related joining a peaceful assembly en route to Alabama's capital to petition for voters' rights. The group was attacked by troopers with clubs and whips, trampled by a posse of one hundred on horseback, and gassed—while white locals roared like fans at a bullfight. When Dr. Martin Luther King, Jr., invited all Americans to join in a new march to Montgomery, thousands heeded the call, among them Roberta.

For years Ezra had refused to marry the girl from Central Park South. "We poor have our pride," he noted wryly. (Roberta's mother helped to change his mind, informing Ezra of the Jewish tradition of wealthy families marrying off their daughters to poor scholars.)

Roberta made a difference in Selma, Ezra said. When the marchers were stopped at the Pettus Bridge, it was she who led the elderly wives of Senators Paul Douglas and Charles Tobey to the front of the march, forestalling a repetition of Bloody Sunday.

That night in a dimly lit restaurant in Atlanta, Roberta recalled, Ezra had taken her hand in his, looked deep into her blue eyes, and exclaimed, "*God,* I wish I were a Negro!"

What, then, turned Ezra into a Jew? The rise of Black Power extremists who excoriated Israel, Dr. King's assassination, and New York's teachers' strike, which polarized the city's black and Jewish communities. Ezra's subsequent exploration of Judaism led to his discovery that Jewish, too, is beautiful.

One holy day he had accompanied Robert and Mrs. Benjamin to temple, whose rabbi preached a sermon so long that countless people throughout the world never survived it. When, finally, he said, "I think I've spoken long enough," there was a burst of applause. Misinterpreting, the rabbi extended his remarks, whereupon Ezra took Roberta by the arm and headed for the door. Incensed, the rabbi demanded their reason.

"Boredom," said Ezra. Lo and behold, a third of the congregation followed him out.

"That's when I decided on entering Ezra in the rabbinate," Roberta said. "In addition to honesty, he's got this tremendous leadership ability."

Ezra, more and more of his time devoted to policing students, left teaching for R.I. after the principal advised him never to go to the men's room by himself.

A perfectly complementary couple: he muscular, stocky, and dark; she soft, lithe, and fair. His sensitivity buttressed by her assurance and determination, her drive and verve channelled by his idealism. I was very fond of them, and they treated me like one of the family, even arguing in my presence. Not that anything embarrassing was ever in dispute. The Farber rows were not like normal couples', but what to do, for example, after the mortician came. Hearing of a former classmate's untimely death, Ezra instructed Roberta not to mourn excessively should he die and to remarry soon afterward.

"You mean," she said, "at graveside?"

Solemn, he made her promise to start dating within three months of his demise. Not to be outdone, Roberta suggested he marry within six months of hers. Ezra refused. But when he finally yielded, she pronounced Ezra fickle and refused to talk to him all night long.

A larger bone of contention was Roberta's charming widowed mother, who spent her days raising money for Hadassah when she wasn't campaigning for grandchildren. Mrs. Benjamin had even posted a ten-thousand-dollar bounty on the head of any baby born to the Farbers, with a bonus for twins.

Roberta should have had enough of kids, teaching thirty-three of them daily. Yet she often returned home to play and chat with a ten-year-old neighbor. On Hanukkah, Roberta gave the child no less than eight little gifts.

Cheryl kissed her. "You're so nice, Roberta. Someone like you should have more children than the old woman who lived in a shoe."

Roberta swept the child into her arms. "She had all the luck," she said wistfully.

Cheryl hugged Roberta tightly. "How come you don't have any?"

Ezra rushed the child to the door.

But Mrs. Benjamin demanded an answer. "I'm dying to have grandchildren and *shep nachas*. When you become parents yourselves, you'll understand."

A lovely Yiddish phrase, to *shep nachas,* to derive pleasure from another's joy and to share in it. In contrast to Hollywood people, who *shep nachas* from each other's disasters.

"Mother," Ezra retorted, "why don't you get married? Then Roberta and I could *shep nachas.* from *you.*"

After the kindling of the Sabbath candles, he chanted the *Kiddush,* then recited from the Book of Proverbs:

A good wife, who can find?
Her worth is far above rubies.
The heart of her husband trusts in her
And nothing shall he lack.
She renders him good and not evil
All the days of her life.
She opens her hand to the needy

[139]

And extends her hand to the poor.
She is robed in strength and dignity
And cheerfully faces whatever may come.
She opens her mouth with wisdom,
Her tongue is guided by kindness. . . .

Mrs. Benjamin could hardly wait for the *Hamotsee* over the challah before accusing her son-in-law of censorship. "You deliberately omitted 'her children rise up and call her blessed.'"

Ezra responded with the traditional blessing for parents, "May God bless our love for one another." But it was through gritted teeth.

Mrs. Benjamin wasn't to be put off. Why should Roberta tend strangers' children when she could have her own? "All your friends are mothers already. Even Betty Turner, and she's single. Don't you *want* children?"

Roberta coughed up the piece of challah that was choking her. "Everyone yearns to create, Mother, for good or for evil. You think men would become artists or soldiers if they could give birth?"

Mrs. Benjamin brightened. "Well, if you're willing and I'm eager—"

Helplessly, Roberta turned toward her husband.

He presented his defense. Of all things, a hymn to *The Population Bomb* by Dr. Paul Ehrlich, one of vasectomy's most illustrious alumni.

What was Mrs. Benjamin's rejoinder? "So *you're* the bottleneck, Ezra."

As he sputtered, Roberta pointed Mrs. Benjamin toward the kitchen and sent her to warm up something there.

"Jews have always been 'a light unto the nations,'" Ezra said. "Now it's up to us to set the example for Zero Population Growth, too."

Roberta stamped her foot. "Never is one so active, said

Cato, as when one does nothing. Ezra, talk of genocide! We're doing it to ourselves. *Imploding.*"

Ever hear such a high-toned dispute? Only, I didn't believe either of them: it takes a deceiver to recognize self-deception.

Eventually, Roberta said, "Ezra, I know I have everything. A husband I love, who loves me. And yet . . ."

The grim look on his face softened. "You're right, of course," he said quietly, "in wanting our child now—"

"Oh, Ezra!"

"—and I'm one hundred percent right in postponing him." He threw up his hands. "That's just the trouble! We're *both* right."

"Suppose we have our first baby now, as *I* want. And the second one we can postpone, as *you* want."

Ezra demurred. "Women now insist, rightfully, on control over their bodies. Well, I stake the same claim over my by-products."

Roberta shot to her feet. I didn't realize how much self-control she had been exerting until she began shouting.

Ezra clasped and unclasped his hands. "Babies grow," he said, finally. "So does anxiety."

"What anxiety? Look at me. We love each other, don't we?"

"Love is not St. George. It takes more than love to slay some dragons."

"Which dragons?"

Ezra stood up and walked to the window and looked out into the night. "If I knew them by name, they'd be pets . . . with leashes on them."

I got up and tiptoed into the kitchen. There, I almost knocked over Mrs. Benjamin, ears cocked.

"What a mouth on that Cato!" she said. "Andrew, you think we're making headway?" Mrs. Benjamin shushed me, and when I tried to close the door, she threatened me with a pot of hot chicken soup. "They're fighting over my immortality."

Something must have got lost in transit, for Roberta was now saying, "Of course, Ezra. That's right. Certainly."

Then, silence.

Mrs. Benjamin sneaked a look into the dining room. "They're kissing! Is that good or bad? How can I tell who's convincing whom?"

"Roberta, you're so damn simpatico, I *knew* you'd understand."

"Yes, everything *will* work out, Ezra. As soon as you heed the Bible's first commandment."

That puzzled me as well as Ezra. "I am the Lord thy God Who brought you forth out of the land of Egypt?" he said.

Ever so softly Roberta quoted, "Be fruitful and multiply."

The next thing heard was the front door slamming. This time I also looked. Ezra had fled, leaving his wife in tears. Mrs. Benjamin rushed to console her.

Roberta wiped at her eyes. "If it's the last thing I do," she vowed, "I'll fix that Dr. Paul Ehrlich!"

. . . Never thought *I'd* consult a psychiatrist.

Couldn't talk to my chaplain—he's part of the problem. So gung-ho on this war, I expect him any Sunday to announce that in lieu of cash, the congregation may drop ears into the collection plate.

I told the psychiatrist of American atrocities. Also, of our allies' atrocities against their own people. Chaining political prisoners in concrete boxes so small they emerge cripples. A jail system bigger than those of all the hospitals, schools, churches, and pagodas combined.

In return I got a lecture on the Causes of Wanton Violence. . . . And, always, the fear of being killed. In such a situation, it's a miracle there are so few My Lais.

So saith my psychiatrist, as well adjusted to this atrocity-inducing situation as my chaplain. So where do I go from here, Drew? If both God and Freud are in eclipse in Vietnam, whence cometh my help?

At school I stayed away from Ezra. Why have him reminded of the quarrel with Roberta? But one day he pursued me. Accustomed to being asked to take sides between my parents and step-, I hailed the merits of both theses. "Quarrels wouldn't drag on if only *one* side were right."

After mulling that over until lunchtime, my friend asked for a critique of Roberta's position. Since he really sought ammunition, I evaded the question. Solicited then for criticism of his own position, I asked why.

"To shore up my stand," he said.

"What convinced *you*? To sterilize oneself for an abstract ideal—"

Ezra became livid. "*Sterilize?*" He jumped to his feet and rushed out of the coffee shop, fork still in hand, leaving me with his bill. I deserved that. What kind of idiot lets himself be drawn into an intimate family argument? Only a bachelor.

I phoned Roberta for advice on making amends. To my surprise, she thanked me for striking a nerve, which had provoked a weekend's marathon discussion recalling their marriage in June of '67. "That," she said in teacher fashion, "may very well account for Ezra's lack of motivation."

She meant their wedding night? Roberta rewarded me with a dinner invitation, mysteriously insisting on my coming early. And what was that reference to exorcising Ezra's dybbuk?

I brought along flowers. Roberta thanked me, then dropped the bouquet on the couch and went about the living room misaligning all the pictures on the wall.

Retrieving the flowers, I took a vase from the table and headed for the kitchen. A sudden cry stopped me.

"What's the matter, Roberta?"

"Andrew, I want you to be the second person to know that—that—that—"

"Yes? Yes? Yes?"

"There's nothing for you to help me chop." She rattled on, uncharacteristically, "What's new with *you*? Andrew, it's so aggravating never having anything new to tell people."

"Why not lie a little?" A better question would have been,

Why so jittery? Eyes popping at my innocuous remark, she slammed her lips down over her tongue. Me, I proceeded to the kitchen, where I banged into something behind the door.

A baby carriage?

Roberta appeared at my side. "Surprise," she said weakly.

Jubilant, I tossed the bouquet in the air, then forgetting about the vase, dropped it when I reached out to catch the roses.

Roberta dismissed my apology. "An old vase."

As I placed the broken pieces on the kitchen table, I asked when she was due.

"Oh, the baby. Well . . . I suppose . . . October."

"Marvelous. October is only . . . *eleven months away?*"

Distractedly, Roberta said, "You confused me. The vase breaking. It's two hundred years old. I meant September."

Both of us counted on our fingers and finished in a dead heat. There were just enough fingers to complete our tally. Had Roberta consulted a doctor or a fortuneteller?

She corrected herself. "I meant, of course, August tenth. *That's* nine months, isn't it?"

Understandable, Roberta's befuddlement. This was her first child. How wonderful, I thought, becoming a parent, being able to improve on your own parents' mistakes. "Ezra must be *thrilled.*"

Roberta took a deep breath.

"Well, wasn't he thrilled? How *did* he react?" There was no answer. "You did say I was the *second* to know."

Finally: "I asked my mother first."

"Asked?"

"Ezra *will* be thrilled. Won't he, Andrew?"

I seized her by the shoulders. "What are you talking about?"

She threw herself in my arms. "Oh, Andrew! I mean . . . *well.* Honest I do!"

Enough was enough. I demanded an explanation.

"Dare I go through with it, Andrew? Is it right to deceive Ezra? Is it wrong to seduce a man—"

Uh-oh. She had insisted on my arriving that evening before Ezra. Yet there were limits even to my duplicity. "I can't do it, Roberta. Much as I'd like to help out," I said at the same time that she finished: "—even if the man is my own husband?"

Another simultaneous exchange. "Do *what*, Andrew?" and "Seduce *Ezra*?"

We broke from our clinch and retired to opposite corners of the kitchen table.

"If I were to tell Ezra, while using this baby carriage as a prop, that I was already pregnant."

So Roberta wanted my nod, not my bod. "Then you're *not*? It's all a . . . a . . . a . . . ?"

"Not a *real* lie, Andrew. I'd just be . . . anticipating." She faltered. "You think it's wrong, don't you?"

"Maybe I'm just unimaginative. Roberta, there must be *other* ways. I mean, look at all the birth announcements in the *Times*."

"There are dozens of ways. But this way, if Ezra starts banging his head against the wall, I can always laugh it off as a practical joke."

"*Trial parenthood?*"

Crestfallen, Roberta took the carriage and wheeled it from the kitchen to the front door. There she paused, the picture of dejection. "The store agreed to exchange this for an electric pants presser if I wasn't satisfied."

Don't ask why I burst out, "Wait!"

"What else can I do, Andrew?" In her agitation she rocked the carriage back and forth as if it were occupied. "Ever since June '67, Ezra's been feeding me the Pill with my morning orange juice. As if I were a junkie on methadone. And that was years before Dr. Ehrlich's bomb."

"What's the connection with '67?"

"We were married on the eve of the Six-Day War. That so traumatized Ezra, he was . . ." Roberta searched for synonyms and failed. "Let's just say our honeymoon got off on the wrong . . . leg. I shudder to think what would have happened if Israel had not triumphed. Night after night Ezra kept saying, "The whole world wants us dead.'"

I still didn't get it.

"Ezra postponed . . . things. Exactly as he's now postponing our children . . . our future." Her eyes showed a lot of white as she recited, "Ezra may have internalized what he considers the world's hostility against the Jewish people. Those are the psychiatrist's exact words." Roberta slumped against the carriage. "Some individuals find it difficult to withstand the death wish of others."

"That's *voodoo*."

"Voodoo, schmoodoo. It works like a charm," she asserted. "Why do you think Ezra married me in the first place? Because I *willed* it."

"You think you can will a *baby*?"

She looked at me as if I were one. "Of course. Mother has agreed. It's men who make wars and men who make peace, she says, but it's up to us women to carry on through both."

A conspiracy!

"But Mother may be slightly prejudiced. As a man, Andrew, what do *you* think?"

"Me pass on your morality? That's ridiculous! Still . . ."

She broke in to thank me. "You think it'll work?"

That answer I knew. "Only a madwoman would think up such a scheme, Roberta, but only a maniac would think of doubting it. As for your means, though—"

Too late. The doorbell sounded.

Roberta pushed the carriage at me and told me to hide it. "No, not in the kitchen. Ezra always heads for the refrigerator." She shoved me and the carriage down the foyer.

Opening the first door encountered, I wheeled it into the master bedroom. Its unmade bed unnerved me. What if Ezra found me there?

Presently, voices came through loud and clear. No doubt Roberta wanted me to hear how the scene played. Perhaps, if the going got rough, to step in with a cry of *"Cut!"*

"What do you mean, Ezra? 'The world is on its way out.'"

"You haven't seen today's newspaper?"

"Know what I think? You're *afraid* to become a father. Having a baby means to stop being a baby yourself. That's what the school psychiatrist said—"

"Hold on! You discussed me with a *child* psychiatrist?"

"What's the difference? Boys will be boys."

"For crying out loud, Roberta, let *me* call the shots around here!"

"By flying out the door in the middle of arguments—"

"I do the honorable thing under such circumstances. Run like hell."

"Same here, Ezra. Because every mature wife yearns to be called *Mother!*"

Evidently thinking herself paged, Mrs. Benjamin, who must have been sweating this all out in her own room, suddenly joined the dialogue. "Oh, I'm so happy! So happy for you both."

"What for?" said Ezra.

"What for?"

"Not yet, Mother. You've . . . jumped the gun."

"Oh!" A door slammed.

"Roberta, what was *that* all about?"

"Our baby."

"Ye gods! . . . With war brewing for weeks in '67, Roberta, what did the U.N. do? Pulled its troops from Sinai. And when Egypt blockaded Israel and threatened to slaughter every Israeli? Pope Paul issued a statement: 'Please don't harm our religious shrines.' My poor cousin Jimmy! Usher at our wedding on Sunday, volunteer in Israel on Monday, hamburger on Thursday. . . . And nobody gave a damn until Israel started to win. Then everyone ganged up to force her to quit. And you want to bring another Jew into a world that wants us all dead?"

"Ezra, my darling."

"Yes?"

"Fuck the world."

With the approaching denouement requiring Ezra's entry into the bedroom to see exhibit A or my wheeling it out, I decided to make the bed. Unmade, it might upstage the fictitious fetus. Before I could finish, however, a male voice sounded behind me.

"Andrew! What are you *doing*?"

I dropped a pillow. "On my way back from the john . . . time on my hands—"

Roberta darted to the carriage. "Ezra, look!"

He threw back his head and laughed, then picked up a tray of coffee cups and saucers. "Your mother and her bargains. Last week it was a dozen earrings without mates."

"This is no bargain." She took the tray away.

"Mother must be slipping." He took the tray back and disappeared into the foyer.

Roberta called after him, "Mazel tov, Ezra. You're going to be a father."

Crash!

Roberta sallied forth, trapping me behind. I couldn't leave now without stepping on her big speech.

"Tell me, what do you think? I mean, how do you *feel*? Ezra? Are you there?"

"There" was not the living room. Wrong guess. I ran right into Ezra, speechless and immobile.

Roberta wrung her hands. "Okay, Ezra. No baby. We'll just forget the whole thing."

"Huh?"

Her final appeal. "Tell me now . . . while there's still time . . . how you feel. . . . Nothing? Oh, Ezra! I honestly thought you wanted our child, and if I waited for that realization, our baby would be old and gray at birth. But now I see . . ." Tears started to her eyes.

Instinctively, I went to Roberta. Reason, however, kept me at arm's length. Ezra might still be puzzling over my presence in their bedroom.

"Ezra, what I told you just now . . ." To steady herself, Roberta picked up a glass of wine from the table and drank.

Ezra grabbed the glass away so swiftly, some wine splashed on the tablecloth. "Want to pickle our son?"

"Our son?" Roberta turned toward me. Then back toward Ezra. "Really, I could drop the whole thing. What do you say?"

Ezra pushed me aside to get to his wife. "Let's name him after Cousin Jimmy." His eyes glistened as he embraced her. "*We* want our Jewish baby alive."

"Oh, Ezra!" Roberta's voice cracked. "You make me feel so . . . so . . . so . . . acquitted."

I took another wineglass from the table and held it aloft. "A toast! To the joy of creation."

Mrs. Benjamin, who had slipped in unnoticed, exclaimed softly, "Let us pray."

TWELVE

I never should have answered the door that morning.

"Excuse me, Drew." Levi's father opened his fist. "Excuse me . . . excuse me for . . ." He handed me a crumpled piece of paper. Reluctantly, as if it were a disease he didn't want to communicate.

Nor did I want to catch it. Unread, the telegram couldn't report what I had feared since that last meeting with Levi. I couldn't even bear to question Mr. Simon. If not for my friend and R.I., that message might have gone to Terri and Dad. All of a sudden I was flooded with anger. Why hadn't Levi listened to me! *Why?* I'd never forgive him for having wasted his life. And for what? In another year or two, who on earth would even be able to spell Thieu?

". . . Well, Drew? *Will* you?"

"What?"

"Or do you think I'm a crazy man? . . . You typing letters to my wife and me and signing Levi's name."

"Letters?" From the dead? I smoothed out the crumpled piece of paper. Three words leaped out at me: ". . . *missing in action* . . ." A chance, then!

"Levi may still be alive, the army says. A prisoner of war." On account of his wife's heart condition, Mr. Simon wanted to await further notification. Fake letters would spare Mrs. Simon the uncertainty that's more agonizing than knowing the worst. "I got the idea from Levi. Though his letters came from England, the army said he'd been in Vietnam all along. I've tried faking a letter home from Levi, but . . ." He bit his lower lip until it turned white, then red. "Tell me the truth, Drew. Am I a crazy man?"

I promised to write the letters, do anything else he asked. Even go to Vietnam to search for Levi myself. Crazy talk, though I meant every word.

Mr. Simon seized both my hands, and suddenly my eyes overflowed. I cursed myself, for instantly he burst into tears. "I don't know what to pray for, Drew, I swear I don't. First I prayed for Levi's life. But remembering my own experiences in the camps, those amusement parks for monsters . . ."

By the time Mr. Simon left, I convinced him that the North Vietnamese were not Nazis, and he convinced me that Levi was alive and well in a P.O.W. camp. Never were two people more desperate to be convinced.

I immediately began a letter to the Simons, cannibalizing Levi's last one to me. "The world is full of such beauty," he had written. "Isn't it a pity that instead of taking advantage of the beauty, people take advantage of each other?"

Pity, indeed. For it had been Levi's first happy letter.

Remember that psychiatrist I consulted, Drew? Well, he left for the States yesterday—six months before the end of his tour of duty. Scuttlebutt has it that he was shipped home for erupting with statements like "Only beasts accept alternatives foisted on them" and "Call me Doctor, goddamnit, not Major."

He volunteered to help me get back earlier to the States, too. But I declined. Don't be shocked. My hitch ends soon and right now I'm busy organizing an orphan asylum. It will also shelter children of Vietnamese women and vanished American servicemen, who are scorned by the natives—and if black, despised. You'd think life was tragic enough, but no. Even the oppressed enjoy oppressing.

That includes the Vietcong, who execute village leaders and others indiscriminately. Some war. It has no side to root for. Only victims.

But at least sleep no longer eludes me like mercury. Doing something in atonement has made me feel like a new man. A decent one, a *mentsch*.

1972-3

THIRTEEN

O to be a painting by Michelangelo, a sculpture by Rodin, any opera by Mozart. Finished, complete, instead of still in progress.

It was painful corresponding with the Simons as Levi. Mr. Simon, forgetting himself on occasion, wrote as if Levi were the recipient. Gallant man, hiding his grief, perhaps suffocating in it. And Mrs. Simon kept anticipating Levi's separation from the army and his settling down with wife and family.

I often left the Simons' mail unopened for days—bills I didn't want to pay. And the nights I replied, I never slept. Mounting depression finally drove me to seek out Dr. Tchernichovsky.

He listened sympathetically, then said, "Thanks to my great erudition, Baron, I can answer every question under the sun except one. Why do the good suffer?"

"But if *you* don't know—"

The professor seized me by the wrist. "*Nobody knows.* Not only doesn't religion provide answers to all questions, it's a *challenge* to all answers. So we must live on faith. Only, remember that faith is hope, not necessarily belief, certainly never knowledge. If you think God lets nearly all saints and heroes die forsaken—you're absolutely right." He squeezed my wrist hard. "Yet it's the saints and heroes who confer meaning upon this defective world. They sanctify it by assuming burdens for others. Never count their sacrifices as waste, however. For they enrich God, inspire Him, the world, too, even as He does us."

Levi's orphanage in Vietnam came to mind. Yet I'd never have swapped it for his life.

The professor's grip loosened. "Be kind, Baron. God too

needs our compassion. Our forgiveness as well for being help-less to avert so many tragedies. Just as you need His forgive-ness for your sins."

I started. "*My* sins?"

He held up both palms. "Mine, then. When I think of all I could have accomplished during my lifetime . . ."

Regrets? Yet his favorite *midrash* was that of the elderly man ridiculed for planting acorns. "Old man," laughed a pass-ing youth, "do you actually expect to see those acorns grow into trees?" The old man replied serenely. "The world was not barren when I entered. So I plant for those who shall come after me."

Dr. Tchernichovsky's hand fell to his side. "Sorry, Baron. You've caught me at a bad time. I've just come from my doctor." His face took on a distant expression. "The romantic allure that death holds for the young grows slack in the aged." A deep sigh. "Everyone's *second* greatest wish is to die well. But . . . is there a bad mother or a good death?"

Suddenly, the professor reminded me of a play in its final performances. One could almost see the closing notice posted backstage.

Speaking with desperate urgency, he looked deep into my eyes. But I felt he was addressing his own reflection there. "As all of us need forgiveness, we must grant it to a heartless universe that knows not what it does. If you can't forgive, Baron, at least don't give up hope. Isn't the survival of our people the greatest argument against despair? The continued existence of the Jews attests that life is not meaningless, that people can indeed affect the course of history. That's the ulti-mate heresy—despair. For it spells the defeat of God. Always remember, Baron—the world goes on only because of those who disregard their own existence."

With grades high enough to qualify for Columbia's Ph.D. program, my plan for the seventies was progressing more successfully than Nixon's peace plan for '68 ff. But suppose I got ordained before he Vietnamized the war or remaindered it. To continue as a 4-D I'd have to take a synagogue. Unthinkable! Unless the war dragged on. Then all things were possible. Levi was one sacrifice too many to Mars.

In August, my annual pilgrimage out West. This time I inquired about Dad's family background, barely mentioned before. Now he spoke tersely of his parents running away to America after World War I to escape pogroms in Eastern Europe. They never learned to speak English or made a decent living. Dad worked his way through college only to find himself barred from medical school, those being the days of Jewish quotas.

First I'd ever heard of his wanting to be a doctor. "Restricted because of your religion. How cruel."

"And I wasn't even religious!" Dad exclaimed in a rare show of emotion. "At least I've spared you that, Drew. The burden of Jewishness. But the army appreciated me all right. You have my medals. And the business world considers only the bottom line. So I have no complaints."

"None? What about your dream of medicine?"

His mouth flew open. But not a word. He pressed his lips together, and after a moment, said in a flat tone of voice, "That was a long time ago."

Dad had questions too. The draft. Why hadn't I been called up? My supposed 4-F bothered him. He wanted me to consult his physician. Whether for my sake or the army's, I couldn't be sure.

"I have a doctor of my own in New York."

"Not a psychiatrist, I hope," said Dad. "They're all nuts."

Terri was now into kundalini yoga. "God is a crock," she explained. "Everything lies within the person. The spinal column is the channel through which the yogi can lift his psychic energies, symbolized by the serpent goddess coiled at the base of the spine."

Terrific comeback for the serpent after having been kicked out of the Garden of Eden on its belly.

Terri was enjoying a comeback of her own. As a result of her identification as Suzie the Sniffer, a T.V. series had signed her for a continuing role, a black family's domestic. Some irony—Terri could be considered a housekeeper only insofar as after her last two divorces she got to keep the house.

To prepare for her T.V. role Terri now made her own bed and dusted an occasional room. In the process she happened on a letter of mine to the Simons. "'Dear Mom and Dad.' Mom? *And* Dad? What's this, Drew?"

I must have wanted to share my anxiety. Else why leave that half-completed letter in full view? The talk with Dr. Tchernichovsky, revealing his illness, had further depressed me. "This friend of mine is missing . . ."

"That's so terribly sad. Awful," she said. "Sounds like *Love Letters* with Jennifer Jones and Joseph Cotten."

My two-year-old secret had to out then too. I alluded to someone's masquerade as a Jewish divinity student in order to beat the draft. And when Terri nodded and said something about *Some Like It Hot,* with Jack Lemmon in drag in an upper berth with Marilyn Monroe, out came my R.I. student identification.

Terri flopped into a chair. "Like Bogart as a priest in *The Left Hand of God!*" She chortled.

What a relief! I could have kissed her. "You're not ashamed of me?"

"Why? You're *acting.* An inherited trait. Runs in the family," she said. "Look at it this way, Drew. Nixon and Company have *their* game plans."

"But I'm deceiving so many good people."

"Make-believe," said Terri. "It's the cornerstone of films as an art form."

Perhaps her reaction made it easier to return to R.I. that fall. Or perhaps for someone at loose ends, half a belonging is better than none. In any event, seeing Dr. Tchernichovsky in good spirits—an operation during the summer had gone well—buoyed mine.

But then, the Palestinian massacre of eleven Israeli athletes in Munich's Olympic Village. How the crowd of 80,000 in Olympic Stadium roared approval of the next morning's announcement: "The Games must go on!" Other than Israel, only Holland and the Scandinavian countries withdrew.

Surely, there'd have been more of a worldwide commotion if Mark Spitz had shit in the Olympic pool.

That evening Mrs. Simon had a heart attack.

The nurse in the cardiac-care unit would admit only members of the immediate family. Mr. Simon's telling her I was like a son lost a great deal in the transmission, for inside I found Mrs. Simon expecting Levi. Yet the woman was happier to see me instead.

"I made my husband promise not to tell Levi," she said. "Why should he aggravate, him so far away?"

They certainly were a family for secrets.

One ray of sunshine. After the gestation period of an elephant, the Farber baby put in an appearance. Ezra woke me with the news, incoherent, having waited up for his son for months. Happily, its thirteen pounds and six ounces furnished an alibi for the unaccounted interval.

To Roberta's first words afterward, "You *are* glad about the baby, Ezra, aren't you?" the happy father responded, "Asking that! As if I were an Indian giver."

The Farbers asked me to be the *sondek*, the godfather whom an infant is purported to grow up morally and intellectually to resemble. Parents usually choose a pious, God-fearing man to hold the infant in his lap during the *bris*. But someone like me could be *sondek* to nobody but Pinocchio. So on the eighth day I called in sick. Then I read through the ceremony at home and toasted the new Farber an easier time inside the world than he'd had in breaking and entering.

Afterward, Ezra wondered about Dr. Tchernichovsky. He had prayed that the next time the infant came to the hospital should be for his own son's *bris*. But then the professor remarked, half to himself, "Lucky child. *His* last operation for years and years."

"Did you hear about the mother inspecting R.I. to make certain the school's good enough for her son?" Perry Davis asked me one morning.

"Okay, I'll bite."

"No gag, Baron. The woman's here. Sophie Portnoy lives!"
Reports flew hourly about a Mrs. Goldberg from out West.
So pushy, she had bombarded the homiletics class with
suggestions on the fine art of communicating with congregants, her example being *The Godfather*.

I caught a glimpse of the woman, swathed from head to foot
in boots, a leopard pants suit, turban, and sunglasses as large
as a windshield. Perhaps, like the Invisible Man, when she
removed an article of clothing, nothing showed.

Except for a tongue. To several freshpersons who criticized
her for reinforcing the stereotype of the overprotective Jewish
mother, Mrs. Goldberg retorted, "Frankly, my dears, I don't
give a damn." Everyone felt sorry for her sonny boy, some
speculated on her also enrolling at R.I. to keep an eye on him.

She was sitting alone at a table in R.I.'s *sukkah* when I
entered for lunch. Something familiar about her gave me a
turn. It must have been my imagination, though, because she
took no notice of me.

Then, someone asked Mrs. Goldberg to join the others, and
a voice as familiar as my own mother's said, "Thank you. I'm
waiting for Dr. Furth."

The woman *was* Terri! Inside the Rabbinical Institute of
America, my mother the *shiksa*. I must have broken the record for the ninety-yard dash getting to her. "*What are you
doing here?*"

She pointed to her pancaked face. "My T.V. pilot is being
taped a few blocks away," she whispered. "Smile, Drew.
People are watching."

"That goofy disguise—"

A whisper: "Everyone in America with a toilet knows my
face." Loudly: "Thank you. So nice to be here."

"You'll *ruin* me. Why on earth did you come?"

"All those stories in the press about youngsters brain-
washed. Besides, I'm playing a mommy in the series. And I'm
a Method actress. Why I've sold so much disinfectant on
T.V."

"Life isn't *I Love Lucy*. If you blow my cover—"

"You have any idea how long *Lucy's* been running? Oh,

stop worrying, Drew. I'm really very good. Dr. Furth asked for a date."

"You didn't accept!"

"Well, I'm between husbands. And they say Jews make the best. Who knows?"

I returned to my classmates. Terri, of course, was putting me on about Dr. Furth. And yet . . .

Everyone else enjoyed the lunch and a remark of hers on entering the *sukkah* made of evergreens and decorated with fruits and vegetables: "So this is the forest primeval." They nudged one another when Dr. Furth quoted to her from Song of Songs, and winked when Terri removed her jacket and flared her nostrils.

I darted back to her. "Mrs. Goldberg. Your plane to L.A." I rushed her out of the *sukkah* and into the street.

There, she removed her sunglasses and pulled off her turban. Out tumbled her thick streaked mane. She gave it one toss after another.

Donald Stein came running over with the leopard jacket. "You forgot . . . Say! Haven't I seen you on television? Aren't you . . .? Yes, you are!"

A broad smile. "That's right." Terri flared her nostrils and sniffed Suzily.

So she had had in mind something more important to her than seduction. Recognition. Poor Terri. She had turned in the best piece of acting in her life, and nobody would ever know.

FOURTEEN

"Peace is at hand," Henry Kissinger declared on October 26.

Several weeks before, Levi's two-year army hitch had ended. I had him immediately enrolled at Oxford, but Mrs. Simon wondered why he was never in when she phoned and she always out when Levi called. Would he please come home for the winter recess? I wrote back that England had none. Meanwhile, Mr. Simon and I kept assuring each other that the war would surely be over in 1973 and Levi a survivor.

At the inaugural Nixon took the oath of office on two family Bibles opened to Isaiah 2:4: "They shall beat their swords into plowshares . . ." (Only seven verses later, however, the prophet vowed, "The lofty looks of man shall be brought low, and the haughtiness of men shall be bowed down.") There were six balls that night.

Two days later Nixon appeared on television to announce he had achieved "peace with honor." So ended the longest undeclared war in U.S. history. Times Square saw no mob scenes, only knots of drunken servicemen cursing. "They make a desolation," one cried, "and call it peace."

On the day of the cease-fire, Defense Secretary Melvin Laird announced the end of the draft! But no amnesty for war resistors, whom many thought guilty only of premature morality. "We cannot provide forgiveness for them," Nixon stated. "Those who deserted must pay their price . . . a criminal penalty for disobeying the laws of the United States."

Now, what if Levi's name did not appear on the released list of American P.O.W.s? Mr. Simon, frantic, reproached himself for not having prepared his wife all along for the worst. If Levi hadn't survived, the sudden shock might kill her. Me, I caught myself praying. Actually, wheeling and dealing. Save Levi, and I'd return the favor tenfold, a hundredfold. Whether or not there was anyone to uphold the other end didn't matter. Let my friend live, I implored, and I'd never lie again. The ultimate sacrifice.

The very next day the phone rang insistently. So naturally the door key slipped from my fumbling fingers. When the door was opened, no more rings. Certain that it was Mr. Simon, I didn't return the call. Instead, I washed the week's dirty dishes. Again, the phone rang. By the time I decided to pick it up, it went dead.

I called the Simons, but the line was busy. And it remained busy for an hour. Unable to bear the suspense, I drove to

Manhattan Beach. Once there, however, it took me fifteen minutes to make it to the door.

Mrs. Simon herself answered. She looked all worn out, yet luminous. "Drew!" She embraced me and burst into tears.

Mr. Simon appeared in the foyer. "We've been calling for hours, Drew. Mrs. Simon told you . . .?"

My heart skipped a beat.

He threw out his arms and fumbled for words. "It's a . . . a . . . a . . ."

"*Miracle!*" Mrs. Simon corrected herself at once. "But that's selfish. When I think of those *not* coming home. . . ."

I fell into the nearest chair. Having steeled myself for the worst, I was unprepared for the best. "He's *alive?*"

Levi had called from Clark Air Force Base in the Philippines. He'd been held prisoner all this time in a jungle camp in South Vietnam.

Mrs. Simon waved a finger at me accusingly. "I should have guessed those letters weren't Levi's. All those quotations from the Bible and Talmud, a regular Jewish *Bartlett's*. How can I ever thank you, Drew? To agonize for nineteen months that Levi might be dead." She turned toward her husband. "My poor dear. How did you ever live through it?"

It was after midnight when I left, far too excited to sleep. *Levi was alive!*

Now for my part of the bargain. Even without the vow, I'd be quitting R.I. Not the very next morning, of course. I wanted to bow out gracefully. It would kill me if my hoax went public. Nobody respected a liar, least of all myself.

As if to assure me that there were worse people, a Russian woman doctor turned up that week at R.I. to speak on the Bolsheviks. Hard to believe that a superpower would bother getting Jews fired from their jobs for applying for exit visas to Israel, remove their phones, intercept mail, jail them for "jaywalking" or "jostling strangers on the street" or "saying dirty words in public," then mete out additional sentences for "resisting arrest."

Though the Soviet Government wouldn't allow anyone to hire the doctor or her physicist husband, they faced imprisonment "for maliciously evading socially useful labor." Only after his nervous breakdown was the family allowed to leave the country. Hundreds of thousands of others, however, still remained trapped. Like mice in a cathouse, Dr. Q. said mistakenly, but nobody laughed.

Why, she was asked, did her family emigrate?

"In the Soviet Union, we could be neither good Russians nor good Jews," Dr. Q. replied. "Of all the peoples in the country, only the Jew's religion is stamped on his internal passport as his nationality. But Jewish culture is outlawed. And when Jews try to leave, they call us traitors."

What made the refuseniks, those refused exit visas, now want to live as Jews?

"The Six-Day war and the death of our God. You are surprised that atheists like us believed in God? Well, we did— his name was Education." After the Bolshevik Revolution, learning became the golden door to opportunity and advancement. Shedding their ethnic identity, Russia's Jews felt, was a small enough price to pay. But in recent years the doors of learning were slamming shut in their faces, entry into institutions of higher learning being reduced to the Jews' percentage of the Soviet population. Less than two percent. "Once the most universal of peoples, we are now forced to return if not to the faith of our fathers, then to their culture," Dr. Q. said. "For who can live on nothing? Only fools and men of the spirit."

What could we do to help?

Dr. Q.'s reply came in staccato bursts. "Go to Russia. Visit refuseniks. Keep their cause alive. Contact your Congress. Demonstrate. Don't let the world look the other way *this* time."

A score of students and faculty volunteered for a trip to Russia. The number dwindled when Dr. Q. forbade lying on the visa application, which inquired about one's occupation and family history. Surely, Russia would bar the daughter of the famous rabbi most active in Soviet Jewry's cause.

Isaca turned to me and said in a loud voice, "I envy you, Andrew, being also a student at Columbia."

A great idea. With my days as pseudo-Semite numbered, a trip to Russia would requite Jewry for sheltering me from the draft. Besides, I loved to travel.

Mrs. Simon, inviting me over after Levi's return, said that the army psychiatrist had advised against asking P.O.W.s about their experiences. "And please don't comment on Levi's appearance."

"Anything else?"

After a pause: "Are you disturbed by long silences?"

Despite the preparation, Levi's cadaverous appearance shocked me. Body emaciated, skin blotched, face drawn like a skull's, he might have been recognizable, if not for his eyes. They were vacant, as if nobody were home. Nobody would ever again mistake us for each other.

The Simons and I kept the conversation rolling, Mrs. Simon exclaiming several times over my having learned Hebrew just to forge letters for him.

"Uh-huh," said Levi each time, without interest.

The evening was a great strain—all that chatter with no expression of true feelings. Later, Mrs. Simon apologized. "We know what Levi is going through. In some ways the months after release are worse than the years inside. People can get used to almost anything—but afterward they have to make some sense out of all the agony. And who can?"

No more invitations followed despite my many calls. When I finally asked why, Mr. Simon said it wasn't fair to burden me further. Had anything happened? No—and that was the matter. What did the army psychiatrist counsel?

"Patience," said Mr. Simon. "But he doesn't see Levi sitting alone in his room day after day watching television with the sound turned off. It's giving my wife nightmares again."

The following Sunday I paid the Simons a surprise visit, bearing in mind the injunction not to try to comfort the mourner while his dead are still with him. And Levi's were all inside.

In his room the T.V., playing silently, gave the impression of living wallpaper. Levi wouldn't let me turn off the set or turn up the sound. "Can't stand being alone. But I can't take talk either." Did he want me to go? "I didn't mean you, Drew. I meant . . ." His hands fluttered aimlessly in the air.

Levi picked up a blanket and spread it over the bed, then folded it exactly in half. Fifteen minutes later he was still folding the same blanket. When I finally called it to his attention, he remarked, "Gives a feeling of accomplishment. . . . In camp we did anything to block out thoughts of past, present, future." And the tin cup and spoon beside his bar mitzvah photo? "At my bar mitzvah I became a man; chained to a bamboo cage in Vietnam . . . something less. Training ants to kill beetles isn't what you'd call man's work."

I suggested a walk.

Though the day was overcast, Levi put on a pair of sunglasses before going outside. "Don't want to see anyone," he said.

We walked slowly in the direction of the ocean. Now he said, "I like the beach in winter. No people."

"Your parents are people."

"No. They're freaks."

"Freaks?"

"They've never harmed anyone in their lives. Know what's a hazard to health, Drew? Human beings. Vietnam made a true believer of me. In Original Sin," he said. "And the war's real villan? Everyone. South Vietnam is like that baby brought before King Solomon. But South Vietnam was *nobody's* baby. Neither side preferred it saved rather than destroyed." Suddenly, my friend stopped dead in his tracks, staring ahead in alarm.

"What's the matter?"

Levi pointed at the beach that the morning's downpour had

turned into a huge mud pie. "My nightmare," he mumbled. "Sinking in a swamp, unable to wash myself clean." He fled.

Why is it, I wondered, that only the innocent feel guilty?

Since the money for my trip had to come from my parents, each had his say. Dad was all for travel, World War II having made a man of him,. But not to Russia, which was overrun with Communists. Terri was disturbed by a brief news item about the detention of two American tourists "for agitating the Jews of Russia." The complete article in *Nedalya* reported that the couple had also been charged with defecating on the carpet of their hotel room in Moscow, then smearing their feces all over the walls! What kind of country fabricates something so ludicrous?

To add to my anxiety, Isaca inquired if my trip to Russia was still on. When I asked why, she replied, "I'm *sure* you'll have a safe journey. But you will be careful, won't you?"

"What do you mean?"

"I don't want to frighten you," she said. Friends of her father's had just returned after being held incommunicado by the K.G.B. for thirty hours for taping messages from refuseniks. Finally, with their money and plane tickets confiscated, they had been expelled to Poland.

"Oh," I said, "is *that* all?"

Isaca hesitated. "Well, no. Russian television is now superimposing Ben Gurion's face on Hitler's. And recently, another Jewish tourist . . . Oh, Andrew! I didn't wish you any harm, getting you to go to Russia. It wasn't spite."

"What . . .?"

Her explanation made me sick to my stomach. I felt like something unclean. *Orthodox Jewish law prohibits a descendant of the priests from marrying a divorcee.* For over a year, then, Isaca's chances for marriage had been impaired. "But we never . . . consummated."

She flushed. "Makes no difference."

But Isaca *wasn't* a divorcee. "I have a confession to make. You'll hate me when you hear. Isaca, I . . . I . . . I . . ." The words wouldn't come, however, with her there in person. Soon, I'd be dropping out of R.I. and sight. At *that* time—"I'll write you, Isaca, explain everything."

"You mean from Moscow? No, Andrew! Promise me you'll cancel the trip."

Not the sort to force my attentions on girls who don't appreciate them, why should I do so on a country? "If it'll make you happy, Isaca."

I phoned Dr. Q. my decision without faking a sick mother or a dying father. See? No more lies. Violence practiced by others revolted me, I said. When directed against myself, it scared the hell out of me.

"I understand," Dr. Q. said. Her family had lived in fear for thirty-one months. K.G.B. hooligans had beaten up her husband five times. "Will you tell Perry Davis? The Soviet Union does not allow last-minute substitutes, and I will not let your classmate travel there by himself."

"Why not?"

"Too dangerous."

"Dangerous?"

"Did I say dangerous? My English is limited. Thousands of people have visited safely with refuseniks. For one very good reason. Russia needs hard currency. The refuseniks, you see, are one of Russia's best cash crops. . . . Any chance you will reconsider?"

I told Dr. Q. yes, but myself never. I hadn't evaded jail in America for almost three years just to end up inside one in Russia.

A phone call from Levi indicated progress. He planned on taking courses to prepare himself for medical school. How about meeting in the city?

Perhaps our last encounter in front of the Metropolitan triggered my friend's opening remark. "I kept my promise, Drew. I never harmed anyone in Vietnam. . . . So why do I feel as if there were wounds in the universe that I must atone for?"

Again, we didn't enter the museum. "I thought Jews don't believe in vicarious atonement."

"We don't. And yet . . ." Recent news stories preyed on Levi's mind. As we walked up the avenue, he suddenly spoke of his capture.

His chaplain, who regarded the Vietnam War as a *jihad* against the yellow anti-Christ, had insisted on bringing his word to the soldiers at the front. But with no lines demarcating one side from the other, the two men had blundered into an enemy enclave. Wounded by Vietcong, the chaplain was left behind and Levi seized, stripped of his uniform and boots, then beaten and marched in shackles to a camp in the jungle. There, not only did the prisoners suffer malnutrition, medical neglect, and overwork. Their captors forced on them statements denouncing the war, while an American major threatened those signing with courtmartial.

I sought to reassure Levi.

He stopped short in the middle of the street. "Don't you think I knew that!" Yet the major pressured most of the P.O.W.s, including Levi, to submit to unnecessary beatings. Some died as a result. In the end they all signed statements anyway. The major, too.

Knowing the confessions to be nonsense, why did Levi resist?

"I was the only Jew there. Couldn't have the others think me a coward or a traitor." A harsh laugh. "Speaking of images." Levi pulled a large envelope from his pocket and showed me the engraved invitation inside. From the White House, no less. A gala in honor of the returned P.O.W.s on Thursday, May 24.

Perry Davis accosted me in the coffee shop. "It came as a great shock," he said. "You don't look it."

"Look what?"

"Chicken. You wouldn't back out of our trip, would you, and sink me too?"

Precisely the wrong approach, drowning cocky Perry Davis

being a mighty temptation. He had the knack for making people feel like all sorts of diseases in the presence of a Christian Scientist. Not only because everything came easy to him. Perry exuded too much self-assurance. A discussion with him invariably provoked me to statements *I* disagreed with.

Quoting Dr. Q.'s "dangerous" only incited him. "What a great *adventure!*" he exclaimed, all italics and exclamation points. "A testing of the *spirit!*"

"So is Russian roulette."

"Judaism is deed, not creed. To demonstrate concern for Russian Jewry is a *mitzvah.*"

"There are so many other commandments neither of us observes . . . " I glanced at his ham sandwich.

Perry regarded me with disdain. "Andrei Sakharov, knowing he'd get arrested for it, demonstrated at the Lebanese Embassy in Moscow to protest the Olympics massacre. Foolish of me to expect you to behave as bravely as a righteous Gentile."

Shame did it. And wanting to leave R.I. with my conscience laundered. "Okay, pardner."

Before I could renege, Dr. Q. invited us for a briefing late at night in a ramshackle midtown office that had no name on the door, but four locks.

A close look at the intense chain smoker revealed a middle-aged brunette with a face like a tropical fish and one breast more buxom than the other. After giving us the names and addresses of several refuseniks—always referred to by first names in case of eavesdroppers—she advised us to put all important papers in money belts. Several tourists had been pickpocketed by the K.G.B. Without prepaid travel vouchers, no hotel would accept us, and without passports the Soviet Union would eject us. On the other hand, without exit visas, she'd never let us go. We'd forever remain men with a country—Russia.

"Why would Russia want to hold on to us?" Perry asked.

A sigh. ". . . Now, then." She reached into her bodice and

pulled out a parcel the size of a slim brick. It was to have been delivered, after the exchange of passwords, to a forty-year-old Soviet Jew whose photo she produced. But at the last minute Russia had denied the American courier a visa. "Will you take this to Ivan? No hard feelings if you refuse."

Perry accepted at once. Not over my objections—there was no time to make any. I protected myself by not asking what the parcel contained. So if the Russians caught us with a small nuclear device, I could always honestly claim ignorance.

I did ask Dr. Q. to turn her chair around, however, without explaining that our lips could be read by anybody across the street with binoculars. Her effusive thanks disturbed me—paranoia confirmed is reality unnerving. When Dr. Q. said, in reply to Perry's query about the parcel's contents, "Even those with top security clearance are never told secrets they don't *need* to know," I excused myself to go to the john.

Minutes later Perry joined me there.

"Andrew," he shouted, "this is going to be a great *adventure!*"

"Think so?"

"I *know* so! A *great* adventure!" Already caught up in it, he unzipped and rezipped only his windbreaker.

Together we returned to lap up Dr. Q.'s advice.

"In every other country, the visa is attached to one's passport. Not in Russia. So it can be lost if the authorities so wish. On your arrival they will take your entrance visa. If in the process your exit visa disappears, *leave on the next plane.*"

That gave me the idea of destroying my exit visa before the trip. On discovering its absence in the Moscow airport, I would return at once to the States.

"Expect your hotel room to be bugged and yourselves to be followed. Now, in case you are picked up for questioning—"

Perry and I turned to look at each other.

Radio and television kept running accounts of the P.O.W.

gala, most spectacular party in White House history. At the urging of the Simons, who hoped to dislodge Levi from his extended depression, he attended.

I had also encouraged him, saying he should bring back the lowdown on Watergate.

That afternoon, after former aide Jeb Magruder agreed to be a witness for the prosecution, Nixon received a standing ovation in the State Department auditorium. At his first inauguration in 1969, the President said, the United States suffered from "a lack of national pride, a lack of patriotism. . . . The nation was torn by riots and hundreds of campuses were in flames. I say it's time for a new sense of responsibility in this country, a new sense of dedication by everybody in the bureaucracy."

In the evening, the ex-P.O.W.s assembled in black tie in a huge, candlelit yellow and orange tent on the south White House lawn, which a steady all-day rain had transformed into a bog. Among the colors presented was a small flag patched together from odds and ends and threads of prisoners' uniforms that were stitched to a man's handkerchief in a prison nicknamed the Hanoi Hilton. During dinner Les Brown's band played; afterward, Bob Hope entertained and Irving Berlin sang "God Bless America." When several P.O.W.s honored Nixon with a plaque that read: "To our leader, our comrade, Richard the Lionhearted, for his fortitude and perseverance under fire," I snapped off my T.V.

A call to Mr. Simon at his place of business brought his partner to the phone. The Simons, he said, had been called to Washington.

"What for?"

"Levi took an overdose of Valium."

The phone nearly fell from my hand before I learned of the successful pumping of Levi's stomach.

Next afternoon, I stopped by the Simons'. Not for their sake, but mine. How inconsiderate, though, to drop in without phoning. For the incident had transformed the family.

This time my visit embarrassed the Simons, quiet and depressed. Levi, however, never stopped talking, using my presence to reassure his parents.

The swamplike White House lawn had triggered flashbacks. When he had dirtied his bar mitzvah suit, Mrs. Simon had comforted him with "It's only clothing. Doesn't matter. So long as the stain isn't on the soul." The mud also revived memories. So Levi had taken tranquilizer after tranquilizer, then lost count. His panicky roommate, in the morning, called an ambulance. "But I didn't take enough to—"

"Of course. Certainly," said his parents. Moments later Mr. Simon showed me a photograph intended for Levi. Of a synagogue in South America established by former inmates of a Nazi camp. "See the name of the shul, Drew? *Lamros Hakol.*"

Levi flushed. We left the house and headed automatically for the beach, he in dark glasses. No, he hadn't enrolled in those prep courses for medical school. What were his plans, then? Levi chose, however, to answer the question I hadn't asked.

"What happened in Washington, Drew, *was* an accident."

"I know, Levi, I know. You'd never hurt your parents . . . Would you?"

"There are things I wouldn't *say* to them, much less do. Still, if they hadn't raised me to feel indebted to America for being so good to the Jews, I'd never have let myself be drafted. Everyone's been screwed. Judaism is much too naïve—people *are* born tainted. The only cure for this world is oblivion." He gestured toward the crowded beach. "Tell me, what do you see?"

Sunshine, trees, water, swimmers. Children building sandcastles. Basketball teams. Families barbecuing meals. Elderly people sunning. "A beach-party movie."

"Look again," Levi said. "Those fellows over there? Dealing in drugs. Hard stuff. Yet a few yards away police taking no notice. No, Drew, no hope at all."

A second look confirmed his words. Several men nearby were exchanging little bags. Still . . . "Is that what you were looking for, Levi?"

"What do you mean?"

"We have *two* eyes. Maybe in order to see both scenes at the same time, mine as well as yours. The trick, someone once told me, is to find reason to rejoice. Perhaps even if you have to invent one." I added disingenuously, "That synagogue's name. What's the translation?"

"*Lamros Hakol?*" He hesitated. "In Spite of Everything." Levi turned to face me. "I'm *trying*, Drew. I swear to God. . . . Look." He yanked off his sunglasses. Done with such force, they flew from his hands and fell to the concrete walk.

One lens shattered. I wondered which—his or mine.

FIFTEEN

Three days before departure for Russia someone broke into my apartment. Though it was thoroughly ransacked, the only thing stolen was the lock on my door. "The burglar wanted cash," said the cops.

Then why hadn't he taken forty-six dollars from my night table? Was he after coins only? Fortunately, I hadn't changed jackets, and Dr. Q.'s parcel was still in the same pocket I put it in after being handed the hot potato, which Perry didn't take from me.

Coincidentally, the doorman in Perry's apartment house had admitted a man from the gas company to check the oven. Only, his was an electric range.

"K.G.B.?" I said, and both of us laughed.

Being R.I.'s first duo to go to Russia, the school gave us a heroes' send-off. Alas, the party reminded me of the ballyhoo of the Vikings as they put the torch to ships bearing their brave dead out to sea.

Isaca, looking as delicious as a condemned man's last meal, took me off into a corner. "Andrew, if anything happens to you," she exclaimed, "I'll never forgive myself."

I hugged her. "If anything happens, Isaca, I won't forgive you either."

Heeding Dr. Q.'s warning to beware of eavesdroppers, once aboard our 747 I hid behind a sleeping mask and ignored Perry, who addressed me in Hebrew. Evidently the reason he was served kosher food. Not yet in Russia and already marked men. I worried, until Perry told of having ordered the special meal.

"How stupid can you get!"

Coolly, he referred to reports that many kosher flight meals, tastier than others, are ordered by non-Jews. Nevertheless, I don't think anybody was fooled by his turning the tray sideways to make the Hebrew letters run up and down like Chinese. The next moment he warned against dozing simultaneously lest one of us talk in his sleep.

"Perry! You're nervous too."

"Of course," he said. "I'm no hero."

"Then why—"

"Look, Andrew." He switched back to Hebrew. "My grandfather fought in the Jewish Legion, which helped to liberate Palestine during World War I. And my father fought in World War II, which the Six Million lost." Repeated requests for the bombing of the railroad tracks leading to the death camps were turned down by the Allies. (In the war for mankind and democracy, special privileges could not be granted any single group.) "Three million more Jews can't be allowed to go down the drain in Russia. As eyewitnesses, we'll be able to speak with authority on conditions there. Rouse people, Congress." Perry tapped my midriff. "Meanwhile, this will be of immediate, concrete help."

Did he know something I didn't? Yet neither of us had opened Dr. Q.'s parcel.

Moscow appeared too soon. A journey of eighty days would have been more to my liking. As instructed, we mingled with a large group tour to get through customs unnoticed. But the

Intourist representative waved through an iron-mesh gate and called us by name. How did she pick us out of the crowd? Simple. All the others were Oriental.

A private car, we were told, was waiting to take us to our hotel. Which one we didn't know—tourists to Russia aren't informed beforehand. What a boon for indecisive travelers: no choice.

The stony-faced guard checking passports dropped ours on the floor behind his desk. But he picked them up and returned them together with our exit visas, leaving us with no alternative but to proceed deeper. There was no reason on earth for anyone to be suspicious of us. Except, perhaps, for Perry's demanding the return of the exit visa that he held in his hand.

Behind a nearby table stood the customs inspector, a pile of *Playboy* magazines beside him. In perfect English he asked us to open our suitcases. "Any books?" All the religious material that R.I. gave us to distribute he confiscated.

I protested. "The Bible contains no centerfolds."

The officer grinned. "A sense of humor is very American. . . . Mr. Baron, you have many friends in the Soviet Union?"

How did the man know my name? "My first visit. No friends at all."

"Don't make any," he said, still smiling.

Scary!

The officer checked our custom declaration forms. "Wallets and money belts, please."

Perry aged as quickly as the girl who became a crone while fleeing Shangri-La. But when my money belt was given back, he made a face that said, "Shmuck! You forgot to bring along the parcel?"

As our suitcases were examined, I crossed my legs. All that sweat could unstick the adhesive tape that held the parcel to the inside of my right thigh.

The inspector dropped my clothing on the counter.

"*Spasibo*," he said as jackets slid to the floor. "Get your things together. Quickly. Look at the long line behind you."

"*You* look! It's your fault." Was that *me*? "Is this how Russia greets foreign visitors? This is an outrage!" A first for me, *outrage*, and having used it, I couldn't stop, though Perry tried to shush me. "The most outrageous . . . outrage I've ever been . . . outraged by."

The officer was amused. "You are keeping twenty people waiting."

"They'll just have to wait for me to fold everything." By then I was unable to discern between genuine outrage and acting, and how much of both was induced by fright. What would the next week bring? "I happen to be a very neat person."

But Perry grabbed my clothing and dumped it into my suitcase, then tossed his and mine onto a cart, all the while apologizing for me.

Our driver, asked if he knew English, shook his head and said "*Ya ne panemayo*." Still, when Perry fretted aloud about the meticulous search, I cut him off. On the palm of his left hand, he wrote in the script of a thousand-year-old man, "*They're on to us*." Then licked off the ink.

Automatically, my legs locked together. Yes, the brick was still there. For good or for evidence.

During the ride along a mediocre replica of Queens Boulevard's highrises, Perry heaped praise on everything not seen. The lack of traffic congestion (evidently Moscow has few cars). No advertising billboards (all businesses are state owned). The immaculate streets (probably no dogs and plenty of jails for litterbugs, not a bad idea to emulate). Ingratiating himself with the driver in case he did understand English.

That puzzle was solved when an automobile drew up alongside ours with individual flowers glued over the entire chassis and a doll on the hood, and I exclaimed, "Look over there on the right." Before Perry moved a muscle, our driver faced right.

The liar deposited us at the gargantuan Hotel Rossiya, where we were taken to a room directly opposite which sat a beady-eyed female floor monitor at a phone. The bellhop fussed just as deftly with the fixtures as his American counterpart until tipped. As soon as he left, Perry cried, "I tell you, Andrew, they're *on* to—"

I clapped one hand over his mouth and motioned with the other to our ears.

He nodded. "The whatchamacallit—where is it?"

"Toilet's over there." Silently, I pointed out the brick's location, then worried that the room might also be televised.

Downstairs in the lobby, we lined up to convert our dollars into rubles. There was a half-hour wait for the clerk in the adjoining room to stop picking her nose, possibly friends' too. Then another fifteen minutes while she counted coins and bills. It took fifteen more minutes to transport the money to the counter, which she did denomination by denomination. By then, there were forty-six people on line. Apparently not enough to discomfort, for the clerk disappeared. Ten minutes later she returned with a glass of tea and a piece of sugar sticking out of her mouth. Still, we were lucky that she didn't have a smaller mouth and a longer nose.

Red Square—so named because the Russian word for beautiful is the same as for red—*is* beautiful. Spacious and cobblestoned and carless, bounded by the fortresslike Kremlin, the longest department store in the world (GUM), the State Historical Museum, and St. Basil's Cathedral with colorful, swirling pineapple- and onion-shaped domes straight out of Walt Disney. One thing spoiled the plaza. An ugly squat red- and black-marble pyramid without a point, Lenin's Tomb.

In front of it, on the hour, Ivan would be waiting.

Two guards popped out of the Kremlin, swinging bayonetted rifles, and goose-stepped along the red-brick wall to the tomb. As the bell tolled, they changed places with two other sentinels, who marched off. Not much different from the changing of the guard at Buckingham Palace, except for the Russian royalty inside being dead.

Two sets of guards later, our blind date still had not put in an appearance. Alas, we knew neither Ivan's address nor a substitute recipient. In Russia, Dr. Q. said, every group of ten contains a K.G.B. informer.

Finally, Perry stated the obvious. "He's not coming." No mistaking the note of relief in his voice, nor the anxiety a moment later when he reflected aloud, "What do we do now?"

We fared no better the next morning while taking pictures every hour on the hour of each other and of the mile-long line of people waiting to enter Lenin's tomb. Even bridal couples came to visit straight from the wedding. One would have thought the tomb had been found empty after the third day.

A woman asked how the Polaroid works, and while Perry demonstrated the camera, a stocky bystander with a shopping bag sidled up to me. "Cut yourself shaving?" he asked.

Not the exact password, but close enough for one who resembled the nondescript Ivan of our photograph. I touched the Band-Aid on my left cheek. "What was that?"

"You cut yourself shaving?"

Perry whirled around and replied, *"Kol od balevov penimah."*

The Russian stooped over to tie a shoelace that was already tied. After a pause, his words wafted up, *"Nefesh Yehudi homiyah."*

Now to pass the goddamn package and enjoy our trip. "Where can we go . . .?"

"For lunch? Yes, almost one o'clock." Perry grabbed my arm and hurried me off. A block away, he explained, "That Russian may know 'Hatikvah'—but not the password, which is the last line. He recited the second line. That isn't Ivan."

"Who else . . .?"

"I don't know. But there was a microphone inside his shopping bag."

Ian Fleming revisited! And if arrested and exposed as an imposter, who in the United States would demand my return? Neither the Jews nor the Gentiles.

Since mail in Russia requires the writer's name and address, I immediately dropped a post card to James Reston of *The New York Times*.

Dear Scotty,
    Russia is everything you said it was. I'm picking up lots of local color for a warm human-interest article.

Moscow was at its most impressive underground. Subway stations are palaces of marble and bronze bedecked with paintings, mosaics, murals, sculptures, crystal chandeliers, and—wonder of wonders—no graffiti. It would be a pleasure, I said, to be mugged amid such splendor. Gravely, our guide stated that unlike in America, there were no muggers here. Who told him so? *Pravda* and *Izvestia*, which never reported any plane crashes either.

I felt unreassured. Were we being followed throughout Moscow by a Gothic caricature of the Woolworth Building? No, Stalin had erected seven identical skyscrapers that resemble castles built with dripping sand. Presumably, at first he had not succeeded.

Our fifth meal in Russia was every bit as good as its predecessors. Mineral water came in a rust-encrusted bottle with matching rusty cap—evidently the Soviet Union recycled its rust. And the food tasted as if it had passed through other alimentary canals before mine.

On Saturday morning we found our way to Moscow's Great Synagogue on Arkhipova Street a few blocks from our hotel. No Ivan inside, however. All the congregants were the age of Medicare. And despite our guide's denial of the existence of slums, unemployment, or poverty, most people were shabbily dressed and missing teeth. The synagogue itself was well kept and freshly painted. A Hebrew prayer for the welfare of the Soviet Government in large letters on the front wall suggested why. This shul, whose officers were in the state's employ, served as a showplace for foreign visitors, unaware it was the only synagogue allowed for Moscow's 300,000 Jews.

Neighbors extended a warm welcome, then asked in Yiddish about Israel and America. Alas, neither of us knew the language. "*Dubra, dubra . . . spasibo, spasibo.*"

"*Dubra* means good—and *spasibo,* thank you. They want you to know they appreciate your visit."

The speaker, a fortyish, Slavic-looking man in the pew behind us, claimed to be a New Yorker. But what adult American Jew wears a windbreaker and stubble to synagogue? Or refers to John Lindsay as New York's current mayor when he'd been succeeded?

The real action, Perry and I discovered, took place after the service. So many people of all ages clustered on the sidewalk, they spilled over into the street. Dozens descended to ask us in English about America, how Jews fared there, how strongly our government supported Israel, Senator Jackson's chances of becoming President—all things picked up from the Voice of America. But how could people tell our origin?

"You are strangers," said a patrician-looking woman with white hair and chiseled features. "Everyone else we know, as this is our only gathering place in all of Moscow."

"On Rosh Hashonah and Simchas Torah thousands come," said a fellow my age. "Sometimes the police break up the crowd and send us home, or to the hospital."

"A fine thank you!" exclaimed a middle-aged man with a twisted leg. "In World War II, over half a million Jews fought in the Soviet Army." Another added, "Over two hundred Jews became generals, and almost that many were honored as Heroes. Many more than the Byelorussians and Ukrainians, who outnumber us by millions." A third continued, "But since the war Jews are denounced as shirkers."

One man, coming upon us unobserved, shouted, "Liars! You defame the great Soviet Socialist Republic."

The group bristled. But only the patrician woman spoke up. "I am too old to lie anymore."

The interloper's retort in Russian put the woman to flight. I followed after her.

"He didn't *say* anything," the woman replied bitterly. "He only asked if I do not have have a son and granddaughter." She rushed off.

A quick glance revealed only one person there who resembled Ivan. The man who had approached us in Red Square. "Yes, I know him," the cripple said when I pointed him out. "K.G.B."

My skin crawled. "But he knows some Hebrew."

"So did Eichmann."

Casually, I inquired about a host of Russian writers, plus some characters from *War and Peace*, sliding in Ivan's name among them.

"His father is very sick," someone said. "He went to visit him in Leningrad."

Luckily our next stop, for Russia permits no change in itinerary. Perry, however, said without a moment's thought, "Do you know the address of Ivan's father?"

More crawling flesh when someone remarked, "So it is Ivan you two are looking for."

"Nobody Russian is alien to us," I declared, and ticked off the names of several cosmonauts.

Afterward, when I berated Perry, he snapped, "Who appointed *you* captain of this team? Just unload that damned parcel before—"

But he never finished the sentence.

Dear Billy Graham,

The churches here are really something. St. Basil's Cathedral is a delight! And painted on the front wall of the Great Synagogue is a beautiful prayer for the U.S.S.R.

My best to the family,

Off that night to the first family on our list, Perry and I

passed up the taxis in front of the hotel—their drivers were police informers, Dr. Q. had warned—and flagged down one half a mile away. We showed the refuseniks' address written in Russian with the number 96 substituted for the correct one, 22. Arriving, the driver made a big fuss. The street numbers ran only as high as 39.

Inside in place of pictures or paintings on the wall, there were large white sheets of paper with carefully handwritten words: *I, you, he, she, we, they, I have, you have, he has, she has, we have, you have, they have,* and numbers *one* through *one thousand*—all in Hebrew. The family's proudest possessions. They had little else.

No, Yuri and Galina hadn't expected us (which meant they weren't intimates of Ivan, to whom the parcel could be entrusted). He had been fired from his job as physicist and Galina from hers as English teacher after applying for exit visas. Yuri's subsequent job as elevator operator lasted only a month. "My supervisor did not think I could learn the route," he remarked wryly.

Not wishing to deprive them, I declined the refreshments that were served on stacks of books covered with a sheet. "What do you live on?" I asked.

Yuri pointed to the bare room. "Our furniture. We are eating it for thirteen months now," he said. "We also do like my grandfather's pious rabbi. If not for his weekly fasts, my grandfather said, the rabbi would have died of starvation."

Galina burst out, "If only the police did not constantly threaten us! Parasites they call us and our son here. All this pressure . . ." Her hands beat the air. "It turns even the most happily married couples against each other." She excused herself to go into the kitchen.

I slipped ten twenty-dollar bills under a plate.

Perry asked, "What reason does the government give for not letting you go?"

"State security," said Yuri. "They say I know important government secrets. When I showed American scientific journals proving that in my field Russia is ten years behind, they told me, *That's the secret.'"*

Galina, returning with tea, spoke of the early days after the Revolution. "All nations will disappear, there will be only one mankind. Those were the slogans my Communist father taught me. But reality was knocks on the door and midnight arrests. World War II killed two million Russian Jews—many with the collaboration of Russians and the Ukrainian police."

Yuri continued. "And after the war, what happened? The government deprived us of our identity. The Chukchi tribe of ten thousand in northern Siberia has a publishing house, books, schools, a teachers seminary, medical school, and musical institute—all in their native language. But for thirty years now the government bans all Yiddish culture. Those caught with a Hebrew grammar are sentenced to ten years in jail."

The teen-ager spoke up for the first time. "The Nazis made my parents Jews, and the Soviet Government makes us Zionists."

Perry couldn't understand why Russia persecuted the refuseniks.

"As a terrible example. You think Jews are the only ones wishing to leave this paradise?" Yuri said. "The Russian word for *dissident* is 'anyone who thinks differently.'" For fourteen years the director of a laboratory of forty technicians, he had worked twelve hours a day, seven days a week. "Being a Jew, I would lose my job if I worked less." Sorrowfully, he added, "So instead I lost my family. My wife says I destroyed our life."

Galina flushed, but did not contradict him. She asked about Israel. "It is our destiny to go there, I believe that. And I say it even if it embarrasses my family or you gentlemen. *God* means us to go to Israel."

Perry gave a funny laugh. "Embarrass? Impossible. My friend here is studying to be a rabbi. And so am—"

Yuri turned to me, appalled. "You are?" His hands flew to hide his face. "Here my wife and I spend the entire evening talking only of our troubles, and never once do we ask about yourselves. Such bad manners."

When we left, Yuri invited us to the weekly seminar of the refuseniks, their only forum for scientific discourse. Would Ivan attend? Galina didn't think so—his father was very sick. But she supplied his address in Leningrad.

Outside, Perry became enraged when I expressed regret for not having more money to leave the family. Had I forgotten that departing tourists had to account for every dollar declared at customs? We could be arrested for trafficking in money. He calmed down only when he saw the street deserted. "At least we weren't tailed here. No car followed us, I'm sure."

"Tailed? Nonsense." And nonsense it was, I realized on engaging another taxi. Nobody had followed us, we had followed him. For our driver sported three moles in the same configuration on the back of his neck as did the one who took us to Yuri and Galina.

It was a mistake to tell Perry, already jittery. Without my knowledge he had sprinkled sugar all over the floor of our suite. Now he pointed in alarm to footsteps everywhere. But the K.G.B. would reason that only those with something to hide would have pulled that trick. Trading charges of stupidity, we almost came to blows. Grown men scribbling insults at each other on Magic Slates. Still, it was the closest we had come to converstaion since our encounter at Red Square. With our room bugged and possibly another microphone in one of the shopping bags outside, we were afraid to communicate. Inseparables, each on a solitary journey through Russia, now on a collision course of swearwords.

"*En garde!*" Perry wrote, finally.

I retreated to the bathroom. But with the parcel taped to my thigh and no extra tape should it be removed, I could neither bathe nor shower unless I did headstands in the tub. What stopped me from flushing the damn thing down the toilet was the thought of its draining directly into police headquarters. In this country, where no individual was sacred, why would bodily wastes be?

Dear Mother,
So happy to read that your new television show is among the Top Ten. That makes you a real Superstar, doesn't it?
My trip is fabulous. Loving every minute.

The Kremlin was our sight for the day, and guess what our guide showed us inside. Churches! The government had spent fortunes to refurbish these opulent nonfunctioning houses of God for the tourist dollar. Just like any good capitalist country.

The guide responded to our request for a functioning Russian Orthodox church with "Churches are only for old women." Why, then, did the government find it necessary to repress Baptists and Roman Catholics? "Why," said the guide, "are you Jews so interested in church?"

She knew our religion!

Two tranquilizers later, Perry exclaimed, "I tell you, Andrew, they're *on* to us."

On meeting Yuri and Galina that evening, my friend told of our having been followed to their apartment, and probably now as well.

Yuri smiled.

Perry's jaw dropped. "You aren't frightened?"

A shake of the head. "The K.G.B. knows everything about us. But that makes us the freest people in Russia." Yuri thanked us for the money. He had distributed it to unemployed refuseniks with even less furniture than he to sell. "Do you know the old Soviet joke? Under capitalism, man oppresses man. Under communism, it is just the opposite."

To escape Perry's scowl, I took Galina by the arm and walked on ahead.

"My husband is not entirely accurate. Refuseniks do have something to fear. Self-destruction," she said. "Some succumb to recklessness. Do something lunatic. Anything to end the agony of limbo."

Yet a few blocks later, Galina added, haltingly, "What I said just now about the Soviet Union, last night too. I should have kept quiet. I love my country even though she is a prison. You cannot understand unless you love someone who hates you."

Oddly enough, I thought of my parents, though, of course, they didn't hate me.

"And what will I do in Israel without my language? Russian, I was born to, live in, write poetry in. Russia is my home. The home that doesn't want me, yet won't let me go. No, do not look for reasons. Anti-Semitism is the greatest mystery. Jews are hated not because we killed God, but because we *conceived* God. They have never forgiven us for that. . . . Still and all—" she threw up her hands—"I cannot not love the Soviet Union! Am I too not a lunatic?"

The seminar was held in the apartment of Yevgeny, a Hero of Socialist Labor, whose cherubic face radiated serenity. The thirty other refuseniks there exhibited comparable grace.

One, the suspicious man in the pew behind me in the Great Synagogue, was introduced as Rabbi Seymour Siegel.

"Since when," I asked, "does a rabbi dress like a hippie?"

"Since Aeroflot lost his luggage," he said with a grin. "And what New Yorker doesn't know that Beame is now mayor?"

"That was *your* mistake."

"But I was only testing *you*."

A professor of microbiology lectured on the interaction of tumor-causing viruses with genetic material in human cells and the role of viral enzymes in the development of cancer. An attendance book was passed around in which were dates, the names of dozens of American scientists and several rabbis and their lecture topics. Since I considered everyone in attendance a hero and each page an honor roll, I presumed to add my own name. Honor by association.

Perry glared at me and passed the book along without signing. A moment later he sent me a note. "We might miss connections in Leningrad tomorrow. So how about giving the whatchamacallit to Yevgeny?"

I nodded, then tore up the note into little pieces and swallowed them.

Following a tea break, Rabbi Siegel lectured on Jewish history, after which he asked for questions.

A handsome man with dark eyes and a mustache raised his hand. "I am twenty-one years past thirteen," he said gravely. "If they let me leave here one day, can I be bar mitzvah at my advanced age?"

Rabbi Siegel swallowed hard and nodded.

Yevgeny took two coins from his pocket. "These were found among the ashes of those murdered by the Nazis." He handed one to the microbiologist and the other to the rabbi. "Mementos of this evening. With our gratitude."

A shudder ran through me as the memory surfaced of the cultural programs put on by Jews the night before being exterminated. I examined the rabbi's coin. On one side it read *"Der Aelteste der Juden in Litzmannstadt, quittung uber"* and *"10 marks"* on the other side. *"Getto 1943"* under a Star of David. Strange. The coin felt hot to the touch, as if it smoldered still.

Suddenly, there was a series of sharp thumps at the door. Moments later two florid-faced men entered. Yevgeny rose to greet them with a faint smile. Yet they couldn't have been friends. Something about the cruel set to the faces, the coldness in the eyes, the words issuing from thin lips in barks and growls.

Nobody else said a word. The expressions of loathing and defiance and fright and resignation spoke for all. Here in person—the dread K.G.B.

My legs locked together. Somewhere between the apartment and the street, I'd have to untape the parcel from my thigh and get rid of what could endanger the entire group. Slowly, very slowly, I unzipped my fly.

As Yevgeny took a jacket from an armoire, one of the intruders picked up the register, and, after glancing through it, pocketed it. Yevgeny said a few words in Russian to the group, then kissed his wife and daughter. Moments later the agents hustled him away.

Only when the front door slammed shut did I realize that the rest of us were safe. Shame flooded me for feeling such relief when Yevgeny had been arrested. "And do you know what the charge is?" Galina said. "Sowing discord among the races."

My right hand hurt. I unclenched my fist to see the German ghetto coin. Imprinted on my palm as if branded was the Star of David.

There was no way of determining Yevgeny's fate before leaving for Leningrad the next day. Who do you call when the police are the kidnapers? And the refuseniks had no phones. I recalled the would-be bar mitzvah's words: "The K.G.B. believes everything they can prove, and they can prove everything."

Perry and I traveled to Leningrad in steerage, otherwise known as Aeroflot. The airline's seventy-minute flight took seven hours, counting the six-hour delay in the Moscow airport, during which we tried to wrest information about departure, another of Russia's secrets. "The plane will leave when it is ready," said the clerks. And when would it be ready? "When the plane leaves."

Seats were cramped, and refreshments consisted of rusty mineral water and a piece of hard candy. What separated the cockpit from the cabin was a shower curtain, and something resembling a bath mat covered the floor.

Leningrad posed another problem. The desk clerk who took our hotel vouchers denied having received them. Backed up by his supervisor, both advised us to take the next flight back to New York. Yet without having seen our vouchers, how did they know our city of origin? Everyone always tells me I don't look New Yorkish.

The matter was settled to the Russians' dissatisfaction when Perry took from his money belt a Xerox of his voucher, which also carried my name. Soon the original vouchers turned up in the file of the Scotland-Soviet Peace and Friendship League where, the clerk said, they must have accidentally fallen.

In our suite Perry burst into his theme song, "They're *on* to us!"

"Why not think of it this way?" I whispered. "We're on to *them*."

He turned on me. "It's all your fault! Signing that register at the seminar. Did you want class credit for the lectures?"

Pills put him to sleep, while I despaired of completing our mission without making a detour to Siberia.

Over breakfast I daydreamed of being back in the United States, untailed, where nobody but the draft board gave a damn about my goings and comings. Not entirely a dream, for everyone around me was speaking English. Members of the Scotland-Soviet Peace and Friendship League, they said, touring Russia by day, putting on musical performances for workers at night.

Then an idea. Could I attend their concert?

"Of course," said Mr. McPherson.

Our tourist pose probably fooling nobody by then but other tourists, Perry and I proceeded with our scheduled tour of Leningrad. Russia's window on Europe, built on 101 islands in the Gulf of Finland, was a magnificent city of gilded domes and low buildings of yellow, green, and ocher. All dated to the time of the Czars, the most splendid the work of an architect named Rastrelli.

"Rastrelli?" I said. "Isn't that an odd name for a Russian?"

"Yes," said our guide.

"But not at all odd for an Italian," Perry said before asking, "What beautiful things have been built *since* the Revolution?"

The guide frowned. "The Union of the Soviet Socialist Republics." She took us into the Hermitage, Catherine the Great's Winter Palace which fell to the revolutionaries in 1917. "The finest museum in the world," she declared. "Over two million works of art inside."

I didn't stop to count, but the museum was indeed glorious.

For the first time since arriving in Russia, I forgot to be frightened. The breath-taking *objets d'art* made one lose all sense of place. Even the floors and doors were exquisite. What brought me back was the guide's calling one of the Rembrandts *Portrait of an Old Man*.

Perry corrected her. "You mean *Portrait of an Old Jew*."

"Jew?" The guide took another look at the haunting painting of an old man in phylacteries and prayer shawl. "You are mistaken." Clearly no lie. She was only repeating what had been taught her. ("Someday," Dr. Q. had said, "the Czars' jewelry collection will be known only as the Crown Els.")

Perry objected to my using the Scottish troupe. Too James Bondish. "There's a much simpler way to sneak off." Returning to our hotel, he jumped up on a sill—"Look" and disappeared through the open window.

"Perry!" I ran to look outside, heart in my mouth, having forgotten for the moment that our room was on the second floor.

But a pudgy man in black outside knew all along. He emerged from an alley to follow Perry at a discreet distance.

My friend the jock, now that he had incited stricter surveillance over me, too, said on hearing of his tail, "So go ahead with *your* plan, Andrew."

Was it possible that Perry . . .? Of course not. He *couldn't* be in the employ of the K.G.B.

After dinner I went to McPherson's room. Could he imagine my companion's astonishment at seeing me in a kilt? The Scot looked dubious. The expression on Perry's face would be worth a jar of caviar, I said, and McPherson replied, "Two."

With my legs a foot longer than the Scot's, his kilt was my mini. And when I moved, one could see where the parcel, now bulging in my money belt, had been taped.

McPherson blinked his eyes. "Peculiar. I've never before seen man or woman or beast with one thigh hairy and the other smooth."

"Runs in the family. We call one Esau and the other Jacob."

Perry overdid his surprise—"Is that really you, Andrew? I

thought it was Tony Perkins in *Psycho*"—before confessing himself a victim of the scourge of Leningrad, diarrhea. An excuse for returning to our room. The floor lady would get word to Pudgy. Having been inseparable since our arrival in Russia, everyone should assume we were inside together.

Hunched over and with a tam-o'-shanter pulled down to my eyes, I hid behind bagpipes as the Scottish troupe proceeded to the bus. In response to queries, I won everyone's heart by denouncing America's intervention in Vietnam and holding my tongue about Russia's everywhere else. Puzzling, selective outrage. Why is it always the *other* fellow's hunchback that one sees?

The troupe's destination was one of those churches converted by the Soviet Government to secular use. There, hundreds of Russian workers gave us a standing ovation. During the opening number, I slipped away.

It wasn't hard to find a taxi, two, even three. But all off-duty. When the fifth one passed me by, I finally caught on. No taxi driver would pick up what appeared to be a six-foot-two mustached transvestite.

I turned around to find a policeman staring at me.

Automatically, I said, "I work for *The New York Times*."

He tapped his foot. "*Dokument.*"

The passport came out of my money belt without dislodging the parcel. When the cop glanced back and forth from the passport photo of me in a shirt, tie, and jacket to my bare knees, I motioned him to follow me inside the ex-church. Seeing his compatriots applaud thirty other males in kilts, he broke out into a smile.

Now when I pointed to the address of Ivan's father, the cop nodded. He took me outside and hailed a cab.

At my destination I paid the driver and, after tipping him handsomely, held up five fingers. "Please wait. Okay? Five minutes. Five. *Dubra? Spasibo.*"

He shook his head and held up five fingers of his own, waved them, and—under the impression we were exchanging fond farewells—sped off.

Ivan's father's flat was on the fourth floor in a dark building. To conserve electricity, each floor had a switch that lighted the hall for a minute, just enough time to make it to the next switch. Only after knocking on the door with the correct number did I finally breathe a sigh of relief.

A short one. There was no response from within.

Another knock, harder, summoned nobody. Yet a very sick man would have an attendant. Somebody *had* to be home. I banged at the door.

Finally, a door opened. One down the pitch-black hall. A neighbor appeared in silhouette.

I grunted, "Ivan?" As in "Does Ivan live here?"

The man shook his head and growled.

"Ivan?" As in "Then where in God's name *is* Ivan?"

"*Parkhaty zhid umer.*" And he slammed the door.

Terrific. No Ivan. No idea where he might be. Nothing but panic and me. Downstairs, I couldn't even find a taxi to pass me by.

Striking out blindly, I reached a main thoroughfare. Eventually, it led to a metro built like all Russian subways, not in the bowels of the earth, but in its heels. The woman in the change booth, who couldn't see my kilt, looked at my piece of paper with the church's address and pointed to the right, then held up all ten fingers. Another long escalator ride delivered me to the station itself, where riders eyed my attire in disbelief. A preview of coming attractions—on the train the titters turned into snickers. Though I yanked the kilt down until my bellybutton was exposed, passengers kept pointing me out to newcomers at each station. What could I do but bury my eyes in darkness?

The noise level rose steadily, then suddenly fell. Why? Opening my eyes, I found a young tough before me, smirking. Even before he started spouting Russian, I recognized the confrontation scene from a thousand movies.

A fight didn't scare me. Who would know if I lost? But fearful of getting picked up by police, I tried to stare the hooligan down. That wasn't his choice of weapons, however.

He grabbed at my kilt, and when I slapped one hand away, the other replaced it and got slapped too. I felt like a girl defending her virtue.

Shifting sights, the hoodlum grabbed my tam-o'-shanter and carried it off to the other end of the car. How could I explain the tam's disappearance to McPherson? Tossed up in the air to hail his performance, the tam had never returned to earth? He'd make a stink that would expose my charade. So pride being far more digestible than terror, I went to the hooligan and ransomed the tam.

"*Spasibo.*" He pocketed my rubles.

"May you always have plenty of money," I said. "For doctors."

I got back in time for the finale. Some workers congratulated me, too, afterward. I told one who spoke English that a limited knowledge of Russian kept me from appreciating their leader's opening remarks. What, for example, was the meaning of "*Parkhaty zhid umer*"?

The man gave me a funny look. "Nobody say that tonight."

How could he be sure? What did it mean? Perhaps I should ask the leader.

"No!" He restrained me. "It means . . . 'died.'"

Died? My heart sank. *Who* died? "All those words. Must mean more."

"Now I know you do not hear correct," the man declared. "Nobody here say 'The dirty Jew died.' Are not all of you Scottish?"

Perry had long since run out of things to say while engaging himself in conversation for the benefit of buggers. My news, coupled with Ivan's probable return to Moscow, must have unhinged him. He proposed telegraphing Ivan under the name of a fictitious doctor to return to Leningrad, a new diagnosis presumably having diagnosed his father to be still alive.

Not that I was in complete control. Else why would that anti-Semitic remark have hurt when I was a Gentile? Worse yet, I found myself not so much bothered by the demise of Ivan's father as envying him.

Next morning was my turn to climb the walls after Perry went off to ask one of Dr. Q.'s refuseniks, a sociology professor, to contact Ivan for us. Not only did my friend insist on going alone. Though Perry had no parcel to hide, he pulled a newly purchased oversized hat down over his ears, penciled in a mustache, and stuffed a pillow inside his coat. When I said that would draw attention and excite further suspicion, Perry swore at me.

"Goddamnit! You wore a kilt, I can wear a pillow." He sneaked out of the hotel, looking as if he were smuggling me out *in utero*.

Pudgy spotted him at once—who could miss a shifting body? He said something to a companion, who limped after Perry.

Would my friend turn around to see whether he had escaped detection? Certainly. Then he looked upset enough to throw up his pillow.

> Dear Senator Javits,
> How very nice of you to send your own personal limousine to take me to the airport. Russia is truly a fascinating country, and the people have a wonderful sense of humor. They adore Mark Twain.
> My best to Mrs. Javits and the children.

"American?"

An attractive older young woman, with wintry blue eyes and ruddy cheeks and Slavic accent, sat down at my table with a glass of tea. "I can tell from your plaid pants. You like the Soviet Union?" Before I could answer, she was rounding third. "You are alone?"

"Well . . . no."

She looked at me reproachfully. "There is old Russian saying: A traveler should never take along his own samovar." (English translation, I suppose: "You teakettle spout, Me cup.") For a footnote, she placed a lump of sugar on her tongue and sucked her tea through it.

I blushed. Yet a side-glance around the room revealed others with lumps of sugar. Men, too. "Just happens . . . nobody's with me now."

"Oh?" She took another few drags of tea. "You like your room? Nice? Large?"

I nodded.

She pushed away the glass. "Show me."

It happened much too fast, of course. Maybe not for Sean Connery, but certainly for eight o'clock in the morning and no eye contact.

She stood up and straightened her skirt.

What the hell. I got to my feet and led her out of the dining room. "What's your name?" My contribution to the word count.

"Why?" she said. "Do you keep a diary?"

Only after taking her into my room did the parcel come to mind. Damnit! Leaving on my bulging money belt would raise as many questions as welts. "Let's first get to know each other," I faltered. "How about a date?"

The woman with no name flushed. "Russians do not do such bourgeois things." She reached deep into her bodice and pulled out what I took to be a breast. It turned out to be a beige chamois bag, however. From it she extracted a coin.

She wanted to *pay* me?

"I sell to you this gold coin and more." The woman's voice was loud and distinct, perfect for reproduction on tape.

"Sell? Gold?" Trafficking in foreign currency or gold, Dr. Q. had warned, got people twenty to thirty years in jail. "That's *illegal*."

A wave of the hand. "So is taking woman into room." She opened her pocketbook. "Also, I have documents for sale."

At the top of my voice I shouted, "Asking to use my toilet, young woman, and now proposing all kinds of illegal activities. That's . . . not nice!" I yanked her to the door and shoved her outside.

A torrent of Russian resounded in the hall.

I don't know how many hours passed before Perry found me in bed in the fetal position. No, the professor knew nothing of Yevgeny's arrest, and yes, he'd send a telegram to Ivan with an offer to buy his late father's effects, contingent upon his immediate return to Leningrad to close the deal. Though even if Ivan did return, how could we transfer the parcel without getting caught in the act? By now I had lost all faith in immaculate reception.

Our schedule called for an afternoon trip to Petrodvorets, Peter the Great's spectacular yellow and white summer palace on the Baltic, which would have delighted Cecil B. De Mille and Busby Berkeley. Natural pressure from springs thirteen miles away operate fountains by the dozens, some playfully hidden under rocks; and gorgeous formal gardens stretch out a mile or more to the sea. At the bottom of two cascading staircases there is a huge semicircular basin with a giant figure tearing apart the jaws of a lion.

"That represents the military glory of the Soviet Union," said our guide, unaware that the figure was Samson of non-Book fame.

The Cathedral of Our Lady of Kazan, converted in 1932 into the State Museum of Religion and Atheism to discredit all religions, had Greek and Roman statues strewn about in a manner that suggested a garage sale. Judaism was represented by a couple of small showcases displaying one placard in French, "*Judaism est Racism*," and another in English, "Golda Meir Is a Murderer." Translating from the Russian at our request, the guide read that the Zionist movement heads a huge international conspiracy to subvert the Communist regimes, the independent states of Africa and Asia, and national liberation movements everywhere. Also the United States.

"How many Jews in the world, do you suppose?" Perry asked.

"Hundreds of millions," said the guide. "And they have the best jobs."

That many would have come in handy for shopping for supper. One must wait on three lines for each purchase. To find out the cost of each item, to pay the cashier, then to exchange the receipt for one's purchase. Ingenious. People who spend so many hours shopping will never have time to rebel.

After dinner Perry wanted to return to the professor's by himself.

"Nothing doing." Hard up for companionship, I might invite a girl into our room. And not all policemen were pudgy or male. When Perry scoffed, I showed him the fresh scratches on my hand.

He blanched. "As if I didn't have enough troubles. A fucking sex maniac!"

"You take tranquilizers."

The professor's spacious apartment on Nevsky Prospekt reflected the high station in society he had forfeited by applying for an exit visa. A tall, sandy-haired man with a craggy face, he had alert blue eyes that seemed to prick up the way some ears do. Though a fellow sociologist, he hadn't been one for as long as his sixty years led one to assume. Sociology had to wait till Stalin's death to be born in Russia. And then it was strangled shortly after, when studies showed that the Soviet Union, instead of being a classless society, was growing increasingly stratified. Pitifully few blue-collar or rural children attended universities. Russians' alienation toward their work probably accounted for the high rate of alcoholism, fifteen percent of the average salary going for drink. And the youth were as materialistic, career-oriented, disdainful of physical labor, hedonistic, and apolitical as in the West.

The government's reaction to these studies was to fire the institute's director, forty percent of the researchers, and most of the Jews, among them the professor. Sociology then declared a Party science, impartial research was banned. "A very efficient way of practicing sociology. And so economical," the professor noted dryly.

Among those assembled there were the professor's very pretty nineteen-year-old granddaughter and a little boy, who amused himself with ten Magic Slates. They said Soviet Jews had such great faith in America that with the announcement of Nixon's 1972 visit to Russia, tens of thousands wrote to beseech his help in leaving the country. Members of the Moscow seminar volunteered to supply him with the names of all those imprisoned for applying for exit visas. Women appealed to Mrs. Nixon, prisoners' children to Tricia and Julie. "The Jewish people's belief in good is inexhaustible," said the professor's wife.

Response came swiftly. From the Soviet Government. Preventive detention for some, others held incommunicado during the presidential visit. Activists were called into the military reserves to expose them to supposed military secrets, additional grounds for denial of visas.

The professor recalled *Pravda's* report of President Nixon's toast to the triumph of the principles of peace and justice at his meeting with Soviet leaders. "All of us imagined how everyone there applauded and cheered," he commented.

"Good old Tricky Dicky," I remarked.

The group took great offense. Exclaimed an elderly doctor, "If not for the United States, all of us would be in jail. To us America is—is—"

"—the hope of the civilized world," concluded her sickly husband, who, earlier, had discounted their chances of ever seeing their son and family in Israel.

America the hope of the world? I had grown up with that belief, just as people once took it for granted that the world was flat.

This group's composite history was no less depressing for being familiar.

"My work in astrophysics is so vital to Russia," said one man, "that the K.G.B. confiscated my telescope. Now I am a watchman in a dairy where all night long I gaze at udders."

"To read a foreign newspaper or the Bible, you need a

security clearance. There are people who have been detained in the Soviet Union for having read the *Washington Post* or about Noah's Ark."

On second thought, perhaps the world was flatter than I had realized.

"The facts, if made known abroad, can set us free," an agronomist insisted.

"Is that why all of you want to go to Israel?" said Perry. "To live a freer life?"

"Freer?" An engineer threw back his head and laughed. "No, not freer. *Free.*"

Following the professor's application for a visa, forty people had been promised exit visas in return for testifying that he had formed an illegal Jewish underground organization, a crime punishable by death. And he had been locked up in a psychiatric hospital, along with many other dissenters, dissent in Russia being viewed as an expression of mental illness. There he had been force-fed chemicals to cure him of his pathological delusions about freedom. "By the time they declared me sane," he said, "my heart went crazy and I had had three heart attacks."

"You should write all that down," I urged. "To inform the West."

The professor and Perry exchanged glances.

Half of those present had been jailed in accordance with Beria's dictum "Just give us the man, and we will find the crime." The mathematician got three years for writing articles explaining the Jewish holidays and passing five carbon copies to friends. For cheering the Israeli team at the World University Games, the woman engineer was beaten up by the police and detained for thirty days. The metallurgist spent a year in jail for knocking a sausage out of a woman's hands. For defending him, his lawyer was disbarred and sentenced to six months. Lye had been sprayed on another's legs and genitals—

"Enough!" cried the professor's wife. "How much can our guests take?"

Nina, her granddaughter, served tea and cake and cheese and bread. With black hair and lustrous large eyes set behind thick lashes in milk-white skin and the manner of a startled faun, the girl was exquisite.

"You're beautiful," I said. "How about coming away with me?"

Everyone but her grandparents laughed. They looked so wistfully at each other, it was easy to read their minds. I felt terrible.

The group sang Hebrew songs while the little boy danced around the room, spilling his Magic Slates behind him. Whence so many? From American tourists who used them in hotel rooms. "But having nothing to hide, we never use Magic Slates," said the father, "though our apartments are also bugged and searched."

Perry, who had wanted to leave the parcel with the professor, turned pale. Invited to join next evening's meeting with a visiting congressional delegation, he spoke vaguely of a previous engagement. When the professor mentioned the possibility of a surprise visit by a mutual friend, I accepted for both of us. What better place to unload the parcel than in the presence of U.S. Congressmen?

In the morning, Piskarevskoye, a cemetery memorializing the one million Russians who died during the nine-hundred-day siege of Leningrad. Dirge-like Muzak played as we walked past an eternal flame toward a huge sculpture of a Russian woman with a sad face and a garland of oak leaves.

"The Motherland." The guide translated the words carved into granite. "No one and nothing has been forgotten . . ."

"Where," Perry asked, "is the cemetery for the millions that Stalin killed?"

A toss-up who was shocked more, the guide or me. Would my friend, who had breakfasted on tranquilizers, also mention that Stalin, completely paranoid toward the end of his life, was preparing to place all Russian Jews in concentration camps?

"Stalin made mistakes," the guide conceded.

Perry persisted. "Twenty million mistakes? Haven't you read Khrushchev's 1956 denunciation?"

She wrinkled up her pert nose. "Stalin may have been ill-advised, but Khrushchev was a clown."

I asked to be dropped off at a taxi.

The guide refused. "You cannot leave me. I am responsible for the two of you."

So. She was also our keeper, her function being to spell Pudgy and Gimpy.

Deposited at our hotel after more palace-hopping, Perry went out to shop. With our departure scheduled for the following afternoon, I'd be damned if I got caught smuggling out of Russia the same contraband I had smuggled in. Aside from the danger, I'd feel like a fool.

On his return, Perry rushed me into the bathroom and opened all the taps. A prelude to telling of his visit to the American Embassy to ask an aide there to hold our parcel until it was picked up.

"But the embassy is *bugged!*"

So, Perry related, the aide wrote on his own Magic Slate when refusing to serve as a drop. Moreover, soldiers posted outside the embassy bar all Soviets from entering.

"Goddamn idiot!" I felt like drowning Perry in the toilet bowl.

He bristled. "Think you're smarter than me, don't you?"

I, easily Perry's match in idiocy, readily agreed. "You bet your ass." But there was a way out. I ripped open my money belt.

"What are you doing?"

"Flushing our albatross."

Perry stayed my hand. "You *mustn't!*"

"Give me one good reason."

He stared at me. "You don't know what's inside?"

Dumbly, I shook my head.

He sat down heavily on the edge of the tub. "After Dr. Q.

wouldn't say what pig was in that poke and you left the room—well, I insisted."

"What *does* the parcel contain?" All that kept me from opening it to see for myself was hysterical paralysis.

"Why do you think I've been so anxious ever since customs gave us that hard time?" He stood up and paced back and forth, moving his arms jerkily. "I wanted the suspense ended. One way or the other. *Anything* is better than waiting to be caught, wondering whether we'll be jailed for twenty years or thirty."

Twenty or thirty *years*? That settled it. Into the toilet with the evidence. I slit the package open with my penknife. Oh, wow! In my hand lay more American currency than I had ever seen in my entire life.

"Nobody can eat furniture forever," Perry said. "Ivan *has* to show tonight." He begged me to reconsider. Yet he never relieved me of a single bill.

In the end my debt to Jewry tipped the balance. Back into my money belt went the parcel.

As insurance, we left our suite. So long as Pudgy was following us in an aimless walk, nobody could contact him to order us searched.

At eight o'clock we went to the Hotel Leningrad. No Ivan. Should he arrive later, the professor whispered, Nina would direct him to us.

Here in Russia—what a difference geography makes!—I looked upon the eighteen congressmen I wouldn't have crossed the street to meet back in the States as my saviors. It was all I could do to keep myself from blowing them kisses.

Now, would the refuseniks explain their circumstances?

"Things are going very well for us here," the professor began, wryly, "like for saints in this world." He presented his own case in a matter-of-fact fashion, and the others followed suit, some through an interpreter.

On occasion, hearing a name, some congressman said, "Oh yes, we've heard about you." And the refusenik would rejoice as if his reservation for life had been confirmed. Clearly, to be unknown in Russia was to be in peril.

Suddenly, the congresswoman, taking down all the statements, pointed her pen at me. "We haven't heard from *you*."

"But I'm not a refusenik, I'm sorry to say. Drew Baron from New York."

The mistake amused my countrymen, but not the professor. Upset, he pulled me aside and berated me for endangering my mission. "The K.G.B. is present."

"Here too?" The hairs at the back of my neck stood up. "Who . . .?"

"I do not know." With sorrow the professor added, "Do not judge informers too harshly. Once, during his eight years in prison, in order to save his life, even Solzhenitsyn. . . ."

Shaken, I turned to the nearest congressman and blurted out in a loud voice, "When you get aback to Washington, please give my love to Barbara Walters."

Naturally, he was impressed.

"Haven't you caught me on Barbara's 'Today Show' on television," I nearly shouted, "which is watched by forty million Americans every weekday, including the President and Congress?"

At the meeting's close, the professor hymned the representatives, all Christians but one, in words that recalled "America, America, God shed his grace on thee," which had thrilled me as a youngster. Funny. The America that many thought had died in Vietnam was alive and well in Leningrad.

The lone congresswoman, warmly acknowledging the professor's words, asked if there was any message the refuseniks wished transmitted to Soviet officials.

"Only one." The professor drew himself up to his full height. "Kindly ask them not to inflict on us all that we may be able to endure."

As Perry told the professor to have Ivan, should he arrive, meet us in the Hermitage in front of Rembrandt's *Portrait of an Old Jew*, there was a sudden tug at my sleeve.

A congressman's wife. "About the 'Today Show.' I've been trying to get my husband on it for years. Perhaps a note from you to Barbara . . ."

Our luggage had been searched, so adroitly it escaped Perry's notice. How could I tell? My jars of black caviar no longer alternated with the pearl grays. So I hid the parcel on the ledge outside our window, hoping that *The Lost Weekend* had not been shown in Leningrad.

For hours the phone rang at odd intervals with nobody answering our hellos. Obviously to check our whereabouts or drive us crazy. Either way a brilliant success. Perry took so many pills that soon he spoke of spending the night on the window ledge also, while the two that I took knocked me out. In the morning we could barely wake each other up.

At the Intourist office I ordered a car to take us to the airport that afternoon, while Perry muttered, "We should only live so long."

We killed some time at the spectacular St. Isaac's Cathedral, of forty-three different kinds of marble and with gilt enough to paint the sun.

"Does anyone come here to pray?" Perry asked dreamily.

"What for?" said the guide.

"Tranquilizity."

Back to the Hermitage to unload my treasure—maybe.

To establish an alibi, every few minutes I went to the john while the guide waited outside. So when she tired of playing chaperone, where did I head? Back to the john. Terror had seized me in its jaws and was shaking me, cramping my insides and refusing to let go. How on earth did Mata Hari ever survive the runs?

By the time I weaned myself from the toilet, I was late for my appointment. Two men in the room with Rembrandt's *Portrait of an Old Jew* resembled Ivan's photograph, but neither asked about my Band-Aid. Perhaps just as well—a third man there resembled the K.G.B. agent in Red Square.

"Hello, Andrew Baron."

I whirled around. The professor's beautiful granddaughter, this time looking me in the eye.

"Good. You seem happy, as when a boy meets a girl." The professor, who wasn't feeling well, had sent Nina to tell us that no word had come from Ivan.

I felt too disspirited to reply.

Then: "If the package is so important—" She checked herself as a man brushed by. "Come. We leave."

Dumbly, I followed her down the long sweeping staircase.

"We go to the park . . . No, never look behind."

A shy girl, Nina. Her mother had died when she was fifteen, and her father last year, fortunately. She asked for a Hebrew lesson.

I thought of *She sells sea shells by seashore.* Oddly pleasing. What was it that Isaca found so inspiring? Continuity.

In the middle of a past participle, Nina said, "I should explain my 'fortunately.'" Her father had divorced Nina's mother when informed that her religion barred his advancement. Nina never saw him again until her mother's death, a few months before the girl's sixteenth birthday, when she'd be issued an internal passport. As his daughter, he reminded Nina, she could declare herself a Russian. After she identified herself as *Yevrai*, a Jew, he refused to grant her permission to emigrate, required of every applicant. So long as her father lived, therefore, Nina could never leave for Israel.

Her story perplexed me. "You *chose* second-class citizenship?"

"My mother always taught, Better to be among the persecuted than the persecutors."

As we entered a park, the girl took my hand. "You must act as if you want very much to be alone with me." But when I bent over to kiss her, she pulled away. "Too much."

The path we took was lined by beautiful trees that looked as old as the city. Such surroundings made it difficult to think of harm befalling anyone.

"Here, Andrew Baron, we stop for embrace. But not large embrace. Not done in public."

When I put my arms around her, she forced a smile before leading me off the path into a green cave of shrubs. "Lovers come here. Not me. I see them enter." We burrowed deeply into the underbrush. "Look. Can we be seen?"

People could be heard walking nearby, but I couldn't see anyone. "No."

Nina got down on her knees and with her bare hands dug into the earth.

Swiftly I knelt. "Let me." I took out a penknife and dug into the ground. When burying the parcel at last, it felt as if I were disposing of my Siamese twin.

"A brilliant idea, hiding the package here."

The girl flushed. "I am not brilliant."

"It wasn't your grandfather's idea?"

Nina shook her head. "How would a man his age know a place for lovers?"

A chuckle died stillborn. Maybe the professor hadn't suggested this because it was unsafe. If we were followed and the package discovered! I reached out and hugged the girl tightly.

She yielded for a moment, then struggled. "Please!"

I released her at once.

She turned away. "It is not only this place I have not visited. I have never been . . . anywhere." She bowed her head. "I do not know how to behave."

"Nina, Nina. What makes you think *I* do?" My own experience was more limited. I had never known anyone to jeopardize her life for a stranger and for a country she had never seen. "I've got an idea! There *is* a way." Having spoiled one life, maybe I could now save another. "Marry me."

Her eyes widened.

"A temporary marriage. In name only."

"Temporary. In name only."

"That means—"

Softly, she said, "I know temporary, I know in name only. It is my life here. Why I must leave. But no, Andrew Baron. I will not allow the Union of Soviet Socialist Republics to make me a liar."

I flinched. "Come. It's late."

But returning to the path, she shyly suggested a kiss—in case we were being watched. We kissed, noses bumping, then hand in hand strolled out of the park while reviewing Hebrew's possessive pronouns. Anyone seeing us could only think, Here's a couple very much in love.

Given a few more days, he would have been exactly right.

Happy fade-out on Nina and me walking off slowly into the sunshine? Ah, but Perry.

As soon as I set foot back in our hotel room, he started yelling without the accompaniment of so much as a single drop of water. Why didn't I return to him and the guide earlier at the Hermitage? Where had I been? Had I any idea what he had gone through? Or that the desk clerk insisted on seeing us? And what about the whatchamacallit?

I pulled Perry into the bathroom and turned on all the faucets, though a tidal wave couldn't have drowned him out. I kept saying during every flush of the toilet, "Everything is okay. Relax. Everything's fine. Take it easy."

The only response was additional shouts.

"Perry! Did you take any more pills?"

"How do you think I've managed to keep my cool?"

Filling the tub with water, I pleaded with him to jump in. Somehow—either I slipped or he pushed—the wrong man ended up in the tub. Okay with me. Alone in the bath, I couldn't be yelled at. So I got up, dripping, ejected my friend, locked the door, undressed, and got back into the tub.

Bang! bang! bang! The desk clerk wanted to see us, Perry shouted, even though we had already checked out. His call followed the guide's report of my disappearance.

Frightening! But not even the K.G.B.'s millions of

employees could bug everybody in Russia live, I had been told. So conversations in hotel rooms were often put on sound-activated tapes and played back at night. By then, Perry and I would be over the Atlantic. If I didn't strangle him first.

Bang! Bang! Bang!

A more pressing concern was to get my friend to the plane without a gag. He terrified me. Wonderful. Now that we had nothing to fear, we had each other.

BANG! BANG! BANG!

I got out of the tub and dressed. But there was still no talking to Perry. As a last resort, I wrote on a Magic Slate:

1. Pass completed.
2. All's well.
3. Absolutely nothing to fear.

When he pointed to the first two statements and I nodded, so did my friend. But he wouldn't buy the third: it followed too logically. Clearing the Magic Slate, I wrote, "*WHAT* IS WORRYING YOU?"

His face registered a big blank. That he did not know worried him. Perry hadn't even packed. It was as if he was expected to remain in Russia forever. Call it panic, call it terror, call it an overdose of tranquilizers. He was out of it. Worse, the way Perry was carrying on, soon he'd have company out there. Me.

Suddenly: "*Hava nagila, hava nagila* . . ." His joy was short-lived, however. After a few choruses, he wrote on the Magic Slate, "*CUSTOMS!!!!!!!!!*"

I whispered in his ear, "We have nothing to hide now."

"Suppose," he whispered back, his eyes wide open as possible, "they plant something on us."

"Don't be silly." Yet the question gnawed at me while I packed. By then, I too felt we were the only people in Russia worthy of scrutiny. That would enable the K.G.B. to concentrate all its agents on us. What if hundreds had followed Nina and me into the park and dug it up?

Perry put his lips to my ear. "I'm . . . apprehensive."

Arguing would have been counterproductive. Perhaps if I agreed, acknowledged the validity of his anxiety, shared his all-too-human fear. "So am I, Perry."

"You *are*? My God!"

The porter who came for our bags took us straight to the desk. As soon as the clerk spoke of a grave matter that had come to his attention, Perry entered a plea of innocence, protesting loudly enough to convince no one.

The clerk cried, "Enough! We have the *proof*." He produced two broken glasses. "If you do not pay one and a half rubles—"

I paid up, then marched us outside, and pushed my groggy friend into the car. Soon we were on our way. Unfortunately, the car stopped for a traffic light at the corner, and there, pretending to look in a shop window, stood Nina.

I caught my breath. It hurt terribly to desert her.

Nina was watching us, face expressionless. No sign of recognition. But the color rose high in her cheeks.

Suddenly, Perry cried, "Look! Hey!"

She turned white. Throw caution once to the winds in Russia, a refusenik had said, and they threw you to the wolves in Siberia.

Not even a swift kick silenced him. Why, he yelped, did I do that? I warned him in Hebrew about our driver. Speaking Hebrew would arouse his suspicions, Perry retorted in English.

At last the light changed, and the car moved on without my chancing a last look at Nina. I would never forget the chalky whiteness of her face nor forgive Perry, now prattling about refuseniks. There was no diverting him. But he didn't mention Nina's name or Ivan's and references to the whatchamacallit made little sense. Eventually, he lapsed into limericks. Limerick, rather, for he sang the same one thirty-nine times.

At the airport, when our driver left to report our arrival to Intourist, Perry's jitters started up again. "Customs," he kept repeating as if it spelled doomsday. To calm him, I opened my hand luggage and pointed to empty caviar jars I had scavenged from the hotel dining room.

He glowered at me. "I'm losing my mind, and you're worried about getting your deposit back?"

The caviar would account for the missing two hundred dollars for which I had no receipt. Barely was the explanation made than my alibi was dashed before my eyes by some burly idiot who blundered into us and knocked the canvas bag from my hand. All those jars hitting the sidewalk sounded like *Kristallnacht* in Russia. "Stupid sonofabitch!" An exact self-portrait—in my haste to retrieve the broken pieces, I cut my fingers.

"Band-Aids are best . . ." said the hit-and-lingerer.

My Band-Aids being packed away, I licked my wounds.

"For shaving cuts," said the man, "Band-Aids are best."

As my fingers froze to my tongue, Perry sputtered, *"Kol od beleivov penimah."*

"Eretz Ziyyon vi-Yerushalayim" came the response.

Ivan! The man in our photograph.

Perry poked me in the ribs, a stricken look. "But you said the pass was completed."

"Yes. But a lateral, not a forward."

He shook his head as if to clear it. "Then give it to him now. Quick!" Suddenly, Russians were bearing down from all directions. Perry's voice rose to a shout. *"Give it to him!"*

So I did. A wild swing at Ivan, my open hand connecting with his jaw. There was just enough time to say Nina's name twice before being seized.

Though I took the blame and apologized for my bad display of temper, Pudgy hustled Ivan away. Gimpy led Perry and me to customs, his eyes fastened on us. Ah, but we were clean.

After a meticulous search of our luggage—long needles were stuck through the lining!—Gimpy hustled us into an office where an officer greeted us with a smile big enough to remind me of a refusenik's comment: "In this country they kill you, smiling." The officer said that nothing had been found on our friend.

"Friend?" said Perry weakly. "We never saw that man before in our lives."

With a grin the officer asked for our jackets. "Perhaps in the scuffle something slipped into your pocket. Unknown to you, of course."

I took off my jacket at once.

Perry, however, recoiled. "Dr. Q. said—"

Not to allow a body search without an American official present. But waiting for his arrival would make us miss our plane, thereby extend our stay in Russia beyond the time allotted by our visas. And what if the embassy sent over the aide Perry had contacted?

"We have nothing to hide," I said, ostensibly to the officer, and grabbed at Perry's jacket. As I pulled it off, the air crackled. The sound of fear. Since there was nothing to incriminate any of us, my worry now was a drugged Perry's going to pieces, thinking the money still on me. Swiftly, I stripped and dumped my clothing on the desk. "Search away," I said.

Perry gasped. And when I told him to strip too, he reacted as if he now imagined the package was on *him*. In another moment he'd confess all. So quickly I sat down, took a pencil and pad, and copied down the sign in Cyrillic on the desk.

The officer's smile developed a twitch. "Why are you writing my name?"

"For my article in *The New York Times* travel section."

He scoffed. "You think you can deceive me?" A tap on the folder before him. "You are a rabbinical student."

I forced a chortle. "My friend is the rabbinical student. Me, I'm not even Jewish." From my wallet I extracted my *Times* calling card. "Now if you want a war with *The New York Times*—"

Perry quavered, "Androo-*oo* . . ."

The anger I felt with myself for disowning the Jews I directed at the only one of them there. "Come on! The sooner you undress . . ." I got up and pulled at Perry's shirt.

Now, his teeth crackled too.

Suddenly: "Out of here! Both of you!" The officer shook his head. "But you behave so guilty. It is in all the reports."

Jackets in tow, Perry and I left the office. Our reservations had been canceled, so sure had someone been of catching us red-handed. After making new ones and surrendering our exit visas, we sat in the departure lounge for fifty minutes without exchanging a word. Only when our plane was over Poland did I reveal the parcel's hiding place.

And then my friend swore at me. "If that officer had called your bluff!"

Perry didn't know it wasn't my first bluff. But it would be my last.

He opened his shirt—that same crackling sound again—and took out dozens of typewritten pages. A manuscript Perry got on his visit alone to the professor. Memoirs of his lengthy imprisonment in a psychiatric hospital which named the psychiatrists involved. "Why do you think I've been popping pills?" Perry clasped his hands together until the knuckles turned white. "In only one week they made you deny your heritage, and me they very nearly drove mad. Andrew, how on earth do the refuseniks stay sane!"

"God bless America," I said.

SIXTEEN

R.I.'s annual ordination, inside Fifth Avenue's Temple Emanu-El, was just the right time and place to say *shalom*. I had already moved to a new apartment in order to leave no forwarding address.

Now to complete the painful letter that explained to Isaca why she was no divorcee and I a dissembler. O how the truth hurts when you're the one who has to tell it.

To Dr. Diamond I wrote simply, yet evasively, "Personal

reasons force me to leave." That letter I mailed in full view of the temple's great rose window which, recessed within a high arch over the entrance, suggested the eye of God.

It never blinked. I hoped that meant no hard feelings.

I wasn't the only non-Jew present. Several people sported Roman collars and nuns' habits. Probably friends of Rabbi Zion, who was receiving an honorary degree. Skullcaps were also in evidence, a decided change from the days of early Reform. Decades before, a famous Protestant minister happening into the temple sat through an entire service without realizing it was Jewish. Now, the temple's choir accompanied the processional with a Hebrew hymn, and increasing numbers of students at R.I. wore yarmulkes.

Reform had undergone other changes. There was a growing call for *halacha* to define standards of religious observance, a code of thou-shalts and thou-shalt-nots to replace the current whatsoever-you-dig. Little more than velvet curtains now separated Reform from Conservative.

The dim lighting encouraged one's thoughts to wander. Or perhaps it was the occasion, my silent farewell. The three years at R.I. had proved not bad at all. Subtract my guilt, maybe good.

Certainly, the rabbinate compared favorably with other professions. At the hospital Bernie and I overheard residents and internes refer to a ward of stroke victims as "the vegetable garden" and discuss whether to specialize in anesthesiology ("Seventy-five thousand dollars a year and no sweat") or dermatology ("Perfect—your patients never die and they never get well"). Not to mention a doctor or two who must have gone through medical school on football scholarships, like the one who tried to abort a virgin. And then, all those lawyers who, elected to take crime off the streets, installed it in the White House. As a group, lawyers must be as dedicated to justice and public service as Con Edison is to providing illumination.

The Vietnam War having mortally wounded America's civil religion, my classmates would figure prominently on the

American scene. Also in supporting Israel and Soviet Jewry. Yevgeny had been released after several weeks in jail, but the professor, summoned for daily interrogations in an office up six flights of stairs, had suffered another heart attack and died. The government had granted his body an exit visa for burial in Israel. Poor Nina, still held prisoner there. Had any of my letters gotten through?

". . . for bearing witness that Judaism knows only of the holy and not-yet holy . . . Dr. Isaiah Zion."

Accepting the honorary degree, Rabbi Zion quoted Abraham Joshua Heschel. "Religion begins with the certainty that something is asked of us. Unlike all other values, moral and religious ends evoke in us a sense of obligation. Thus, religious living consists in serving ends which are in need of us."

I wished for such ends myself. Sociology, I strongly suspected, could survive without me. Others could with equal ease refrain from questioning the truth of ideas, and instead analyze their causes, functioning, consequences. Hurray for those rabbis who, citing biblical laws about slave labor, had declared California grapes unkosher.

"Will the class please rise?"

Dr. Worenz, who put in three more appearances at R.I. per year than God, ordained the men. Now I knew more about him. He hadn't been born to the purple, but to the poverty-stricken Orthodox. During the Depression he had enrolled at R.I. for the same reason poor Catholics entered the clergy in the Middle Ages and blacks in modern times. Afterward, just as Archie Leach invented Cary Grant, Worenz created the great sophisticated archaeologist.

The president's voice broke during the parting benediction. Yet, while addressing the ordinees minutes before on his deep and abiding faith in a personal God, he never glanced their way, his gaze seemingly fixed on the long ago and far away.

I bid a final unvoiced *shalom* to R.I., teachers, and classmates. But no *l'hitraot*, till we meet again. That was reserved for the Simons, my adopted family.

The temple was so crowded, it took a while to work my way to the door. In solitary. Not a new experience for me. But now I felt very much the outsider, soul pressed to the window. How comforting, then, to hear my name called on Fifth Avenue even as a warning bell.

Mrs. Simon loomed before me. "What are you doing here? Wasn't Rabbi Zion marvelous! Too bad Mr. Simon won't set foot inside a Reform synagogue. Look. There's Levi." Her face lit up. "A healthy sign, isn't it, his dating again. Oh, what a gorgeous rabbi she'll be."

A gorgeous *rabbi*? I mumbled something about feeding a dime to the parking meter. Mrs. Simon grabbed my arm— this was Sunday. The car had been parked on Saturday, I said, and broke away. No need now to finish that letter. All these years the gun waiting to explode in my face had been Isaca.

"Drew!"

I plunged into the crowd, as if somewhere in its midst my self-respect could be located. Like a bullfighter with a death wish, I crossed against the light, dodging the cars on Fifth Avenue. Word had probably spread already about me. So many stares.

Jumping the low wall into Central Park, I ran through the underbrush. What a rotten, undependable world. Just when you need the earth to open up and swallow you whole . . . not so much as a crack.

1973-4

SEVENTEEN

Well, I got my wish, almost. Though the earth didn't quite swallow me whole, it did yank. The night of the near confrontation I got so drunk, it took weeks to sleep it off. That's all I did. Sleep. And feel exhausted. And watch television. And tell myself that tomorrow I'd get myself together. Maybe throw out the garbage. But tomorrow never came, not that month. Fire or flood would have moved me, but only together and tomorrow.

Missed out on Columbia's summer session for the first time since 1970. Too busy rationalizing my hoax to the Simons and Zions and R.I., who haunted every waking hour. Funny, how one can lie with few qualms so long as nobody knows. Now I couldn't bear to stay in the same room with myself. Damn! Just when life was at last returning to normal for every other American, I alone was out of sync.

The annual western sojourn provided a welcome change of venue. This time I went first to Beverly Hills, feeling I needed—promise not to laugh?—a mother. Also a home. Where, when you slink back wounded, even if self-inflicted, they must take you in.

Terri, opening the front door, swiftly put on the chain. "*Drew*? What's happened?"

"Nothing," I explained. "Except for quitting R.I."

"That straggly beard. So thin and sallow. You look like the picture of Dorian Gray."

Disgusted with myself, I soon picked a fight with dear old Mom. Over just that, calling her Mother.

"Why Mother now?" Terri said. "When you're old enough to be a father. Which'd make me—good Lord—a grandmother."

"But you play a mother of four in your T.V. series."

"I play a mommy. All four are nine years old. You're not breathing right, Drew."

Terri rushed me over to the Rebirth Clinic, her newest discovery. There, people lying flat on their backs were urged to experience anew the birth trauma, taking their first breaths and exhaling their fears at being thrust against their will into a painful world. Those mastering the dry-land procedure were equipped with a snorkel and nose clip and submerged in a vat of water, stripped. After reliving the wonderful wet of the womb, now perceived on an adult level, they breathed themselves into life when the plug was pulled and they emerged through the drain.

Several there had been rebirthed more than once: a few skins were permanently puckered. The leader, a woman who resembled Johnny Weismuller, tried to pop me into the vat too. But the way I felt, one birth was more than enough.

On the drive home, Terri said, "What's making you so miserable, Drew? Is it a girl?"

I shook my head.

"Then what?"

"It's . . . a people, Mom."

She glowered at me. "*Mom?*"

At loose ends, I left prematurely for San Francisco. There I didn't have to pick a fight. One was waiting. Dad had found me out. Someone had informed—one guess who. When he demanded my draft card, I didn't even put up a struggle. What was the use?

One look at my 4-D had Dad shouting. "Then it's true! You're no son of mine. Shirked your duty."

A feeling of nausea swept over me. I fought it down and said, "What about *you*, Father?"

Back to the airport, close to tears. Once having thrown up, however, I rallied. Funny, one could deprecate oneself for years, but when unjustly attacked from without, antibodies were activated in self-defense. Dad had indicted me for the one crime I was innocent of. No guilt could accrue to fifteen million avoiders of an undeclared, immoral war, for the Bible commands, "Thou shalt not follow a multitude to do evil." Consequently, it wasn't my ends that were wrong, but the means. I wrote all that to Dad before the plane left for L.A. Stand up for yourself, Isaca had urged. Well, I would.

Terri was out for the evening. So I got some cartons from the basement to pack up all my belongings—books, mostly. Then I sat down at my desk and put my feelings into words.

On the twenty-ninth of August in the year 1973, I do hereby grant a bill of divorcement to my parents, Ben and Terri, this being a deed of release according to the Law. Self-rule from now on for Drew Baron!

After a night's sleep and shower, I was ready to return to New York in full charge. No longer only to be acted upon. I'd be actor in my own life. One day, if Isaca proved correct, perhaps even hero.

Terri was standing beside my desk when I stepped out of the bathroom. Something amiss. Her face looked in disarray. "You going to serve me now?" she said.

"Huh?"

She picked up the *get*. "Think I'm totally self-absorbed, don't you? But I did check out that rabbinical school. Something else which you don't know. I've always opened your mail. How many other parents take the trouble to do that?"

I grabbed the paper away. "This wasn't meant to be seen. No insult intended. Only to set myself free." But a moment later: "Terri, how could you! Telling Dad about R.I."

"So that's it. He aggravated so about your draft deferment. Thought up reasons far worse than the real one. It was a kindness to tell him. Or so I believed. But I've made mistakes before. Just look at my marriage record." She walked away.

"Terri, this isn't the first time—"

She turned on me. "I've let you down? Well, *you* try being a woman alone with a child."

"You took me away—"

"I should have stayed in the same community as the *first* Mrs. Baron, the *other* Mrs. Baron, *poor* Mrs. Baron? And all San Francisco had to offer someone like me was a waitress' job. Drew, I'm sorry I haven't been the best mother for you. But at least you had one. Mine died when I was eight. So it was hard to learn all about motherhood. Schools today! They teach you everything you want to know except how to make a good marriage and be a good parent."

My heart went out to her. I took the *get* and threw it into the waste-paper basket. "I'm sorry, Terri." Nobody in this world had it easy. Why should I have been the exception? "I apologize."

"Forget it." She glanced sideways at all the cartons. "You won't be coming home anymore?"

"Sure. To visit. You're still my . . . Terri. But not home. Have to make my own now."

"Of course. I understand." There was a catch in her voice. "Let me make you breakfast. . . . Drew?"

"Yes, Terri?"

"The time left. I don't mind your Mothering me." She hurried off.

Packing completed, I drove out to Malibu for the day. "Last one to London," I heard myself saying to nobody in particular in the water, "is a rotten egg." Swam myself into exhaustion, then fell asleep on the sand, waking up with a bad sunburn. I returned to Beverly Hills hot and shivering.

And there, as in a feverish dream of childhood, were Mother and Dad together. First time in eighteen years. I closed my eyes, and when they were opened, my parents were still sitting there in the living room like any other normal family. What a handsome couple!

"Drew, you're all sunburned. I'll get you vinegar and water," Terri said, and left the room.

Another family scene came to mind. The mother urging ointment on her son. The father beside himself. The son savagely attacking both.

"I got your letter," Dad said after a long pause. "Then your mother called. Told me to get the hell over here. . . ." On the coffee table before him lay my *get*.

No, of course they hadn't reunited. It was high time to lay that childish illusion to rest. Nevertheless . . . "You came here just to see me? All the way to Los Angeles?"

Dad cleared his throat. "The reason I never came before, Drew. It was on account of, well . . ." He searched for words.

"Logistics. Two other families in San Francisco."

"Sarcasm?" he said, voice rising. "If that's the way—"

"Ben!" Terri had returned with a jar of liquid and a washcloth.

If one doesn't stop regarding himself as a product of his parents or their victim at age twenty-five, *when*? Foolish to continue blaming an orphan and a discriminated-against Jew. If I had been victimized by anyone, it became clear to me now, it was by other victims. Didn't Dr. Tchernichovsky say that all of us need forgiveness? Only a fool would shirk the future. That's where my duty lay now. "No sarcasm intended. I . . . now understand, Dad. I really do, Mother." I picked up the *get* and tore it into little pieces.

Gravity's pull had eased. No, no grand resolution of every single difference with Mother and Dad. Is anything in this world ever resolved? But there had been reconciliation. Isn't that the best life has to offer?

Something still nibbled at me, however. My ulcerated conscience. I identified it at once when a familiar voice sounded my name outside a Columbia classroom one morning. And there stood Levi.

I held my ground unsteadily.

Finding no trace of me anywhere, Levi had waited for the fall to look up my program. He too was now at Columbia—in the School of Social Work. "Hey, remember me, Drew? This is your old buddy."

"Buddy?" I winced. "After what I pulled?"

"Looking after my parents, all those letters to me and to

them. Then posing as a rabbinical student in Russia also. Me, I posed as a soldier only in Vietnam."

I averted my gaze. "What your parents must think!"

"Well, they never heard of a Gentile passing as a Jew. You've got to admit that's a switch."

"And Isaca? She must despise me."

"She doesn't know. That can wait till we're married. Yes, we're talking of next summer. I may have you to thank, Drew. When I told Isaca that I, a *kohen*, couldn't care less about her accidental marriage to one Andrew Baron—"

I felt a twinge of what-might-have-been. But *nachas* afforded me instant relief. "Mazel tov! Isaca is . . ." Beautiful, desirable, loving. ". . . a tremendously fine person. No wonder you look so happy, Levi."

"Selfish of me. I never did ask about *your* girl, Drew. Too screwed up before. When do I get to meet her?"

"Who . . .?"

"The girl you wrote me about. What was her name?"

"Oh," I said. "Didn't work out. Never stood a chance."

"Don't be so definite," he said. "Look how long it took for Isaca and me to get together."

I burst out, "What I did, Levi. Can you ever forgive me?"

Was it my imagination, or did he hedge? "For what, Drew? You never sinned against me." He added, "How about seeing each other right after the holidays?"

Yom Kippur, when it came, gave me something to brood about. Its very name, Day of Atonement, propelled me back to a synagogue for the obligatory scene. Repentance.

One thing had slipped my mind. Nobody would sell me a ticket, conducting business on the High Holy Day being forbidden. Besides, the temple was sold out. So three cheers for the universal language, a ten-dollar bill. Pocketing it, the Italian guard said, *"That's* the ticket."

The memorial service must have started. Many congregants were dabbing their eyes, some sniffling. I paid no attention to the preaching, being interested only in what *I* had to say. But why so much handholding in temple? As I took a seat, a middle-aged woman to my left, with a handkerchief pressed to her mouth, sobbed something about a son in Israel.

Naturally, I expressed regret. "He must have been very young. What a pity."

The woman gasped. "Must have *been*?" She jumped to her feet and fled. The man sitting beside her followed. Stranger, yet.

A man in front of me turned around. "What's the latest news?"

"The World Series?"

"You didn't hear? Egypt and Syria have attacked Israel. Crossed the Suez Canal, overran the Golan Heights."

"*War*?" This was where I came in. "Jesus!" I left at once for home and radio.

It shaped up like another Holocaust. On the Golan Heights 2,000 tanks, more than Hitler threw against Russia, attacked 180 Israeli tanks. Over 100,000 Egyptian soldiers and 2,000 more tanks overwhelmed the 800 defenders of the Bar-Lev Line on the western side of the Suez Canal. And the Israeli Air Force was decimated. Soon the Syrians were advancing on the bridge that led to the Galilee, from which they could cut Israel in two.

In the U.N., Ambassador Malik stated, to prolonged applause, "Like savage, barbaric tribes, in their mad destruction the Jews have annihilated, destroyed, and tried to remove from the surface of the earth cities, villages, the cultural heritages of mankind. They have ravaged entire civilizations."

But what of the civilized nations? France embargoed all arms for Israel while selling arms destined for Egypt. England withheld tank parts for Israel, already paid for and about to be shipped, and continued training Egyptian pilots. Though Russia was urging Arab regimes from Algeria to Iraq to join in the kill and moving a hundred ships into the Mediterranean Sea and Indian Ocean, America sent no arms to the Jewish State. But on the chance that she might, NATO countries barred all landing and refueling rights to planes on their way to Israel. Sonsofbitches!

Some at Columbia thought me overwrought. Their reaction resembled mine to Isaca's Purim sermon on pogroms. Annoyance.

Predictably, Egypt's religious leader declared the war a *jihad*, a struggle for God promising heaven to all Arab dead. But what was one to make of the Vatican newspaper's seeing the war as an even match, because while the Arabs were employing oil as a weapon, there was "the mobilization of international high finance to the side of Israel"?

Though a substantial number of individual Protestant clergy condemned the Arab attack, most official denomination declarations, particularly of liberal or mainstream churches, were studiously neutral. Many evangelical groups asked the U.S. Government to support Israel, but the National Council of Churches appealed for a U.S. embargo on arms for Israel.

Two years before, Roberta had accused Ezra of paranoia for asserting the whole world wants the Jews dead. Now I thought that any Jew who isn't paranoid is crazy.

If only there was something I could *do*! All I could think of was to demonstrate at the synagogue I had attended on Yom Kippur. That night it was full of a type unfamiliar to me. Mostly white- and blue-collar workers, like the plain, harried people in Moscow's synagogue. Everyone thanked God for the Arabs' miscalculation. The sneak attack had come on the only day of the year when all Israeli reserves are in synagogue or at home and all roads clear for swift mobilization. So if anything would save Israel, it would be Yom Kippur.

A shudder ran through the congregation when the rabbi called Israel the Kitty Genovese of nations. Bitterly, he said, "During the Second World War the Nazis offered to barter Jewish children for trucks. Now the world wants to sell the Jewish State for oil. That's progress!"

Out came the chain I had impulsively bought. Foolish gesture. But many people stopped me on the way out to express gratitude for my being there. One woman touched the large cross around my neck, then pointed proudly to her own.

Why the cross? To show Jews they weren't as alone as they feared.

In truth, were.

The night before our appointment Levi phoned from Kennedy Airport. "I'm leaving for Israel. In case anything happens," he said, "will you please see about *Kaddish*?"

I could barely get the words out. "A father can say the memorial prayer for a son."

"I'm talking about getting someone to say *Kaddish* for my parents."

I cut the conversation short. Time better spent in packing and getting to the airport.

At El Al, however, nothing could get me aboard. All planes were filled with Israeli reservists and their families returning home, newsmen and volunteers, some of them Christian, with skills other than Sunday-school teaching or conducting High Holiday services. How, then, did Levi get a flight?

The Israeli ticket agent shrugged. "He must have *proteksia*. To get into this miserable war, you need pull."

I never did say good-bye to my friend—the Simons and Zions were there seeing him off. *Shalom,* I said from afar. *L'hitraot,* I hope.

That reaction continued to trouble me. "Forgive you for what, Drew? You never did anything to *me.*" The implication, or the one I imagined, being I had done harm to Judaism. The Jewish God forgives only transgressions against Him; all others must be pardoned by those sinned against. But how does one repent to an entire people?

A curious letter in the *Times* suggested the way.

Father Chuck had written the editor defending Father Daniel Berrigan, of all people, against the idiotic charge of anti-Semitism. Since for the life of me I couldn't face Dean Diamond or Dr. Tchernichovsky, I'd confess to Father

Chuck. Then accept my penance, hug my absolution—and that at long last would be the end of that.

It was impossible to get him on the phone, however. Out of order, said the operator.

Father Chuck eyed me warily when I showed up at his apartment. "You've come on account of my letter?" He delivered an impassioned defense of his colleague that made me laugh.

"But I *know* the Berrigans are the greatest clergymen alive."

He threw his arms around me. Then sat me down in front of a typewriter. "Suppose you write that to the *Times*, Drew. I had to take my phone off the hook. The names people called me for defending Dan's speech. And him the Vietnam War's greatest martyr."

"What speech?"

Father Chuck put a sheet of paper in the typewriter. "Go ahead, Drew. Just say what's in your heart."

Easy enough. I wrote of the need for models to pattern oneself after. For me there was no greater exemplar of active moral concern than Daniel Berrigan.

Father Chuck looked over my shoulder. "Fine, Drew, just fine. Now add that you're a rabbinical student."

Swiftly, I asked for a copy of the Berrigan speech. "So I can go into more detail." In place of mentioning R.I.

Following his gaze, I saw a mimeographed manuscript atop a pile of books. His hand beat mine to the copy. "You don't want to make your letter *too* long."

"Right." I slid the speech out from under his hand and read, "Keynote address delivered by Father Daniel Berrigan at a meeting of the Association of Arab University Graduates in Washington, D.C., on October 19, 1973."

"Drew!"

I looked up.

"You didn't hear about the speech at R.I.?" My "No" unsettled Father Chuck. "Bear in mind," he said, curiously agitated, "Dan is a poet. He's published books of poetry. Splendid books."

I chuckled. "The speech is in iambic pentameter?" It might as well have been, for it was hard to follow all the anti-Semitic slanders that Father Berrigan had quoted in order to refute.

> In the space of twenty-five years, this metamorphosis took place. The wandering Jew became the settler Jew; the settler ethos became the imperial adventure . . . the slave became master, and created slaves.
>
> It is a tragedy beyond calculating that the State of Israel should become the repository, and finally the tomb, of the Jewish soul. . . . That in place of Jewish prophetic wisdom, Israel should launch an Orwellian nightmare of double-talk, racism. . . .

Venomous lies and more lies with an occasional half-truth thrown in to make the lies stronger. But where were the refutations? I read further:

> In America, in my church, I am a Jew. I am scarcely granted a place to teach, a place to worship, a place to announce the truths I live by.
>
> I am a Jew, in resistance against Israel.
>
> My church has helped Israel . . . to seek a biblical justification for crimes against humanity.

All of a sudden I burst into sobs. *Me*. Tears ran down my cheeks, dripped onto the speech. No quotes at all, these. The lies were entirely Berrigan's. Far more beautifully composed than Malik's, but the Russian ambassador was no poet.

"Drew!" Father Chuck was shaking me by the shoulder. *"Drew!"*

"My friend in Israel. Still haven't heard from him. And I can't call his family." I rattled on, all self-control lost. "How *could* he? If you knew how I idolized Father Berrigan. If *he* can't be trusted. My God! Who can?"

Father Chuck's hands slipped away from me. "Dan's a

poet," he insisted. "A poet has, you know, poetic license. To be flowery, use rhetoric to make a point."

"You *endorse* this speech?"

He shifted his weight from one foot to the other. "Not the speech. I once spent a summer in Israel. But the man. Dan's a saint. And a good friend. He's no anti-Semite. Believe me, Drew."

I glanced once more at the Berrigan text.

Israel . . . manufactures human waste, the byproducts of her entrepeneurs. . . .

. . . that racist ideology, which brought the destruction of the Jewish communities at the hands of the Nazis, should now be employed by the State of Israel. . . .

No, I never did confess. With perverse logic, I figured it should have been the other way around.

Dear Drew,

First the good news. Three cheers for the good old U.S.A. for finally airlifting arms to Israel! But now, the quadrupling of oil prices. Can't help thinking (a) that was the purpose of the Yom Kippur War, not the result, and (b) that's the price being paid for the Vietnam War. If not for that disaster, America would surely take on OPEC, no?

Not that the personal news is that bad. I've come through scathed, but reparably. Being a Vietnam veteran—no one knew I was only a chaplain's assistant—I got to drive supplies to the Golan Heights till my truck bumped into a land mine.

With the Columbia semester forfeited, I'll recuperate here in Israel. Maybe take courses at Hebrew University's School of Social Work, while lending a helping hand. My wounds serve as a bridge to the other wounded and their families. So that's all to the good.

I miss Isaca terribly. In Vietnam I thought it bad not to have a girl back home. Now I know better. Worse is having a girl like Isaca—six thousand miles away.

The weirdest thing. I've developed this sudden urge to have five or six children, maybe more. Don't ask me why—and don't tell Isaca. Might scare her off!

By the way, I saw you at the airport just as I was about to pass through security. I wish you had joined us. Made me feel sad to see you hanging back, alone. How are you, Drew? At peace with yourself, I hope.

Dr. Diamond did a double take when I entered his office, just as surprised as he to find myself there. Jean Valjean had never dropped in on Inspector Javert. Still, I had to beg forgiveness. And now there was also Father Daniel Berrigan to apologize for. Only then would the slate that was my secular soul be wiped clean.

"You're late, Baron." The dean pointed to his wristwatch. "Classes started three weeks ago. Of course you weren't the only dropout. One sophomore quit, and one junior. Draft dodgers, I suppose. What do *you* suppose?"

My cheeks burned. Come to spill my guts, I could barely untie my tongue. And when I did, it was to deny. "You're charging me with—with—"

"Ingratitude, for starters. After three years together a Dear John letter? Okay, Baron. *Tell* me why you quit."

"Certainly. That's why I came here today. And on account of Father Berrigan."

"*Berrigan?*"

"I left because . . ."

"Yes? Yes?"

"Because of . . . personal reasons. That's it exactly."

"Personal reasons." Dr. Diamond rolled his eyes heavenward. "If brevity is the soul of wit, I'd die laughing now. Never could figure you out, Baron. Well? Is that all?"

The moment of truth. But the *mea culpa* stuck in my throat like a bone.

"So you want to come back to R.I."

"Come back?" Do mice re-enter traps after having made off with the cheese?

Dr. Diamond banged on the desk. "I don't know if I take God on faith. And you want me to take you? What makes Andrew Baron the better risk?"

"I just stopped by to say—well, I'm sorry about everything.

Sorry for Israel. For Vietnam. For Father Berrigan. For myself.. . . . But thanks, my *sincere* thanks for everything I'm *not* sorry about." I strode to the door, relieved to have apologized at long last, though only one of us knew for what.

"*Baron!*"

I didn't turn around. Whatever the dean had to say, I preferred it said behind my back.

"It must have been difficult for you to come here."

I hung my head.

"After that vanishing act, *I* wouldn't have the nerve to face me. And without so much as a rationalization. Such *chutzpah!* Well, at least you didn't lie."

"Lie? *Me?*"

"Baron—" The bell drowned out his words. "Didn't you hear?"

"What?"

"I said you can have another chance. But please. No thanks. If there's one thing harder to bear than ingratitude, it's gratitude. . . . Come along, Baron."

Bewildered, I let myself be rushed out of his office and into class.

"Look!" said Perry Davis. "The prodigal rabbi returns."

Isaca hugged me, then showed off her engagement ring with the same look that had lit up Levi's face.

A thing of the past, whatever she had felt for me. Still, I was very happy for them both. A marriage made in heaven. Two *lamed-vovniks*.

The start of the lecture gave me fifty minutes to sort out the rest of my thoughts. Criminals often return to the scene of their crime, but remaining at R.I. would mark the first time someone came back to continue one. On the other hand, I had nearly earned the degree of Master of Hebrew Letters that would be awarded in June. Of course, if I did stay on, I'd absent myself from ordination and simply fade away afterward. On the third hand, didn't the Talmud observe that a sin repeated seems permitted?

All this I wrote Levi that night, before Isaca could inform on me. He replied, charitably, that while my return to R.I.

puzzled him, so did the theory of relativity. Between the lines, however, I detected a veiled warning not to let myself get carried away and ordained, then practice as a rabbi. "Whatever happened," he inquired, "to Clifford Irving?"

EIGHTEEN

Dr. Tchernichovsky was not at R.I., but in Florida, recuperating from another major operation. The prognosis? Dr. Diamond changed the subject. Would I help Rabbi Brownmiller set up *havuros* within his congregation?

"We can't count on the Arabs to oblige us with a war every few years to galvanize American Jewry," said the rabbi at our meeting. "If the *havura* doesn't work, I may put Temple Shalom to the torch."

Yes, that's what Rabbi Brownmiller said, then explained. "Whenever a synagogue is started, there's this tremendous burst of energy and involvement. But they recede as soon as the building goes up. . . . Well, a fire may be extreme. Perhaps from now on we should build houses of God that are biodegradable."

Within a month I organized ten *havuros*. Meeting biweekly, every cluster of six to ten families slowly evolved into the extended family that many people had moved from the city to escape. Nothing so new, I suppose, as an idea whose time came and went a generation or two before.

Would the *havura* bring its members closer as well to all those Jews outside the congregation?

Rabbi Brownmiller replied, "Before a person can figure out who he is, he has to know *whose* he is." A gesture downward. "Or isn't. Look. No more Adler's Elevated."

Something else was bothering him. I figured out it was me when the rabbi went on endlessly about my achievements.

Finally, I asked him to cut the praise and let me have it straight.

"Praise? That was criticism, Andrew. Remember what I told you after your first reading on Rosh Hashonah?"

"No. Oh, yes. To read with less expression."

"That's what the *havura* also needs. You're doing good, Andrew, with a vengeance. Take it easy. Be the resource person instead of prime mover. The more you do, the less others will. The trouble now with congregants. They turn over Judaism for safekeeping to the rabbi, today's high priest."

It worked out that way, as soon as I stopped directing. Me, I chalked up the experiment as a success when Sheridan, divorced now, asked that a *havura* be set up for singles. Surprisingly, he didn't mind my leading it.

"You were right," Sheridan said at our first meeting. "Lloyd does hate me."

"Well," I said, "that makes two."

"You hate me also?"

"Of course not. I meant *you* were also right. To turn Lloyd in. A cult is a sick extended family—an *anti*family. How's he doing?"

"Out of the army as of last month. Now he's in therapy. We all are. Family therapy." A grimace. "Only, we're not a family anymore."

I sought to reassure him. "Nothing lasts forever, Mr. Sheridan. Not even hostility. Look at the two of us."

He allowed himself a smile.

Nor was I the only one to concede error that month. Father Chuck wrote another letter to *The Times*, which restored my faith in men of God and my affection for one in particular.

> I believe now I erred in voicing approval of Father Daniel Berrigan's speech about Israel. As he, who has been an inspiration to all people of goodwill, erred. Perhaps he confused Vietnam with the Jewish state, which I and my brothers in Christ wish well.
>
> It is our sincere hope that both sides in the Middle East will

let bygones be bygones and make peace with each other at long last. Surely, the fairest solution is one that recognizes the rights and aspirations of all parties concerned. I pray for the day when Israelis and Palestinians transcend their differences and join in forming a binational state like Lebanon.

In the spring Dr. Tchernichovsky returned from Florida and asked the seniors over. Those who had completed a hospital course on death and dying debated how to treat the professor until Bernie List finally reminded them, "He invited us in for coffee, not a consultation."

Impossible to decide on a class gift, obstructed as we were by unspoken desires to hit on something that would stay the inevitable. Everything was suggested but repentance, prayer, and righteousness, which, according to the liturgy, avert the dread decree. In the end we voted for individual presents. Strength—and health, we prayed—through numbers.

A stranger never would have taken Dr. Tchernichovsky for sick. True, he now almost looked his age, but the only concessions the octogenarian had made to illness were sallowness and loss of weight. Spirit intact, he stood as erect as ever, eyes larger now in proportion to his drawn face, as he directed us into his study. All four walls lined with volumes piled two and three deep, it gave one the impression of having entered the Book of the People.

The professor eased himself into a recliner and responded to all the greetings with a smile. "Shakespeare was wrong. There aren't seven stages of man, but four. Hello. How are you? How's your family and work? Then finally, You're looking good."

He expressed joy over my return to R.I. So to forestall queries I produced my gift at once. A happy letter from Levi, whose psychological problems the professor knew about, now well and settling in the Jewish state.

"Thank God," he said, pleased. "At least the Lord never smites with both hands."

But Isaca exclaimed, "*Settling?*"

The class followed my lead over Dr. Tchernichovsky's protests. "What's all this—the gifts of the Magi?" He accepted Bernie List's copy of a new Bible translation and Hank Brenner's copy of *Phaedo*, which describes the last days of Socrates. "Splendid combination. The guide for living, and one for stopping."

Isaca gripped my hand.

Ezra Farber showed photographs of his baby and announced that Roberta was pregnant again. Or since it was so soon, perhaps still. What Ezra couldn't bring himself to say, since Jews usually name children after the dead, was that the new Farber baby would bear the professor's name.

Perry Davis offered letters from Yevgeny, recently released from another fifteen days in jail, which described the growing numbers of Jews assembling at Moscow's Great Synagogue. Donald Stein gave the professor galley proofs of the forthcoming *New Union Prayer Book*, and Samson Finn handed over a copy of *On Death and Dying*. "I do hope," said our host, "both have happy endings."

Seth Astrachan presented a gift certificate to Saks Fifth Avenue, plus the name of a specialist who came very highly recommended. "I'm glad," said the professor gravely, "some members of this class are practical."

Trust Isaca to come up with the best gift—for all. Permission for Dr. Tchernichovsky to ordain the class.

The news delighted him. "You phoned Dr. Worenz all the way to Jerusalem? Such extravagance." His eyes took on a new sparkle.

"Professor?" Isaca said. "Would you ordain us now?"

"Yes," everyone clamored, "now."

"*Now?*" The word came out in three syllables, and Dr. Tchernichovsky's eyes dimmed. It was painfully evident that no one there expected him to live till June.

"How thoughtless!" Isaca exclaimed, and burst into tears.

"Dear Isaca." He beckoned her forward. "It's been a long time since I've made a woman cry." Gently, he brushed away her tears. "Don't you think I understand your eagerness to be ordained? A rabbi's sins are forgiven on the day of his ordination, just as they are on his wedding day and on Yom Kippur." He stood up with some effort. "Nothing will keep me from graduation, I promise. But by all means, you sinners, ordination now."

The class surrounded Dr. Tchernichovsky as the sons of Jacob must have crowded around the patriarch for his deathbed blessings. O how I wished to be in their number. Not to be ordained, but to be pardoned.

His fingers brushed against a prayer book. "The synagogue is the portable Jewish homeland. So a rabbi has the greatest of responsibilities," said the professor. "For thousands of years the Jewish people invested their lives in the Portfolio of Judaism by studying the Torah and practicing its precepts. That accounts for our passion for social justice, the disproportionate numbers engaged in civil rights and antiwar, and why American Jews, as a group, consistently vote against their pocketbook. In recent decades, however, acculturation and assimilation have slowed Jewish investments to a trickle, even while the cashing in of our resources has continued apace. One need be no prophet, therefore, to forsee the approaching depletion of our heritage . . . by default. So it's incumbent upon rabbis to itemize the *mitzvos* to congregants, to instill them with learning as well as pride in observances. Only then shall we augment the Portfolio of Judaism, which is our sole security as Jews, and the only treasure we leave our heirs."

Dr. Tchernichovsky searched out each face. "Judaism, remember, is the covenant of mutual obligations between God and the Jewish people. As the end of our partnership cannot be realized for generations, it becomes a partnership not only between those now living, but between those who are living and those who are dead and those yet to be born."

He laid his hands on Isaca Zion's head and whispered something, then directed his attention to Bernie List. Nobody could overhear the professor's words, but their effect was plain whenever an ordinee straightened up. Perhaps the group contained no creative genius to blaze new religious trails. But there was a need, as among all people, for talents to connect and sustain. And we were, by and large, a gifted group.

So mesmerized was I, Dr. Tchernichovsky's hands reached out for the head beside mine before I realized what could happen. A Gentile rabbi! But one promise that had to be kept was the one to myself. So telling Ezra to make my apologies for having been taken suddenly ill, I left. A difficult feat, deserting such a father-figure.

An hour later the phone rang. It was Isaca calling to ask how I felt, but not waiting for an answer. Did Levi write me that he was *settling* in Israel? No, not in so many words. He must have mentioned *something*. Well, Russian isn't that hard to learn. Why is Levi studying Russian? To help settle Soviet Jews in Israel.

There was a long pause. "How can Levi do that while living in the States?"

"That's why I jumped to the conclusion—"

"I'll write Levi tonight. In America he can agitate for Russia to lift its ban on Jewish culture and religion. That's equally important. Why write off all those Jews remaining in Russia? . . . Meanwhile, Andrew, keep August open."

"For Tisha B'Av?"

Well, at least that got a laugh.

"Silly! For a wedding."

The next morning everyone else inquired after my health. It was fine until someone also asked about ordination. *Then* I got sick. So busy patting my integrity on the back, I hadn't realized that Dr. Tchernichovsky would be expecting me back for his blessings. What but interment could account for my continuing absence? To snub the professor now would be to hurt his feelings for the rest of his life. How could that be avoided without confessing my ruse? It couldn't, after he called to set a date.

"I'll stop by tomorrow, Professor." For his curses. I expected nothing less.

Entertaining the class must have taken tremendous effort. Though it was early afternoon when I called, Dr. Tchernichovsky was in bed. Resting, his housekeeper said, after having undergone chemotherapy. An excellent excuse to defer confession.

But he made me stay. "It's not good to be alone," he said, "even in Paradise."

The profusion of volumes lying about recalled all the food on Yom Kippur Eve prior to the fast. It occurred to me that if allowances could be made to take books along, the professor would probably never notice himself going. He made me sit down, though I had been determined to stand, at least, upright. Not one to rush to judgment, I asked how he was.

"The question is no longer how am I, but where," he mused dreamily. "I live in memories now, mingling with those already gone. My wife. My son and *Kaddish*. Old friends. I hear my mother's last words, 'Be a *mentsch*, my son.' I seem to be drifting in and out of death. . . ."

Outside, it began to rain. I couldn't help likening it to tears. True, the professor had lived a decade beyond the biblical threescore years and ten. Still, if it takes hundreds of years to grow a giant redwood, how long before a Tchernichovsky could be replaced?

He roused himself. "Glad you came, Baron. It's a lonely business, dying. Now I understand why the Egyptians buried the wives and servants of dead men with them. Me, I find myself dreaming of the deaths of those very close to me who are still alive. So they can welcome me, I suppose, on my arrival yonder. Can you imagine such selfishness!"

"Oh yes, Dr. Tchernichovsky, yes, yes, yes."

"You can?"

"Not yours. Mine. All mine."

"Oh?" He searched my face. "Since you're here, you must feel better. But you look awful, Baron. My talk disturbs you? Forgive me."

"No, no. What bothers me is . . ."

"Yes?"

"The truth."

"Which truth is that? Every day now so many are proclaimed, it's hard to keep up."

"About ordination—"

"I see." Dr. Tchernichovsky looked away. "You don't want me to ordain you. That's it, isn't it? The way you stared at my hands the other evening. As if they were cobras."

"Well . . . you see . . ."

"No need to explain, Baron. The day you spoke to me about your friend, hours after the doctors revealed my condition, and I despaired. Then my surly reaction to the request for immediate ordination. As if I felt entitled to live forever. When death approaches, everyone feels he's lived but a single day. Still, my wife, toward the end, she granted me permission to seek satisfaction elsewhere. Of course I didn't. Couldn't. But that she could think of others at such a time, whereas I, when you came to me, thought first of myself. . . . You must be very disappointed in me, Baron."

"No, of course not, certainly not. I want to tell you . . ." Another lie! "I don't want, I *must*." Fixing my eyes on the *mezuzah* on the doorpost, I blurted out the truth, naked and unadorned.

The response was the harshest criticism of all. Silence. So prolonged that recalling the Talmudic saying that the tongue has power over life and death, I sneaked a look. Indeed, the professor's eyes were closed.

"Dr. Tchernichovsky!"

His eyes opened. "Then there *is* something new under the sun."

The shock hadn't killed him. That was to my credit. Alas, that only. Now I waited for sentence to be passed. If Hester Prynne was branded with an A for betraying just one person, I'd have to sport the entire alphabet, Hebrew as well as English. "Well, Dr. Tchernichovsky? What do I do now?"

He turned his black eyes on me full blast. "What do *you* think?"

My God, the worst punishment of all! "Won't you tell me?" I pleaded. "Give me a hint?"

"You don't need any. A man as resourceful as you."

"Your knowing of my fraud. That's the worst punishment of all, Dr. Tchernichovsky. Believe me. I'm so *ashamed*."

He pursed his lips. "Well, that's a start."

"I apologize, repent. Whatever it's called, I do. Sincerely. But . . . how do I make amends?" There was no reply. Only more punishing silence. "I know! I'll convert."

A sigh. "Baron, would you make Judaism the dumping ground for your guilt?"

"That would be selfish. To inflict myself on the Jews."

"I didn't say that, Baron. All kinds of incense were used in Solomon's Temple. Malodorous frankincense, too."

A euphemism for calling me a stench in the nostrils of the Lord. "I'm quitting R.I., of course. I'll call the dean right now and explain this time—" I dashed to the phone on the nightstand.

His hand clamped over mine as it reached for the receiver. "Stop that! Basking in shame, luxuriating in guilt." He snorted. "Many Christian ministers and scholars have attended R.I. for advanced degrees. So you aren't the first Gentile enrolled. Only the first to fly false colors. But it would hardly do R.I. any good, your proclaiming it. Think of the school's embarrassment, the bad publicity." He let go of me.

I stared at him. "You recommend I do . . . *nothing?* After sinning against the Rabbinical Institute?"

Dr. Tchernichovsky sat up in bed. "Baron, the main concern of Jewish law is the person, not institutions. Acts of injustice, sins, are condemned not because the law is broken, but because a person has been hurt. The law's duty is not to punish, but to build character." For the moment he seemed transported back to his own Garden of Eden, the classroom. "From now on, Baron, please bear this in mind: 'Whoever learns something with an intent other than to act, it would have been better if he had never been born.' So use your learning to live like the worker-priests of France, who also are not Jews. At least, I don't think *they* are. Thanks to you, Baron, I take nothing for granted anymore."

"That's *all?*"

He pounded a pillow with both hands. "That's all, he says! If it were easy to live as a *mentsch*, decent and honorable and compassionate, would there be so many *momzerim* in the world?"

As I grabbed his hands and pumped them in appreciation, the housekeeper came running. What was going on? Shouting in a sickroom? Indian wrestling? *Feathers?* I had to leave.

The days that followed were my happiest since the start of the Vietnam War, which is to say since I could remember. Good-bye, guilt; so long, shame. And only several weeks more of sham. By graduation Nixon would probably be out of office. And though no teaching posts in sociology were now available, one might open up the following year, when I'd get my doctorate, on schedule. So no time was lost all these years and no amnesty required. Now I could even marry. If only Nina were released from Russia.

A snag, alas, in the marriage plans of my friends. Levi, who had indeed decided to live in Israel, asked Isaca to join him there. But it was impossible for a woman to serve as a rabbi in the Jewish state. Because of the Orthodox ban on giving one's hand to a woman or looking in her face, Isaca said, observant Jews in Israel have protested the employment of women *bus drivers*.

Not that American congregations were clamoring for Isaca. Thus far, the only offer had come from a temple that wanted her for public relations reasons. So she had turned it down. Of course, the situation would change eventually—one third of R.I.'s entering class was female.

"Why," Isaca said with a catch in her voice, "is Levi's work more important than mine? To abandon the rabbinate now—"

"You chose it on account of a man."

"You mean my father? But that was four years ago. Now I want to be a rabbi on account of myself. Andrew, haven't *you* changed?"

On its twenty-sixth anniversary, Israel made the headlines, alas. Ma'alot's turn to become famous for a day when three Arab terrorists from Lebanon entered that town in the Galilee and butchered twenty-one schoolchildren and wounded sixty more.

At a memorial service, Dr. Diamond quoted a Hasidic

rabbi: "I do not ask to suffer. I ask only that there be a reason for my suffering." Then the dean cited an Arab proverb, which supplied as good a reason as any for Israel's agony: "An Arab is a man who will pull down a whole temple to have a stone to sit on."

During *Kaddish*, my thoughts turned again to conversion. In earnest. The connection? I wasn't sure myself. Something to do with wanting to share in the fate of the Jewish people. Left to my own devices, I sometimes was beset by feelings of incompleteness, deprivation. Could it be that I was suffering from hunger of the soul?

No, I had no fix on God. Possibly, like most things in this world, He too was a lie. But doesn't the world depend on which lies people decide to make good? There's no such thing, I had concluded, as no-God. Everyone serves some sort of deity, call Him what he will or won't. A leap of faith was beyond me, but not a leap of action. So I'd postulate a good and concerned God, then compel His emergence. Bet my life that the Lord Himself was subject to self-fulfilling prophecies. And as demanding as hell. No deity for me that didn't cost anything. Yes, I'd enroll in Judaism. Provided Dr. Tchernichovsky didn't redline me.

The professor heard me out thoughtfully during a return encounter without registering emotion. Then he reminded me of what I already knew. Judaism taught that the righteous of *all* peoples deserve a share of the world to come. "So why convert, Baron?"

You know me by now. When in doubt, quote. "Somehow or other, men must have a sense of the whole if they are to live; they must have something to believe in and commit themselves to."

"But why Judaism?"

"To try to be religious in general is like trying to speak language in general."

Dr. Tchernichovsky drummed his fingers on the book beside him. "B.S.," he said.

"But I mean every word. *This* time. I need to believe in something better than what I see."

"B is for Robert Bellah, and S for George Santayana, whom you just plagiarized. Baron, I read too." He waved a hand at the shelves lining his bedroom.

I spoke then of my experiences in Russia. Of Nina. Of Lloyd Sheridan. Of my *havuros*. Suddenly it hit me. "That's it, Professor! That's me. A *havura* in miniature. Acts provide insight and feeling that theory can't. I've come to believe in my Jewish way of life. Conversion will only be a confirmation. Unless—does my hoax disqualify me?"

Dr. Tchernichovsky shook his head. "Even if one enters into an activity for an ulterior motive, the Talmud says, one may arrive at the correct principle."

"And what do *you* say?"

He sighed. "God knows I've done my duty. Discouraging you, as required."

"But if I *insist*?"

"Then we're yours, Baron, and you're ours."

Ecstatic, I clutched his hand.

". . . your first assignment as Jew," Dr. Tchernichovsky was saying. "Help me get the *halacha* reinterpreted. This will involve research and contacting my Conservative and Orthodox colleagues. Whatever obscure reasons for the second-century ruling that only the child of a Jewish woman is considered a Jew—before that Jewishness had been patrilineal—that practice must end. Makes no sense for religion to be determined by the mother, and lineage and Hebrew name by the father. The offspring of *either* Jewish parent should be regarded as a Jew. Do you agree, Baron?"

"I do, I do!"

A smile. "That's wedding talk. Pity there's no bride to kiss." He leafed through the book at his side before handing it to me. "Ruth will have to do."

I read the Moabite's words to her mother-in-law Naomi: "Entreat me not to leave you, to turn away from joining you. For wherever you go, I will go; wherever you lodge, I will lodge. Your people will be my people, your God my God. Where you die I will die, and there will I be buried. I vow before God that nothing but death could part me from you."

No one at R.I. was told of my conversion. It would only confuse people, Dr. Tchernichovsky said. But he probably only wanted to spare me embarrassment. Conversion? No, adoption. I wrote Levi of my feeling that one was naturalized a Jew, the big difference being that to become an American one needn't surrender a foreskin.

Not a Reform requirement of proselytes. But wanting my adoption to be recognized by traditional Jews too, I underwent ritual baptism and the *bris*. Did it hurt? You must be kidding. Ever bang your thumb with a hammer?

Otherwise, I felt good, whole. Born again!

NINETEEN

I had planned to skip graduation, no relatives being there. Terri did wire a telegram, however—MAZEL TOV—signing it MOTHER OF THE YEAR. And Dad sent a big box of cigars, plus an old wooden shingle—DREW BARON, M.H.L.—parts of it freshly painted. (Beneath the first name and degree the eye could discern BEN and M.D. But then, I didn't expect to put the shingle to any more use than dad had.)

Dr. Tchernichovsky insisted on my attending. "I want to see you walk down that aisle in June," he said.

Legend had it that Adam donated years of his life to enable David to live longer. If only I knew whom to contact.

Quite a change from Columbia's graduation in 1970. Only war clouds then, and the antiwar movement, which imagined all those under thirty were as alike as blue jeans and as interchangeable. Now, the only thing that students had in common was each declaring his or her differences, defining themselves by color, sex, proclivities, what turned you on or off, which guru you followed, dozens of other categories. Out of the mass and into the pigeonhole in only four years.

Such was the spirit of the times that would, if history was any guide, leave those newly wed to it soon widowed. Yet to become a Jew was perhaps to keep a step *ahead* of the times. Only by way of the particular, I had come to believe, can one attain genuine universalism. Even Reinhold Neibuhr had said that no one can be a good Christian until first he is a good Jew.

My class assembled in the temple lounge to don academic robes and, in a show of solidarity with all their brethren, yarmulkes and prayer shawls. Isaca, too, put on the traditionally male attire. On my recommendation, Rabbi Brownmiller had engaged Ezra Farber to be his assistant. Perry Davis had accepted a congregation in Los Angeles, while Gary Himmel would be the Hillel director of a college in Boston. Bernie List was going on for his doctorate in Bible, Hank Brenner for his in Jewish philosophy. My plan to complete a Ph.D. in sociology struck nobody as exceptional. However divergent their paths, all would be wrestling now with the nature of authority for the non-Orthodox and appropriate forms of observances. Me too.

When others in the know extended congratulations on Isaca's appointment, she turned to me hesitantly. "Been meaning to tell you. I wrote Levi day before yesterday." She showed me a letter from a large temple in Manhattan welcoming her as an assistant rabbi, for a two-year contract.

"I refused a congregation of my own out West," she hastened to add. "In case Levi returns to Columbia." She searched my face for a reaction. "Am I wrong not to join him?"

"You wrong? Never. But neither is Levi to choose Israel."

Isaca raised her head defiantly. "Would *you* let anything or anyone stop you from being a rabbi?"

Alas, another what-might-have-been. "Only myself."

"Levi's obsessed with atoning for Vietnam. Israel is the easy way—"

"Easy? He'll have to serve in the army there."

Isaca looked shaken.

Dr. Diamond called me aside. "Think you fooled us, Baron, don't you?" Reviewing the records to decide on the homiletics award, the faculty had found me out. The only graduate in history never to have preached in chapel or anywhere else in the world. "May your tongue cleave to the roof of your mouth during your first sermon. Or do you plan to teach Jewish studies?"

Many such jobs were available in colleges and universities throughout the country. But without ordination I didn't feel qualified. "Dean, one question I've wanted to ask since October. Why did you take me back?"

"Personal reasons."

"Personal reasons?"

"Mine I don't mind revealing. R.I. had more riding on you than you did on us, Baron. You only put in time, we invested hope. And so much learning. You're a Jewish memory bank."

Touched, I vowed never to disappoint him, then did so at once. Asked again about my plans, I could only mumble something about becoming a worker-priest-*mentsch*.

"There you go again!" Dr. Diamond threw up his hands.

The processional got under way twenty minutes late, after a call to Dr. Tchernichovsky's housekeeper. Hours earlier, he had gone to the doctor, but sometimes he was delayed by a bad reaction to therapy. So, alas, graduation exercises had to begin without him. Perhaps just as well, if he couldn't lead us into the sanctuary. Everyone dreaded to see him wheeled to the pulpit.

Bernie and Isaca led the worship service, parts of it created by the class, while I kept on the lookout for Dr. Tchernichovsky. Impossible to distinguish among the thousands of faces in the dimly lit sanctuary, however. The small spotlights a hundred feet overhead played tricks on me, for I imagined seeing all three Simons there. Too bad that wasn't so, for the graduates and their families were asked to rise and thank God together for sustaining, preserving, and bringing us to this happy occasion.

No complaints though, my parents having taken the news of my becoming a Jew rather well. Dad wrote: "A Mexican friend taught me Hansen's Law. 'What the grandparents knew and what the children tried to forget, the grandchildren seek to recall.' So now start worrying about your future children." And Terri: "Judaism must have *something*. If both Elizabeth Taylor and Marilyn Monroe converted."

In his remarks Dr. Worenz twice declared, "Before the Yom Kippur War I never realized how profoundly Jewish I am"—the first time in Yiddish. And graciously explained why he wasn't ordaining the graduates. We—rather, they—had already been ordained by a beloved professor who had tremendous faith in our passing the final exams. Then the president called us one by one to stand beside him before the open Ark, there to be awarded the degree of Master of Hebrew Letters and a personal word.

Isaca drew a spontaneous standing ovation from the class, which the congregation joined. Now there were two Rabbi Zions—someday there'd be a third. Levi's, I hoped.

Soon my name was called, and I found myself before the dashing blond archaeologist. I felt a momentary twinge when he greeted me as rabbi, though it would have been as fitting for me to be ordained as for a hit man to collect on his mark's insurance policy. Dr. Worenz looked deep into my eyes and, voice throbbing, began. "Ezra Farber . . ."

I waited till my president of four years had concluded his personal message before saying, "My name is Andrew Baron."

Dr. Worenz shook my hand firmly. "You're very welcome, Ezra."

Minutes later, the parting benediction and recessional. Free at last in one sense, forever responsible in another. While cameras snapped our march toward Fifth Avenue, I searched for Dr. Tchernichovsky. Just as I gave up, there he was. In the very last row. He had kept his promise. And he was standing.

Outside, relatives surrounded the others. I congratulated Mrs. Benjamin, there with her first grandchild, and Roberta, carrying the next.

"The new baby isn't my doing," she swore. "I almost killed Ezra when I found out. You do believe me, Andrew, don't you?"

"L'hitraot," everyone was saying, "be seeing you."

Could that be Margarita with her child on the other side of the avenue watching the temple as Bernie had the church on her wedding day? When I looked again, however, the two had vanished.

I broke out in a sweat at the sound of "Drew! Drew!" The last time my name had been called in front of Temple Emanu-El—

Mrs. Simon. Now with her husband. Though there was nothing to fear but their displeasure, my adrenaline started flowing.

"Is that nice?" Mr. Simon said reproachfully. "Boycotting us after all we went through together? . . . We've missed you, Drew."

That tranquilized me. "I'll try to be a *mentsch*. As much like Levi as possible. I promise."

Mrs. Simon shook a finger at me. "Such foolishness, Drew. I'm surprised. If you'll be like Levi, who'll be like you?"

I hugged the woman.

"Did you see Levi?"

"*Here?*"

"He wanted to surprise Isaca."

Hesitantly, I asked, "How long will he be staying?"

"Until the wedding. Then back to Israel, the two of them." Mrs. Simon motioned. "The happy couple."

But she must have been looking only at her son, who, despite a limp, radiated joy, not having received Isaca's letter. Her face showed the strain of not having broken the news yet.

Levi chuckled. "Surprised? Isaca nearly fell over. How about that ovation! And wait till you hear about our new apartment in Jerusalem. When are you coming for a visit? After the honeymoon, of course. Isaca, how long will that last?" She turned colors. "You're blushing?" He laughed.

"Levi," she began.

Hastily, I excused myself. "See you later." At their wedding, I prayed. *Hal'vai!*

The sanctuary was nearly empty now. No Dr. Tchernichovsky in the last pew or in any other. But way up front stood an imposing figure with swirling white hair before the open Ark. I hurried down the long aisle. Yes, it was the professor, staring up at the Eternal Light. Reluctant to intrude, I waited for him below the marble pulpit, like the Children of Israel at the bottom of Mount Sinai.

Finally, he closed the Ark, turned around, and descended. One could almost see the two Tablets in his arms.

I stretched out my hand.

Pausing a step above me, Dr. Tchernichovsky reached into a brown paper bag that he carried and took out something. "My gifts to the class. But I came too late. Big fuss at the doctor's over my discontinuing his delaying tactics. He doesn't understand. Sometimes it isn't only life that needs to be affirmed."

My arm dropped to my side.

"Don't look like that, Baron. Death is a law, not a punishment." Entrusting me with the bag, whose contents he wanted distributed to the others, he took my palm and placed an acorn in it.

In Russia the ghetto coin had burned me. But the acorn felt moist. Perhaps because it was seen through misty eyes.

"Andrew, I had a dream about you last night."

"*Me?*"

"I dreamed you were dead."

I couldn't look up. "Dr. Tchernichovsky . . . may I . . . say *Kaddish* for you?"

A long moment of silence. Then: "Yes, I'd like that very much, Andrew. To be continued."

Suddenly, I felt hands touching my head and, startled, heard the Lord's blessings invoked upon me.

"Always remember, it isn't the position which honors the man, but the man who gives honor to the position," he said. "Confer honor upon the name *Jew*. Confer honor upon the title *Rabbi*."

For a moment—the thought was too absurd to entertain for more than a moment without laughing out loud—it occurred to me that perhaps all along the divine scheme had never been mine, but His. So help me God.